PUSH

THE GAME BOOK TWO

Also by Eve Silver

RUSH
THE GAME: BOOK ONE

PUSH

THE GAME BOOK TWO

Eve Silver

KATHERINE TEGEN BOOKS
An Imprint of HarperCollins Publishers

Katherine Tegen Books is an imprint of HarperCollins Publishers.

Push: The Game Book Two

Library of Congress Cataloging-in-Publication Data
Silver, Eve.
  Push / Eve Silver. — First edition.
     pages cm. — (The game ; book 2)
  Summary: "Miki Jones continues to fight the aliens threatening to invade Earth,
but begins to doubt the intentions of the Committee who send teams on these
missions"— Provided by publisher.
  ISBN 978-0-06-219221-9 (hardback)
  [1. Science fiction. 2. Combat—Fiction. 3. Extraterrestrial beings—Fiction.
4. Interpersonal relations—Fiction.] I. Title.
PZ7.S58566Pus 2014   2013038563
[Fic]—dc23   CIP
                                                                  AC

Typography by Carla Weise
14 15 16 17 18 LP/RRDH   10 9 8 7 6 5 4 3 2 1

First Edition

FOR RENA, KRISTIAN, OLIVIA, JORDI, ALI, OSMAN, LAMIA, JOSH, AND REBECCA

CHAPTER **ONE**

"MIKI!"

There's a boy calling my name.

Déjà vu. Sort of.

"Miki," Luka Vujic says. "You okay?"

Wrong pitch, wrong tone.

Wrong boy.

There was a moment weeks ago when a different boy was calling my name, his voice inside my head, where no one else could hear.

That was the beginning, and the end. End of the known and familiar. Beginning of my new reality, where I jump between my life as plain old Miki Jones, and an alternate world where I fight the Drau—beautiful, terrifying alien predators bent on conquering Earth.

I don't understand it. I don't get how it works. All I know is that one minute I was trying to save Janice Harper's little sister from getting hit by a speeding truck; the next I was lying in the road, broken and bloody. Dying. Dead. I woke up in a grassy clearing called the lobby, alive, healed, not hurt at all, lying on my back, staring up at a handsome face and old-school, mirrored aviator shades—both of which belonged to Jackson Tate.

Everything that's happened started because of him. He was the one calling my name inside my head that day in the field behind Glenbrook High. He was the one crouched beside me when I came to in the lobby.

He tricked me, betrayed me, traded my freedom for his, offering me up to the Committee to take his place in the game.

Game. God, I hate that word. I can almost hear Jackson's voice, insisting it isn't a game. He was right. So right.

It's life and death, horror and fear, and dragging me in was his only way out.

Maybe I should hate him for that.

But I think of the way he watched my back and saved me more times than I can count. He made me find the strongest parts of myself deep inside. He teased me, challenged me, believed in me.

He climbed through my bedroom window, made me laugh, made me smile.

He kissed me.

Told me he loved me—

my heart feels like it's being crushed by a giant fist

—and then he—

the pain almost makes me scream

—died—

I force a breath past the lump in my throat

—for me. In my place.

He just needed to hang on for thirty seconds after he took the Drau hit. Just siphon off enough of my energy to hang on for thirty stupid seconds. But he didn't. I wonder if he *chose* not to because it might have meant killing me.

Am I supposed to be grateful for that? Am I supposed to forgive him for leaving?

I snap the thought in half.

I'm not so great at forgiveness.

I glance around, forcing myself to focus on something—*anything*—to help me keep it together. Slate tiles, yellow walls, the smell of cheese and grease, a woman behind the counter, a man making pies in the back. The pizza place is exactly as I left it before I got pulled. That was days and days ago. Seconds ago. Time passes differently in the two distinct versions of my current life.

"Miki," Luka says, urgent now. He's about ten feet away, standing beside the empty booth we were all sitting in . . . before. Before the battle, the terror, so many people dead.

I nod to let him know I hear him, and the tension in his shoulders eases just a little.

I've known Luka since we were kids. We were friends

until fourth grade, until his mom died. I was a clueless nine-year-old who understood next to nothing about loss and grief, and I let our friendship fade away. He moved to Seattle for sophomore year. We lost touch. Now he's back, but we really only found each other again in the game. We've both been conscripted. I don't know how Luka's been balancing the crazy for a whole year. Between the time shifts and alternate realities, the aliens and the body count, I can barely keep it together after just a few weeks.

"*Bam*, we're back," he says, his night-dark eyes focused on me. Three little words that tell me I need to pull my shit together before I give something away. There are rules that say we don't talk about aliens and battles and scores in real life. Breaking those rules might get us killed.

I clench my teeth so hard I swear I shear away a layer of enamel, and I nod again to let him know I get it.

Luka rakes his fingers back through his dark hair. His sleeves are pushed back and I stare at his forearm. No cuts, no blood. Last time I saw him was in the abandoned building in Detroit after the epic battle with the Drau. He had blood on his face, his hands, his arms. His shirt was torn, one eye swollen and purple. Scratches and cuts marred his skin in a dozen places.

Now, he's fine. No wounds. No bruises.

I drop my hand to my thigh, half expecting to find sticky, warm blood and the shattered edges of my bone. But I find only smooth denim, soft from dozens of washings.

Of course.

We don't bring our injuries back with us. Only our regret.

"Hey," my best friend, Carly, says as she squeezes my arm.

With a jolt, I turn toward her. Until that second, I'd forgotten she was there, right beside me. For her, no time has passed. For her, it's been seconds since I jumped up from the booth and darted for the door. But for me it's been days of battle and blood.

The first time I got pulled, a girl on my team—Richelle Kirkman—told me that the hours we spend in the game get banked, that we get them back. We do. We restart our paused lives down to the precise second and reclaim the missing hours.

If we're alive to come back at all.

Richelle was kick-ass, the best player on the team. She made it out every time. But not that last time. That mission ended with Richelle gray and still on the cold floor in a Vegas warehouse, her con full red.

Red like Jackson's con.

Can't think about that yet.

"I'm okay," I mumble to Carly. A lie I need her to believe. I don't dare freak out right now. I don't know who's watching, listening. Judging.

One brow arches delicately in that special Carly way, the pink streak in her #11 Extra Light Blond hair falling forward over her cheek. She just put that streak in a few

5

days ago, but it's already fading. No big deal. Carly'll probably change it to purple or blue before the week's out.

"You're okay? Really?" she asks, the words dripping attitude and snark. It's a front. She's worried, and I hate that I'm the cause. She's been so angry with me lately, our friendship yet another victim of the game and the secrets I'm forced to keep, but right now the only emotion mirrored on her face is concern.

A face so familiar. So special to me. She's not part of my other reality. I never want her to be part of it, to fight, to die. I want to grab her and crush her in the tightest hug, but that would just make her worry more.

"I'm fine," I say, trying to force my brain back up to speed. Missions demand one kind of focus. Real life demands another. This is my real life, the one where I run five days a week at the crack of dawn, vacuum the carpet in tiny, neat sections, iron the bedsheets, and wipe the kitchen counter even when it isn't dirty.

Because I can. My choice. *Mine.* No one else's.

"Do you want to go outside? Get some air?" Carly asks, then glances over her shoulder at Luka, either looking for approval or making sure he heard her.

"You think fresh air'll help?" he asks Carly, but he's watching me, his fingers curled into tight fists, the muscles of his forearms corded and taut. "You're fine, Miki. Everything's fine." He dips his chin to the table beside him. There's a pizza there and four unused plates, a key ring, and some bills that Luka must have tossed down to cover the cost of the meal no one will eat.

Nothing important there to see, so why did he want me to look?

Luka scoops his keys from the table and walks toward us. His gaze holds mine, his expression intent, and he lowers his brows like he's doing a Mind-Meld thing. Problem is, the connection's down at my end.

"Earth to Miki." Carly snaps her fingers near my face. The faint scent of cigarettes carries from her fingers, a reminder of the distance that's been building between us. She knows my history and she's been smoking anyway. A lot of people who get lung cancer aren't smokers, but Mom was. A pack a day. And now she's dead.

Like Gram and Sofu and Richelle. And Jackson.

Everyone leaves.

I swallow, but the lump in my throat stays exactly where it is.

"Miki." Carly tightens her hold on my arm as Luka steps up on my other side. "Breathe. Just breathe. You know what to do. You've done this a million times," she says.

I have. In the two years since Mom died I've had tons of panic attacks. I know the signs, and I'm experiencing a bunch of them right now: the feeling that a sword of doom's about to cut me down, the urge to escape, get out, run. The trembling. The shaking. The vise squeezing my chest.

They're known and familiar enemies, and that's why I recognize the subtle differences. This is no simple panic attack. It has extra special layers: it's me battling for control, trying to balance the game with my life, locking the door against the agony that's scratching to get in.

Jackson.

I can't think about him yet.

"Outside sounds like a plan," I say.

Carly wraps her arm around my waist and I cling to her, aching to spill it all out. The lobby. The battles. The aliens. The scores.

Her pupils are dilated, huge and dark, leaving only a thin rim of hazel green. Because of me. I'm scaring her.

I'm scaring myself.

I feel like I've been through a wood chipper and the slightest puff of air will scatter all the bloody, raw bits of me across the floor. And there, at the edges of my mind, is the numbness that's shrouded my every moment since Mom died. It's crawling back like a swarm of maggots to rotting flesh. Part of me wants to let it, to say: *Yes. Welcome. Wreathe my world in fog. Make me numb. Make me feel nothing, nothing at all.*

But I don't want to be that girl anymore. I've worked so hard to be normal.

You were never just a normal girl. I hear his voice in my head, but it's just a memory.

Jackson's gone. Forever.

I thought I could save him like he saved me.

I failed.

I can't bear it. I can't mourn again, can't do it, not right now. Not anytime soon.

The guy in the back is singing off-key while he makes the pie. The woman behind the counter plants her fists on her hips. Her expression's pretty clear. She'd like us to find the exit, like . . . now. Thanks for the concern, lady.

The few steps it'll take me to get to the door stretch like an abyss before me. I'm not sure that my legs won't buckle before I hit the sidewalk.

Carly shifts my arm from her waist and drapes it across her shoulders. She's afraid I'll crumble. I won't. I refuse. I won't let this break me.

"Miki, it's okay," Luka says, drawing out the last word like he's trying to tell me something. I watch the key ring spin round and round and round his index finger.

"Slow breaths. You know the routine," Carly says, and shuffles us both a couple of steps closer to the front door.

My thoughts are a series of cyclones churning destruction wherever they touch down, then moving on, spinning out of control.

From the corner of my eye, I see the keys go around again. The leather fob angles toward me so I can read the word on the round medallion at the center: *JEEP*.

And then everything stops. No confusion. Just clarity.

Those keys in Luka's hand: they aren't Luka's; they're Jackson's. I remember him throwing them down on the table when we first settled in the booth.

My gaze shoots to the table. Four plates. *Four.*

I stop dead, despite Carly's less-than-gentle urgings toward the door.

"Find Jackson," Carly orders Luka. "Where is he, anyway? We need to go. Like, now."

Go. We need to go. We need to . . .

"Wait!"

I break from Carly's hold and turn to stare at her. She just said his name. Jackson. She *remembers* him. Remembers that he was here at the pizza place with us. My heart stutters, then starts to race double time. He's not here now, but . . . he's not dead.

Because if he were, Carly would have no memory of him at all. That's what happens when you die in the game. Your entire existence from the moment you were conscripted gets wiped out as if it had never been.

When Richelle died in a Drau-infested warehouse in Vegas, everyone in her real life forgot all their interactions with her during the months from the time she was first pulled to the time her con went red. According to her memorial page, she died seven months before I even met her.

The only people who remember those months are the ones who knew her in the game—me, Luka, Tyrone, Jackson. For some reason, our memories of her remain.

If my con turns full red, I'll go back to the moment where I'm lying in the road, my blood smeared on the truck's bumper and pooling underneath me, warm and sticky. I'll go back to my heart beating slower and slower until it stops. That will be the moment that all I am in *this* reality ends. My friends, my family will all forget everything about me from that second on. Like I'd never lived the intervening days, weeks, months at all. Not even memories of me from that time left behind. Just . . . nothing.

For Jackson, his life would be snuffed years ago when he died in the real world in a car crash with his sister at the wheel. In that fraction of a second somewhere in the past, he would cease to exist.

That would mean Carly never would have met him.

He wouldn't have been here with us, out for pizza.

So while Luka and I would remember him from the game, Carly wouldn't even know his name.

But she does. In fact, she thinks he's here somewhere, not gone at all.

A tiny, terrifying seedling of hope unfurls. I clutch Carly's forearm. "Did—" My voice is little more than a croak. I swallow and try again. "Did you see where Jackson went?"

"Would I be asking Luka to find him if I had?" She shakes her head and rolls her eyes. "It's like he disappeared into thin air. Check the can," she orders Luka.

My gaze shoots to his. He smiles a little, holds up the keys, and jangles them. *This* is what he wanted me to figure out.

Jackson's alive.

Tears sting my eyes, threatening to fall. I didn't cry

when I thought he was dead, but now that I think he's alive I'm about to collapse in a sobbing heap. I bite the inside of my cheek hard until I feel like I can keep it together.

Jackson's alive.

Which doesn't make sense because his con was red. He was dead.

I need to find him.

"We need to find him," Luka says.

"That's why I told you to check the can," Carly says.

But Luka wasn't talking to her. *We* need to find him, which means I need to get Luka alone so we can figure out a plan.

"Luka! Go check." Carly sounds exasperated. "I'd do it but, hey"—she waves her fingers in the general direction of her fly—"missing some equipment here. . . ."

"He's not—" With a shrug, Luka gives up and heads off to do as Carly ordered.

But we both know Jackson isn't in the little boys' room.

He's . . . somewhere else.

CHAPTER**TWO**

LUKA UNLOCKS THE DOOR OF THE JEEP.

"Miki, you take shotgun." Carly the magnanimous. "Last thing we need is you having another panic attack."

"Bossy, much?" I mutter, mostly because she expects it. Yeah, she's bossy and unpredictable, argumentative, pissy, sometimes even bitchy. But she's also the friend who steps up when I need her, imagined wrongs forgotten, arms ready to hold me up when I feel like I'm going to fall.

She smiles at me and I want to hug her—for sacrificing herself to the cramped space of the backseat, for being safe and here, in the real world. For being exactly who she is, the friend who's been there for me through it all.

So I do. I throw my arm around her shoulders and rest my cheek against her hair. She rubs circles on my back.

"I know," she whispers.

But she doesn't. She can't.

"Thank you," I whisper back. "For always being there."

She hugs me hard. "Right back at you. BFFs, right? Remember when I got my tongue pierced? You sat there next to me and held my hand."

"And almost threw up."

"All the more reason that your attendance at the event was valiant." She kisses me on the cheek and steps back.

"Hey, I was just about to get in the group hug." Luka waggles his brows.

"You snooze, you lose," Carly says, climbing into the backseat. "So . . . where'd you say Jackson went?"

Luka shoots me a look. "He, uh, went out the back door. To the alley."

"That explanation is majorly sketch. You know that, right?" Carly pops the seat forward again and leans out to look at him. "Who's he meeting there?"

Luka shrugs.

"Luka?" she says as I push the seat back and climb in.

He still doesn't answer, just closes my door and rounds the hood to the driver's side.

I stare out the window trying to come up with something plausible to say.

Undeterred by the heavy evasion vibe hanging in the air—or, more likely, spurred by it—Carly keeps right on going as soon as Luka starts the car. "He managed to disappear without a trace in the few seconds while I got up to follow Miki? That's weird."

She has no idea.

"Can someone answer me?" She unhooks her seat belt and leans forward.

Luka meets her eyes in the rearview mirror. "Seat belt."

Carly flops back and I hear a snap. "Who was he meeting in the alley, Luka? His dealer?"

I pinch the bridge of my nose between my thumb and forefinger. Great. The second we drop Carly off, she'll text Dee and Kelley and Sarah about her suspicions. She'll swear them to secrecy. But they'll tell two friends, who'll tell two friends. Carly won't mean for it to balloon, but rumors have a way of doing that.

"Seriously, Luka . . . what's Jackson into?"

"Nothing," Luka says at the same time I say, "The queen of trying crazy shit is actually asking that question?"

I reach back to give Carly's knee a shove to let her know I'm kidding.

She flicks my shoulder and says, "Is he in trouble? Should we do something?" She pauses, then asks, "Is he dealing? Maybe he's getting his shipment in that alley. We really don't know him that well—"

"I know him that well," Luka cuts her off. His tone's not like anything I've ever heard him use before. It's a threat and a warning and an implacable statement.

"Okay. Fine. But I'm just saying—it's weird." Something in Carly's voice makes me turn. She's looking at Luka with this narrow-eyed, sort of predatory look. Then she sees me watching her and her expression goes neutral.

I press my fingertips against my temples. I need to get things under control. I need a plan. That's the priority right now. Find Jackson. Get answers. Figure out what his absence means in the big scheme of the game. Figure out why things are escalating so quickly, why there were so many Drau in Detroit.

"Hey, you okay?" Carly rests her hand on my shoulder. When I nod she says, "You're right, Luka. I'm sorry. You know Jackson better than I do. If you say he isn't dealing, I'll take your word on it. Sorry. Really." Carly the peacemaker's back online.

"*No hay problema.*" He grins at her in the rearview mirror and she grins back. Then he says, "Jackson took off with some guys he has a group project with. There was no parking on the street so they pulled in back. He asked me to get his car home because they're going to drop him off."

Even I almost believe him. I hadn't realized Luka could improvise with such aplomb. I always thought his inner Boy Scout kept him honest.

"Well," Carly huffs out. "Why didn't you just say that?"

"I just did," Luka says.

We've been driving for a few minutes, music on low, when Carly taps Luka on the shoulder. "What *is* that?" she asks.

"The music? Dubstep."

Carly nods. "I've heard dubstep before, but this is darker, sort of experimental."

"These tracks are old," Luka says. "Maybe from the nineties? Jackson turned me on to them."

"I like." She taps my shoulder next. "You look better. You have some color back."

"I'm better." So much better. Because Jackson's alive.

He might not have made it back from the mission, but he's alive somewhere. The question is: Where?

Then I remember the cave, the gurneys, the clones lined up like cuts of meat in a butcher's case. I think of the girl in the cold room, her brain removed, the shell of her body kept alive by machines. I gasp as my little euphoric bubble of hope bursts. What if the Drau have him? What if they're going to use him as an original donor, create an army of clones from his DNA?

My fingers clench, digging into my thighs.

Luka cuts me a sharp look. I turn my face back to the side window, not wanting him or Carly to catch the resurgence of my panic.

Jackson isn't going to die like that.

I'm going to find him. I'm going to bring him back. I've lost so many people I care about. I won't lose Jackson, too.

This time, I will get a say in how things pan out. This time, the ending of the story won't shatter me. I won't let it.

A few minutes later, Luka pulls up in front of Carly's house. I climb out, pull the seat forward, and hold it as she untangles herself from the backseat. She stares at my face for a few seconds.

"You wanna come do the Friday night dinner thing?"

she asks, not even trying to disguise the plea in her tone. Her mom has this thing about the whole family being together for dinner on Friday nights. She doesn't mind if they have friends over or head out after. But she's non-negotiable on anyone skipping out on it.

Doing the Friday night dinner thing with Carly's family would go a long way toward closing the distance that's been growing between us for weeks, a crack that's becoming a chasm. I hate to disappoint her, but every minute that ticks past could be putting Jackson's life at risk. Getting Luka alone to brainstorm a plan has to be my priority right now, and Carly's just handed me a golden opportunity.

"Maybe tonight's not the best," I say. "I'm not sure I can handle the crowd." Truth. I may be ditching her, but at least I'm not lying. I try to ignore the feeling that I'm letting her down.

Carly skews her lips to the side but doesn't argue. She looks disappointed but not pissed. My explanation's plausible. I never want much company on the tail of a full-blown panic attack. Mostly, I just want my bedroom and my music.

Then she glances at Luka and I have the crazy idea she's going to ask him to dinner. With her parents. And her brothers. Is she kidding? A boy who isn't related to her at family dinner night? They'll chew him up and spit him out. I guess she has the same thought because the invitation never materializes.

"You sure, Miki? I know Mom would love to see you."

That's as close to begging as she'll get.

I almost cave. Then I think of Jackson, trapped somewhere in the game, and I say, "Sorry. Call me after, 'kay? Maybe you'll come over?"

She brightens a little. "'Kay." Then she gives me a quick, one-armed hug. As she does, I catch sight of my backpack, rammed into the corner of the seat. I freeze.

Jackson's backpack. It's in the trunk. I have a place to start, the seeds of a plan.

As Carly heads for her front door, I expect Luka to start talking. When he doesn't, I ask, "Do you know where he is?"

"No." He looks at me, then back at the road, his knuckles white where he grips the wheel.

Disappointment and worry sit in my chest like an unchewed chunk of cold, greasy pizza.

"But he's alive, Miki. I know that much."

"Alive for how much longer? I keep thinking *they* have him. That they're going to use him to make an army of shells. Like that girl in the cold room. The one he"—I break off, then force myself to finish—"killed."

"Terminated," Luka whispers, then says, louder, "No." He shakes his head rapidly from side to side. "No, I don't think so. I don't think they have him. They don't need to keep him alive to make shells. They just need his body, hooked up to machines. If *they* took him, they'd have—" He breaks off, swallows. "He wouldn't still be alive."

"And since Carly remembers him, that means he *is*

still alive . . . somewhere."

"Exactly. So what are the chances that the Drau have him? Slim to none, right?"

I nod. The weight that's been crushing my chest lifts a little, but I'm afraid to hope, afraid of the hard crash that'll come if we're wrong.

Luka touches my forearm, then puts his hand back on the wheel. "We don't have much if we don't have hope."

I stare out the window, thinking about that, wondering if it's true.

As soon as we're out of sight of Carly's house, I say, "Pull over," determined to follow the one possible lead we do have.

"What are you doing?" Luka asks, following me when I get out and head for the trunk.

I drag out Jackson's backpack and start going through the pockets. "Looking for clues."

Luka sighs. He doesn't say anything. He doesn't have to.

"I know the chances of finding anything are slim, but I have to try," I say, pulling out an empty water bottle and a ten-dollar bill. I shove them back in and move to the next pocket.

"There won't be anything, Miki. We can't bring anything back with us when we respawn."

"Got a better idea?" I glance at him.

His mouth compresses in a thin line. He shakes his head and mutters, "Knock yourself out."

I pull out Jackson's textbooks one by one, fanning the

pages in case there's something hidden in between, then stacking the books in a neat pile. "There might be something in here that helps us find him."

Luka's quiet for a minute. I think he's going to offer up more objections. Instead, he moves closer, picks up a book from the top of the pile, and double-checks in case I missed anything.

I move to the smaller front pouch and find a paperback copy of Andrzej Sapkowski's *Blood of Elves*. My copy. The one I lent Jackson.

It's the last thing in the bag.

"There's nothing here." I start to shift everything back into Jackson's pack when Luka reaches over and taps his finger on the textbook at the top of the pile. "What?" I ask.

He stares at Jackson's law book, his dark eyes unfocused.

"Luka?" I ask.

"No, it's just—" He shakes his head. "I swear I thought of something, but it's gone." He waves a hand. "Poof."

"Don't focus on it." I push the rest of the books back into the pack, then shove it deeper into the trunk, wishing I could shove aside my disappointment with it. "Think about other stuff and it'll come to you."

"Yeah."

"You were right," I concede as he gets the Jeep moving. "That was a waste of time."

"Now what?" Luka asks, sounding bleak.

Good question. One I can't answer. But I have to find

an answer. Jackson's life may depend on us.

"We talk it out," I say. "We list everything we know, every possibility. We look for a pattern, or something that doesn't fit the pattern."

"It's gonna be a short list."

"It'll be an empty list if we don't at least try. So what do we know?"

"That he didn't respawn with the rest of us."

"And that he's alive," I say, needing to affirm it as fact.

Luka cuts me a sidelong glance. "If we figure out why he didn't come back with us, maybe we can figure out where he is."

"Maybe because he wasn't *with us* in the first place," I say. "He was on a different team."

"And if his team's still fighting—"

"Then he's still there."

I'm allowed a millisecond of hope before Luka shakes his head. "Our team wouldn't have respawned until the mission was complete."

Which means that even if he was on a different team, Jackson should have come back with us once the mission was done. "What if he got pulled on another mission?"

"Without coming back at all?" Luka frowns. "I've never heard of anyone going directly from one to another."

"That doesn't mean it isn't possible." Luka opens his mouth to answer, but before he can say anything, I contradict myself. "Yeah, it does. We always respawn at the exact second we left."

"And the world moves on from that second," Luka says. "Which means Jackson would have come back exactly when he left, at the pizza place, before getting pulled again."

"Which means we still know absolutely nothing." I slump in my seat, deflated.

CHAPTER **THREE**

"DAMN," LUKA MUTTERS AS WE PULL INTO A DRIVEWAY. "I WAS gonna just leave the keys in the mailbox."

No chance of that now. There's a woman coming out of the garage. She's tall and lean, her honey-brown hair falling loose to her shoulders. She stops and shades her eyes as she walks toward us.

"Jackson's mom?"

Luka nods. "We need to come up with an explanation of where he is, stat."

"So I guess that means we can't ask if she has any idea where her son is."

Luka snorts. "Like your dad knows where you are when you're on a mission?"

"Time's frozen when I'm on a mission, isn't it? I doubt

my dad has a clue I'm even gone."

"Ditto for Jackson's mom. It's a waste of time to ask her."

"At this point, I'm a grab-any-straw kind of girl."

He shakes his head. "I know. But there's no straw here to grab. And asking her anything is against the rules."

The rules that state we don't talk about the game outside the game. Stupid rules that make no sense. Rules we've all broken, but only with each other, never with an outsider. I tip my head back, eyes closed. "You realize that we have big neon zero when it comes to leads. Not an auspicious beginning to our rescue operation."

"Auspicious? Can you spell that?"

I glance over and punch him in the shoulder, trying to match his halfhearted attempt at humor.

Luka pushes open his door and climbs out. "Hi, Mrs. Tate."

"Hey, Luka."

I get out and linger by the passenger door, not sure if I should say hi or just fade into the background.

Jackson's mom walks over. She's close enough now that I can see her eyes—not Drau gray like Jackson's but dark, dazzling green. I've seen that color in my nightmare—Jackson's nightmare—the one he shared with me about his sister and the car accident that dragged him into the game.

There's a hint of wariness in Mrs. Tate's expression as her gaze darts to the Jeep, then back to Luka. It hits me that she's already buried one child and now here we are, in her driveway, with her son's car but without her son. That's one thing Dad always says about Sofu dying before Mom: that it's better he passed before Mom got sick, that parents aren't meant to bury their children.

I stare at my feet. Jackson's mom isn't going to bury another child. He's coming back. I'll find a way to bring him back.

"Jackson asked me to drop off his car," Luka says. "He decided to hang out with some guys."

She's quiet for a second. "Are they drinking?"

Nice one, Luka. Try to shovel us out and instead dig us in even deeper.

"No, no, nothing like that. They already had a car and he didn't want to leave his on the street."

"You didn't want to go with?" she asks, and I hear the questions she doesn't ask: *Did Luka take off because Jackson's involved with a bad crowd? Is he doing things he shouldn't?* I figure every parent thinks those things once in a while, even when they trust their kids.

"It's all good, Mrs. T. It's a group project. I'm not in their class." He's sticking to the fairy tale he already spun for Carly.

The frown fades. Mrs. Tate looks back and forth between the two of us, clearly waiting for an intro. Then she surprises me by smiling and saying, "Miki," as if she knows me. "You're the kendo champion."

I open my mouth. Close it.

Jackson talked about me.

To his mom.

I don't know how that's supposed to make me feel, but I can't deny the whisper of warmth that melts the edges of the ice that's been riding in my veins ever since I realized Jackson didn't make it back.

"Um, yeah. Used to be. Not anymore. I mean, I don't compete anymore. I still practice in the basement, though." Okay . . . could I be any more nervous meeting Jackson's mom? And exactly why am I so nervous?

Luka shifts his weight beside me—right foot to left, then back again. The silence stretches. Mrs. Tate tips her head, like she's trying to figure something out.

"We should, uh, get going," Luka says.

With a backward wave, Mrs. Tate heads for her front door and Luka and I grab our backpacks from the Jeep.

"Shouldn't we give those to his mom?" I jut my chin at the keys in Luka's hand.

He stares at the keys like they have fangs. "Shit."

I expect him to sprint for the door and hand them over. Instead he tosses them to me.

"I don't think I can spew one more lie without breaking," he says.

Leaving my pack on the drive, I jog toward the door just as Jackson's mom is closing it.

"Mrs. Tate," I call. She pauses and looks at me, leaving the door wide. I can hear a phone ringing somewhere inside the house. "Jackson's keys." I hold them up.

She holds up one finger in the universal sign for *wait*,

then gestures me inside and hurries down the hall to grab the phone. Not sure what else to do, I shrug in Luka's direction and step inside. After a few seconds' deliberation, I leave the door open behind me.

Mrs. Tate's voice carries to me, a murmur of sound without words. I wonder if she rushed to answer because she thought it might be her son calling. That's what my mom would have done—run for the phone if she thought it was me.

But I know it isn't Jackson calling.

And my mom will never again run to catch my phone call.

With a sigh I take a couple of steps deeper into Jackson's house, curious. On the outside, it's a few decades old, like mine. But inside, it's been renovated. I think a wall or two has been taken down to create an open flow from living room near the front of the house to dining room near the back. Slate tiles in the foyer. Hardwood floor stretching down the hallway and through the rooms I can see. The walls are the color of cappuccino.

I sidle in another step, my gaze darting to the staircase. I wonder if I could get away with running upstairs, finding Jackson's room, searching it. I could say I lent him some school notes. Or a textbook. Maybe a copy of *Bleach*. Or—

Right. Like I'll get away with that. Back on the driveway, I got the feeling that Mrs. Tate's already suspicious or, if not suspicious, wary.

I take a step back toward the door, which brings me

alongside a narrow, rectangular console table with a bunch of photos with brushed-nickel frames. I step a little closer, wondering if I should just drop the keys on the table and go.

But I can't resist those photos.

Leaning in, I examine each one. A little girl and an even littler boy, holding hands, smiling wide, impossibly cute. Same girl and boy a few years later, standing in the surf as it laps across white sand, bright pails in their hands. A family of four: mom, dad, older sister, younger brother with the Grand Canyon in the background. I'm guessing I'm looking at twelve-year-old Jackson. That would be around the time he was first pulled into the game.

I can't help it. I trail my fingertip lightly over the image of him, then move to the next, a picture of the girl, looking about fourteen or fifteen, sitting in a kayak, smiling at the camera, the sun reflecting off the water around her. Her hair's light brown, streaked gold by the sun, tied back in a ponytail, her eyes hidden by sunglasses.

The final picture is a close-up of the same girl's face—a face I recognize. I've seen it before, eyes closed, skin pale. I'm dragged back to the cave where dozens of clones with that exact face lay lifeless and rotting on rows and rows of gurneys. *Please don't let Jackson be somewhere like that. Please.* I wrap my arms around myself, suddenly chilled.

"We took that shortly before she . . ." Jackson's mom says softly, right beside me. I almost jump through the roof. "Oh, I'm sorry. I didn't mean to startle you."

"No, I . . . I'm sorry." I hold the keys out to her and drop them in her upturned palm. I can't stop myself from shooting a last glance at the picture.

"Lizzie," she says. "My daughter."

I nod. I almost say *I'm sorry* again. But I know how I feel when people say that to me. Why are they sorry? It isn't their fault.

Instead, I say, "Time doesn't heal all wounds. It's a lie people say to make us feel better. Make themselves feel better." As soon as the last syllable trails away, I want to reach out and catch it and take it back. I don't know why I said that.

The expression on Mrs. Tate's face is an odd combination of sad and surprised. "No," she says, drawing out the word, "time doesn't heal all wounds. But it dulls them. Remembering hurts less. The good stays bright and sharp. The bad gets pushed to a place it can't hurt us as much anymore. You'll see." She touches my arm in sympathy.

I open my mouth only to find that I don't know what to say.

Jackson must have told her about my mom. I haven't even told my dad that Jackson exists, never mind anything personal about him.

"Go on, now." A dismissal, but not an unkind one. Mrs. Tate smiles at me. "Luka's waiting."

I take a step toward her instead of away and before I know it, I'm hugging her. Really hugging her. And she's hugging me back.

30

After a second I duck my head, pull away, and bolt.

Luka has his backpack slung over one shoulder, mine over the other. I don't say a word. I just start walking and he falls in beside me.

"I thought of something while you were inside," he says after we've walked a couple of blocks. "That thing I couldn't remember earlier." He rakes his fingers back through his hair. "Tyrone told me about a guy on the team who didn't come back."

"Nothing unusual about someone not coming back. Not in our world."

Luka waits a beat and then adds, "Yeah, but then he did."

I stop walking. "What?"

"Tyrone said he thought the guy broke some rule and he got put on trial or something, and they decided to send him back in the end."

Broke a rule and got put on trial—that's why Jackson's law text triggered the memory.

"Put on trial by the Committee?"

"The Committee," he echoes. "Weird hearing you say that. So . . . every time Jackson made some snide comment about decision by committee, he wasn't just being an asshole."

"That about sums it up."

"So there actually is a committee—"

"With a capital *C*."

"And you've already met them."

I nod. "You haven't."

He shakes his head. A kid's high-pitched shriek of laughter cuts the quiet. Luka's lips thin as he glances around. "Let's go."

My turn to look around. There are other people on the street. Some kids playing basketball in a driveway. Some other little kids riding their bikes up and down the sidewalk while two moms stand on a lawn, talking and watching. Luka doesn't want to be overheard. Can't say I blame him.

"This guy," I say once we're out of earshot, "is he the one who . . . I mean, did I take his place?"

"No."

"Did you ever meet him?"

"No, he was before my time."

Which means he either died in the end or got transferred to another team. Or earned his thousand points and made it out.

"Who put him on trial? And why? What else did Tyrone say?"

"Don't know. Don't know. And, not much."

"Could you be less helpful?"

Luka shrugs.

We walk for a few minutes in silence as I mentally run through scenarios. "So you think Jackson broke one of the endless stupid rules and now he has to pay the price? That there's going to be some sort of trial?"

"Makes sense, right?"

It does.

"But what rule . . . ?"

Luka shrugs again.

"Wait . . ." I skid to a stop, worry uncoiling like a cobra. "If the Committee tries Jackson and finds him guilty, they won't be able to keep him imprisoned indefinitely in some sort of alternate dimension prison. His parents will notice him missing. They'll freak out, look for him. Call in the cops. Our teachers, our friends, they'll all notice he's gone. I don't think the Committee wants that sort of attention."

Luka makes a chopping motion with one hand. "He'll be another statistic. Another kid who ran away." He shakes his head. "But it won't come to that. If they decide he's guilty, decide not to send him back, they'll just make certain that everyone forgets."

Forgets all memories of him from the time he was conscripted to the game. Like everyone forgot Richelle. Because she was dead.

And that terrifies me. But it terrifies me less than the possibility that the Drau have him.

And then it terrifies me more.

"You think they'll kill him?" I ask. I know what the Committee's capable of. They take kids—*kids*—to fight in a war against aliens. Their explanation is that adult brains already have fully formed neural connections, which means getting pulled—making the jump into the game—is too difficult for them. But still-developing teen brains handle the shift much better. Makes sense, sort of. Doesn't change the fact that the Committee's ruthless. Any decisions they make are colored by their single-minded determination to defeat the Drau.

"If they think the rule he broke is worth killing him for, then, yeah, I think they will," Luka says.

I picture Jackson lying cold and lifeless, his gold-tinged skin gone gray, the tiny muscles that make his face so expressive gone slack. Dead. People don't look the same once the spark that powers their cells is gone. They're not really that person anymore, just the wrapping left behind.

I trip over the edge of an uneven paver and grab Luka's arm. "We have to find him. We have to—" Words fail me. I tip my head back and stare at the sky, fighting tears, feeling helpless and impotent and angry.

"Yeah." Luka sounds broken. He sounds like I feel. "And how the hell do we do that?"

I meet his gaze. "I need to see the Committee."

Luka starts walking again.

Stop, start, stop, start. I feel like we're on a malfunctioning conveyor belt—which pretty much reflects my life right now.

"How do we get to see them?"

"I think *I* have a better chance than *we*. But I don't know how I get to them. I don't have a clue. I have to—" I exhale in a rush. "I'll figure it out. I just need to think."

Luka says nothing.

Finally, I break the silence. "No suggestions? No questions?"

"No to the first. As to the second, would it be safe for me to ask? Would it be safe for you to answer? Are you allowed to tell me about them? Jackson never did." He doesn't sound bitter, just curious, and a little concerned.

It's a reminder of the whole cone-of-silence rule. No talking about the game or the Drau in the real world. I remember how earnest Luka was the first time he told me that.

Guess we're breaking all the rules now.

"I don't know. Maybe it's better that you're not asking. I don't want to break any *rules*." Luka might not sound bitter, but I do.

Rules and rules and rules. The ones Jackson told me about. The ones he implied. The ones that make no sense because they keep all of us in the dark when bringing us into the light—illuminating us with knowledge—would surely serve our mission far better than having us stumble around without a clue.

"What rule did the guy Tyrone told you about break? What was bad enough to get him put on trial?"

Luka shrugs. "Tyrone didn't say. Probably doesn't know."

I think about that for a few minutes, sorting through all the rules I've broken personally, all the ones I know other people have broken both in and out of the game. "You and

Tyrone tried to sneak stuff out to try to prove the game's real, right? And nothing happened to you. You and Jackson both talked to me about stuff outside the game, explained things, answered my questions. Rule breaking without consequences."

"Okay. Yeah. So where are you going with this?"

Where am *I going with this?* "You and I are talking about it right now and we're not getting arrested, or whatever. And when we were alone in the caves, Jackson told me a ton of stuff about the game and the Committee and the"— I lower my voice—"Drau. So if he's in trouble for breaking a rule, it has to be bad. Worse than any of that."

"Jackson told you stuff?"

Is he angry? Hurt? His tone's completely neutral so it's hard to tell.

"He told me about . . . them. About their planet. About our ancestors. But none of that's the reason he's missing, not that I can see, because he told me all of that *before* my first meeting with the Committee." And, if anything, they'd been even more forthcoming when I questioned them. So if that was the rule he'd broken, why didn't they discipline him back then?

"So it has to be something more recent," Luka says. "Something that happened in that building in Detroit."

Detroit.

Jackson shouldn't even have been there. He'd already traded me for his freedom, so he should have been out of the game.

But he wasn't.

He was there.

He took the Drau hit meant for me.

And now he's gone and I have to find him before it's too late.

CHAPTER**FOUR**

AT THE CORNER, LUKA HANDS ME MY BACKPACK AND SAYS, "My place is that way." As if I didn't know that. "You going to be okay on your own?"

Usually my hackles would go up at a question like that, but the way Luka asks, the understanding in his eyes, the fact that I know he's as freaked out as I am, makes me accept his concern with grace. I bump his shoulder with mine and say, "My dad should be home pretty soon. You?"

"Won't be on my own. My sister's having this nail-and-hair thing tonight with a bunch of her friends."

I can't miss his aggrieved tone. "Tell me you aren't the chaperone."

"Are you kidding?" His eye-widening grimace screams

horror and disbelief. "Ten twelve-year-old girls under my supervision? Not gonna happen."

"I was babysitting by the time I was twelve. Do they really need supervision?"

Before he can answer, his phone vibrates. He drags it from his pocket and listens, his face going expressionless. He says, "Yeah," and then, "Fine," before he ends the call and looks at me. "My dad. I have to go."

I nod. I don't ask why. It doesn't matter. We're teenagers. We don't always get a say in what we do or where we go. Our parents have expectations, make demands. It's just the way it is. In this case, I think his dad's demanding Luka supervise those girls. I guess I'm not a very good friend because I'm secretly smirking and I'm definitely not offering to come over and help.

As I round the corner of my street, a gust of wind catches a paper cup off the ground and sends it swirling along the road until it disappears around the side of the Sarkars' garage. Usually September in Rochester means temperatures that start out high and drop quickly—you can go to school at the start of the month wearing a T-shirt, and by the end of the month you need a parka. Well, not quite. But close enough.

My arms prickle with goose bumps, and I walk a little faster. The chill feels all the more intense because I'm exhausted, like I've lived a year in the span of a day.

All I can think of is the way I held Jackson as he lay dying from the Drau hit.

I clench my jaw. *Dying*, not *dead*. He's alive, and I'm going to find him.

Despite my resolve, my shoulders sag—not from defeat but from complete energy drain. I came back from Detroit fully healed . . . physically, anyway. But the fatigue I feel is in my bones, my heart, my soul. I've never been a fan of energy drinks, but for the first time, I can truly understand the appeal. Right now I either want to down about five of them or just crawl into my bed and sleep for a month.

But I can't. I have to figure out a plan, figure out a way to get to Jackson. On my very first mission, the one to Vegas, he told me he was going to watch out for me and just hope it didn't get him killed. I remember what I said in return: *Eight years of kendo. I won't let you get killed.*

I meant those words, then and now. I'm going to find him and I'm going to bring him home. I just need to figure a way to get in front of the Committee to argue his case. I know Jackson could communicate with them when he was in this reality. There must be a way I can, too.

I tip my head back and whisper, "Requesting an audience here, guys. Please." I swallow. "Please."

Then I climb the porch steps and drag my key out of my bag . . . and drag . . . and drag . . .

My movements are too slow, like I'm pulling my key through syrup. All my senses explode: sounds too loud, colors too bright. The weight of my backpack on my shoulder is like a ten-ton boulder. The cold air pricks my skin like tiny needles, digging deep. Sensation overload.

I'm being pulled. Panic surges. Again? So soon? I can't. I don't have it in me to fight again. Not yet.

Then another possibility hits me and the panic morphs into anticipation. The Committee. They must have heard me. I guess it was the *please* that did it.

Something bounces off the top of my foot, a sharp flick that quickly dulls into numbness. I glance down to see that it's my key ring. My backpack slides from my nerveless grasp and lands beside my foot with a thud.

The world tips and tilts, my front door falling slowly to the side. Or maybe I'm the one falling.

Dizziness slams me and I sink down onto my knees, arms outstretched, palms planted flat to break my fall. But I don't hit the wood slats of the porch. I hit grass, soft and long. I look up, knowing what I'll see: a wide, grassy clearing surrounded by trees.

I'm in the lobby.

"No," I yell. I'm not supposed to be here. I'm supposed to be in front of the Committee, getting answers that will help me find Jackson.

Instead, I've been pulled to fight the Drau. Another mission.

What happened to rest and recovery?

Rage spills toxic waste in my soul.

That's one thing the game's done for me: pushed through the muting gray fog that's shrouded my emotions since Mom died. Anger and pain always broke through the gray, but now they're so bright and sharp, they make me gasp. Be careful what you wish for.

I let my head fall forward between my outstretched arms, fighting the urge to just lie down and say, "No more." The black strap around my wrist snares my gaze. My con. It measures health in the game—a portable life bar—and just appears whenever I get pulled. Right now it's glowing dark green, shot with swirls of blue and turquoise and light green, sort of like the black opal Kelley's dad brought her from Australia when his company sent him there for a month.

The more damage I take in the game, the more the green will bleed to yellow, then orange, then red.

Full red, I'm dead.

I shove that thought to the bottom of the dark well that holds all the terrors and monsters that would love to crawl free and gnaw at my sanity.

Steer the nightmare. That's what Jackson told me to do. Control what I can and let go of what I can't.

It's the letting go part that doesn't come so easy.

Then again, maybe I shouldn't be taking Jackson's advice to heart. Look where it landed him.

I laugh, a dark, ugly sound. I feel wild and out of control, and hate every second of that. I don't want to be this girl.

I pull out the bag of tricks Dr. Andrews, my grief counselor, taught me: Breathe. Visualize. Focus.

Reaching deep, I plumb my dwindling well of determination.

I push through the pain and uncertainty and fear.

Then I get to my feet, expecting the nausea and the headache that's accompanied the jump before, but other than a slight pressure at the base of my skull, nothing. Guess I'm a pro now. Not exactly a thrilling thought.

Incoming.

The sound tunnels into my brain, my muscles, my bones, vibrating through every nerve in my body. I taste it, smell it. Crazy weird, the way the Committee communicates. Not every player in the game gets to hear them, just the team leaders. Lucky me.

Kendra's the first to arrive. Her eyes are wide, blond ringlets standing out at crazy angles, arms folded across her chest like she's trying to hold herself together. It's a pose I recognize, one I employ often. Doesn't really help when I try it. I wonder how it's working for her.

"No." She shakes her head wildly as soon as she sees me. "I can't. I can't. Not yet." Her words tumble together in a rush. "Why did we get pulled again so soon? I don't want to do this. I don't think I can do this again. Miki—" She breaks off and just shakes her head.

What makes you think you get a choice?

That's a Jacksonism. I keep it to myself. He got away with the whole I'm-a-cocky-asshole vibe. Looking back, I think that in a way, his attitude kept the rest of us from losing it. I doubt I'd pull it off half as well.

Kendra looks around and when she speaks again, her voice is even higher, the words tripping out faster. "Where's everyone else? Why are we alone? Don't tell me they didn't make it—" She runs at me and grabs my arm. "Lien," she whispers.

I put my hand over hers. "It's okay. Lien's okay. She made it. Everyone did." Well, not *everyone*. Just everyone on our team of five. It's a gift I'll gladly accept, but a bittersweet one. There were too many shattered bodies that we left behind at the end of the last mission. We had no choice. But that doesn't make it right and it doesn't make it any easier to live with.

One of the people I left behind was Jackson. And that definitely isn't right.

I swallow and look away as Kendra drops her face into her hands.

From the corner of my eye I catch flashes of movement, other teams gearing up in other clearings—mirror images of this one that I can only see if I don't try too hard. If I turn my head to look dead-on, they disappear and all I see are the trees and grass around me.

Even though they're in a different place or dimension or whatever, it's sort of comforting to know they're there. My team isn't in this on our own.

The fact that I could see them the very first time I was pulled was one of the early clues that I was different than most of the other players in the game. Not only am I one of the oh-so-special group that can hear voices in my head, but I get to see other lobbies and other teams when the rest of my team can't.

Kendra sniffles and wipes her eyes with the back of her hand. The most I can offer is a hand on her shoulder. I don't even have a tissue.

"Okay," she whispers. "I can do this. It's just so soon. I thought we'd get a break."

"So did I." But I'm quickly learning not to have any expectations when it comes to the game, not to think too much. The trick is to just play to survive.

I head for the boulders at the edge of the clearing, where five harnesses lie side by side on the ground. Next to them is a black box with five weapons nestled in foam, and a sword in a sheath lies flat beside that.

I pick up a harness, turn, and toss it to Kendra. She catches it, her chest moving with each shallow, panting breath. I focus on adjusting my own harness, figuring she needs a minute to get her head together. She better do it quickly. A minute might be all she has.

I cross the straps the way Jackson taught me, one resting across my chest and the other sitting low on my hips. Holding my hand over the box, I hover over each of the weapon cylinders in turn until one flies up to slap my palm. I shove it in the holster on my right side.

You want your weapon on your dominant side. You don't want to cross reach. It'll slow you down.

Jackson's words of wisdom. It's like he's watching my back even though he isn't here. I close my eyes, picturing his face, the too-brief flash of his ironic half smile, remembering the way it felt when he held me in the caves and told me to rest, his shoulder as my pillow.

I open my eyes and force myself to focus on this moment instead of all the moments in the past I wish I could revisit. That's not a good direction for me to go. Not right now.

A glance at Kendra tells me she's at least got her harness on even if she hasn't claimed her weapon yet. Her lower lip trembles. If I reassure her, will it make things better, or worse?

I bend and grab the sword that's lying on the ground next to the weapon box. I don't just get a weapon cylinder like everyone else; I get a blade. Perks of leadership. I guess something needs to balance out the downside.

The soft silk wrap and the weight of the hilt are familiar in my hand from all my years of kendo, but the actual blade isn't like any of the swords I've used—or seen—in the past. It isn't a wooden *bokken* or a bamboo *shinai* like I used in practice and competition. This one is a *shinken katana*, a real sword, and while I've seen some gorgeous ones before, none were quite like this. The blade is black, smooth, like glass. It doesn't bend or break, and as I found out in Detroit, it cuts through Drau like they're made of butter.

The thought of that still makes my stomach turn even though it's them or me.

I did a book report last year on *American Sniper*. It was written by a U.S. Navy SEAL about his tours of duty—nine, I think. I remember reading an interview with him where he said he didn't think about his targets as people.

He was killing *people*, but he couldn't think of them that way, couldn't wonder if they had a wife or kids or parents at home. He was there to keep his guys safe. Every enemy he shot meant they didn't get the chance to kill one of his team.

I didn't get it back then.

I think I get it now, though. Them or me.

The ugly irony? After everything the guy had lived through, all the dangers he'd faced, he was shot and killed on a gun range somewhere in Texas.

My breath hitches. After everything I've lived through now, if I die in the game, I'll be hit and killed by a rusted-out speeding truck.

There's some deep, philosophical message in there somewhere.

I don't get the chance to decipher it. The Committee pushes knowledge into my head, sound and texture and scent that exist only in the neurons firing in my brain: *Incoming.*

CHAPTER**FIVE**

TYRONE SHOWS UP WITH JAW CLENCHED AND HANDS FISTED. He's tall and handsome, with smooth brown skin and full lips, his dark, tightly curled hair trimmed close. His eyes—all our eyes—are blue in the game, but mine are the only ones that remain that intense shade of indigo in real life. When we aren't in the game, Luka's eyes are brown. I think Tyrone's and Lien's are, too. Not sure about Kendra. With her pale skin and fair hair, I'd guess her eyes are blue or gray.

Luka's next. He arrives looking bewildered, then pissed, his whole body tensing as he registers that, yeah, we're back here again. "This is bullshit," he snarls.

"Got that right," Tyrone says, then glances at me. "Jackson?" he asks, his expression unreadable. He and

Jackson have been watching each other's backs for two years, and their relationship's complicated—part intense dislike, part respect, part some sort of weird guy version of affection. Tyrone's still mourning Richelle's death. Losing Jackson . . .

I can't think about that.

"I believe he's alive," I say.

"Believe," Tyrone repeats, then shifts his attention to Luka. "You believe that?"

"Yeah," Luka says.

"Then I'll believe it, too." Tyrone walks over and stares down at me, his full lips pulled in a grim line. "You okay?"

I nod, but can't get a single word past the lump in my throat. I glance over at Kendra. She's standing to one side, arms wrapped tight around her stomach, shoulders hunched forward. I'm more okay than she is, anyway.

When Lien appears, Kendra runs to her with a cry and they weave their fingers together, Lien lowering her head as she whispers to Kendra. It reminds me of the first time I ever saw them, how they stood so close their shoulders touched, warding off the world by forming a wall of two. Everyone else on their original team was killed. They're the only ones left. But they're part of *my* team now and I mean to make certain we all stay safe.

A tremor runs through me. How did I end up responsible for four other lives?

I hear snippets of their whispered conversation.

" . . . can't do this . . ."

"... then you jump in and take the ... be okay ..."

"... what if we get caught ..."

Lien catches me watching them and her expression goes completely blank. She runs her hand through her sleek, dark hair, then shakes off the droplets of water that cling to her fingers. "I just got out of the shower." She gestures at her yoga pants and flip-flops. "Guess I'm lucky I had time to pull on some clothes. Can you imagine if I got pulled five minutes sooner?"

Luka looks her up and down and waggles his brows. "I'd like to have seen that."

Kendra shoots him a look I can't read, but Lien's glare carries a clear message.

The rest of us laugh even though it wasn't that funny. Comic relief.

But Lien's question gets me thinking. I *did* get pulled five minutes sooner. Why not Lien? Because the leaders get pulled first? Or because the Committee knew exactly what she was doing—exactly what each of us was doing—at any given second? Do they watch us while we sleep? While we're in the bathroom? The possibility of that sends a shiver down my spine on prickly little centipede legs.

"Got a bad feeling about this," Tyrone says, crossing his arms over his chest as he bends one knee so the sole of his shoe rests against the boulder. "Last mission sucked."

"That it did," Luka agrees.

Kendra nods and Lien huffs a short laugh. Unanimous agreement. I think that's a first.

The last mission was one of firsts: first time any of us had worked with another team; first time there were so many Drau in one place; first time that the battle was truly a battle and not a skirmish.

My first time as leader.

The first time Jackson didn't make it out.

It takes me a second to realize I'm clenching my fists so tight that my nails are digging into my palms.

"We come back healed in body but not in spirit. We need some downtime or we're going to make mistakes. Deadly ones. This is too soon," Tyrone says.

I shake off the feeling of déjà vu. Tyrone said that when we got pulled for the first time after Richelle died. He was standing by one of the boulders, his voice hoarse and raw from crying, and Jackson told us we had a job to do, that we'd do it. He didn't need to add, *Or we'll die.*

"Doesn't matter how soon it is," Luka says. "Obviously they don't care." He sounds angry and afraid, and I have zero doubt that he's mirroring the emotions of the whole team.

I can't let him sink any lower. His life—all our lives—depends on focus and commitment. The pit of despair isn't exactly the ideal place for us to be. Luka needs to get his head in the game. We all do. Being angry with the Committee isn't going to lead to anything good.

"Maybe they don't have the luxury of caring," I say. "You think they get to pick when there'll be a Drau attack? You think they're choosing the time line of this war? I doubt they get a weekly schedule from Drau high command."

Lien snorts. I have everyone's attention, so I forge ahead, spinning an idea as I go, with no clue where I'm going to end up. "They have a mission that needs completing, so they pull a team to complete it. We're that team. But we're not alone." I look at each of them in turn. "How many others were there in Detroit? I lost count, and I guess the actual number doesn't really matter. What matters is that there are others gearing up right now to head out. They're going to fight. Just like us. So the world can survive." I pause. "I know it sounds crazy when I say it. A few groups of teenagers are all that stand against mankind's annihilation. But crazy or not, it is what it is."

"Not so crazy," Kendra says softly. "My great-grandfather was eighteen when he went overseas to fight against Hitler. He was a gunner in World War Two. He used to tell us stories about what he called *the boys* . . . his platoon, or whatever. They were all young. Just like us."

"My great-grandfather was too young to fight." I decide not to mention that he spent part of that war interned in a War Relocation camp. His loyalty and that of his parents was brought into question because of their Japanese ancestry. War has a way of amping up paranoia and hate and prejudice.

"Miki, how do you know there are other teams?" Luka asks.

"You know it, too. You saw them in Detroit."

"I think he means how do you know there are others gearing up right now," Tyrone says.

"I can see them. I can see mirror-image lobbies just like ours and I can see the teams moving around in them."

Luka's brows shoot up. "Seriously?"

I shrug.

"Wallhacks," Tyrone says. I lift my brows and he explains, "In Counter-Strike a wallhack lets a player see through a wall, see stuff that's usually obscured."

"There's a name for this?" I ask. "A gaming term? Weird."

Tyrone shrugs.

Luka cocks his head to the side. "Wait, I remember . . . first time you got pulled, right? You kept asking who *they* were, and I thought you meant Tyrone and Richelle. But you were asking about the other teams."

I nod.

"Why you?" Tyrone asks, pushing off the boulder and coming to stand closer as he looks down at me.

"Genetics." It's as simple and as complicated as that. Jackson explained it to me the night he climbed in my bedroom window. "We all have some level of alien DNA. I get a double dose because I have a specific set of alleles."

Tyrone and Lien nod, but the others look confused.

"Alleles are like different forms of the same gene," I clarify. "So we all have alien genes, but it's like mine are pumped up on steroids."

"Why?" Tyrone asks.

"Luck of the draw?" I spread my hands in an I-don't-know gesture. "I think it's because I have alien ancestors on both sides of my gene pool. My mom's side and my dad's."

"My great-grandfather's stories were usually about boys who died," Kendra says, as if we hadn't moved on from that topic. Her tone sounds odd, sort of singsong, like she's not quite in the same moment as the rest of us. Uneasiness uncoils in my gut as I study her expression. It's blank, smooth. Too smooth. I'd like to see a little emotion there, even if it's fear.

"He told us about how they died. In the trenches. On the beach. On long, cold hikes through enemy territory. They died." She looks at Lien and continues, her tone devoid of inflection, "I can't do this again. I'm afraid. I don't want to die."

The words don't wig me out. Afraid is normal. We all feel it. It's her flat expression and tone that get me. I'm worried she isn't quite present and that could put us all at risk.

"Kendra," I say. "You can do this. You can." *You have to. Or you'll die,* I don't say. I don't need to. She knows.

Her eyes narrow. Her chin juts forward.

"*You're* all still here," she says, her tone venomous now, "but *we* lost our whole team. Everyone is dead. You don't know what that's like!"

I close the space between us in three steps. Kendra shrinks back like she thinks I mean to hit her. Lien shifts so she's half in front of Kendra. I sidestep her and move closer still.

"The only things I plan to hit her with are words," I snap at Lien, then focus on Kendra, my voice low and even. "Do not tell me what I do and don't know. And just to be clear, we are *not* all still here. We've lost teammates, too. I replaced a boy who died. You and Lien replaced more teammates we've lost. Richelle's dead. Jackson's gone. And I knew a little something about loss and grief before I ever got to this game."

Kendra takes another step back. I didn't mean to make her defensive, but I can see why she is. Damn. My team's losing it. I need to do something to stop the fracture, but I don't know what.

I wish Jackson were here for so many reasons, not the least of which is so that I don't have to do this. I'd have thought that after what we faced together in Detroit, this team would be a tight unit, but, if anything, that experience seems to have driven us apart.

Kendra flinches when I reach for her. I ignore that and take her hand—the one that isn't clasped in Lien's—and push my fingers between hers until they're woven together. I hold my other hand out to Luka. He steps up and we both look over at Tyrone.

"I ain't holding your hand, bro," Tyrone says to Luka, brows lifting, head jerking back.

"Afraid of a little skin on skin?" Luka asks with a laugh. He lunges for Tyrone, managing to catch his pinkie finger.

Tyrone grunts and turns to throw an arm across Luka's shoulders as he steps and turns, colliding with him chest-to-chest in a typical man hug. They thump each other on the back. I almost expect them to pull out their clubs and learn to make fire.

"You won't hold hands but you'll go all huggy- and kissy-face?" Lien asks.

Luka puckers up and makes kissing noises until Tyrone slams him with a fist to the shoulder.

"Boys." Lien snorts.

Kendra lets out a watery giggle, then reaches for Tyrone so she's holding his hand and Lien's.

The humor's welcome. They're all letting off a little steam. But we don't have much time. Any second now, the scores will show up and then we'll be pulled into whatever nightmare the Drau have lined up for us.

Luka grabs Lien's free hand. She glares at him but doesn't pull away. I reach for Tyrone, closing the circle.

"It's not about *our* team, *your* team." I hold up my linked hands. "One unit. Get it? All of us are *one* team." I give it a second so they can think about that and so I can get my words straight in my head. I need to say this right and I'm terrified I'll say it wrong. I'm not a leader. I'm not.

I'm a loner.

Even during eight years of kendo, I was a part of the team, but always *apart*. Because I was Sofu's granddaughter. Because I was the only girl. But now I'm not just on a team, I'm the one they're looking at to keep them alive.

I glance at Luka. "I'm not Jackson. I don't have all the answers. But I'm going to try."

I press my lips together, searching for the right words. I understand Jackson so much better now, his whole every-man-for-himself thing. He got everyone out alive by telling them to watch their own ass. Then he put himself at risk every time watching it for them. But no matter how good he was—is—Jackson couldn't save everyone every time. Our battle is with aliens who are faster, stronger, and probably smarter.

"We made it through Detroit," Tyrone says.

"That was more stroke of luck than stroke of leadership genius." When I think of it like that, I don't think we stand a chance.

Which is why I can't let myself think of it like that. Can't let myself think of the choices I may be forced to make, just like Jackson had to choose between saving me or saving Richelle.

And I know there were others he couldn't save before her.

I don't know how he lives with those losses. And I don't plan to find out.

"We are going in because we have to," I say, meeting each of their gazes in turn, taking my time. "The Drau are going down. And we're all coming back out again. We. Are. All. Coming. Back." I need to believe that. Just like I believed I'd win in kendo against boys who were stronger and faster than me. Just like I believed I'd survive Mom's death and the gray fog of depression that followed.

I have to stop the negative flow of thoughts, the conviction that I'm not capable.

I *will* survive.

My team *will* survive.

The whole fricking world *will* survive.

CHAPTER SIX

"SCORES," I SAY, KNOWING THEY'RE COMING BEFORE THEY appear.

I turn toward the center of the clearing, along with everyone else. The air shimmers like it's hitting hot pavement, then a glossy black rectangle materializes and hovers in midair, the front face of it like a giant thin-screen TV. It isn't really there. If I touch it, the shape will bend and contort, then resume its appearance when I take my fingers away—I tried that the first time I saw it, after Richelle died.

A picture of me, bounded by a black border, appears on the screen—not a photo, more of a 3-D rendering of me the way I'd look if I really were part of a video game. 3-D me is wearing the clothes I wore on our last mission—I glance down—the same clothes I'm still wearing now. But in the picture, they're torn and bloodied. The image spins upside down, then right side up, before zooming to the top left corner of the screen. I know it won't stay there for long.

We earn points for taking out the Drau: five for a sentinel, ten for a specialist, fifteen for a leader, twenty for a commander. Extra points for head-shots and multi-hits and stealth hits. We get charged points for weapons and we lose points for injuries. If a player gets a thousand points, they're out. Free. At least, that's the rumor.

We're ranked according to cumulative score, highest at the top. My score won't be the highest, and it doesn't matter.

Because a thousand points or a hundred thousand, I don't get to leave. Leaders don't get that option.

The only way I can get out is by finding another leader to trade in to take my place. I have no idea where to even start looking for someone like me, someone whose human DNA is mixed with that of alien ancestors through both their mom and their dad, like mine. Someone with the exact right set of genes, who can hear the Committee in her head and see the other teams in mirror-image clearings. And even if I did, could I do that to someone? Could I condemn her, or him, to this life?

No. I'm not that desperate yet.

But I get why Jackson did it. He's been running in this hamster wheel for five endless years. I might be that desperate if I make it that long.

The next picture's 3-D Luka, then Tyrone, then Kendra

and Lien. Each time, the image turns end over end and shoots to the corner, knocking my picture down a notch.

Two columns of white numbers appear beside our names. The first is our score from the last mission; the second is a cumulative score for the entire time we've been in the game. Our pictures are lined up with the highest cumulative score—Luka's—at the top, and the lowest—mine—at the bottom. I study the numbers, feeling like something's off.

It isn't because my score's the lowest. Jackson's scores were always at the bottom, too. But despite his crappy score, he was the one who had the prestige badge next to his name—a bronze star with a smaller star at the center—because he was team leader. There's a badge next to my name now. It's a simple bronze circle. Guess I haven't graduated to stars.

After Luka is Tyrone, then Kendra, then Lien. Even though Tyrone's been in the game longer than Luka, he purposely kept his score low because for the longest time, he didn't want out because the game was his chance to see Richelle. And his chance to do research. He was planning to create a video game based on his experiences and get rich off it.

After Richelle died, I think his plans changed.

I hate this. The pictures. The scores. They trivialize us, what we do, the risks we take. Our lives are at stake on every mission. The Committee claims they set everything up as a game because they needed something accessible, something teens could relate to. I sort of bought their explanation at the time, but it just doesn't sit right with me anymore.

This isn't a game. They shouldn't treat it as one.

That's what Jackson's been saying all along.

I study the numbers, trying to figure out what's bugging me. Something's off, but I can't figure out what it is.

Jump in thirty. That's the Committee, mainlining thoughts directly to my brain whether I want them there or not.

We respawn in a room—big, dim, smooth gray walls. Metal? I touch the closest one, then tap my fingernail against the surface. Yeah, metal.

In front of us is a huge corrugated door, the black rectangle centered above it lit with glowing red bars. No, not bars . . . an LED number: seven. Beside the door is a keypad with a slot for an ID card.

"Where are we?" Lien whispers.

I hold a finger to my lips. I want complete silence until we know if it's safe to speak. I point over her shoulder so she'll see what I see. There are two black sedans parked against the far wall. The license plates have three kanji— Japanese letters—followed by a number and, below that, larger numbers. So either we're in Japan, or these cars were imported with license plates intact. I'm not sure it matters, but I store the info away in case I need it later.

Catching Luka's eye, I nod toward the corrugated door

as I pull my weapon cylinder. It's smooth and cool and instantly contorts its shape, conforming to the contours of my grasp. He gets the message and pulls his weapon cylinder. The others take the hint and do the same, backs to one another, alert for any threat. I walk over and rest my hand on the hood of the first car. Cold. Same with the second. So they haven't been driven in at least forty-five minutes or an hour. Again, I don't know if that info is relevant, but I gather what I can.

I check my con. There's a rim of green around the outside to measure my health, but most of the screen is taken up with a live feed of our surroundings. In the left corner is a small rectangle—a map of the room—and within it, a clump of five green triangles. Us. I hold up my wrist and gesture for everyone else to show me theirs—all green, no maps or live feeds. That means I'm the only one getting instructions. The Committee wants us to stick together. For now.

I move to the keypad by the door and stare at the numbers.

"Safe to talk?" Luka says against my ear, so soft I feel the words more than hear them.

I listen for any sound, anything at all. Nothing. If we can't hear the Drau, I'm going to work with the idea that they can't hear us, either. Actually, it isn't just an idea; it's a certainty. Perks of being the leader. The Committee dumps knowledge in my head: *no threat.* Not yet. But they're out there, and they're close.

"Safe to talk," I say.

Lien looks around, frowning. "This place gives me the creeps."

"Yeah." Tyrone nods, and his agreement's enough to snag my attention.

"Why?" I ask.

"There's something familiar about it. Something weird," Lien says.

"Familiar like . . . you've been here before? On a mission?"

"No." She shakes her head. "But I feel like I've *seen* this place before. Does that make sense?"

"Does to me," Luka says. "I feel the same way."

"*Resident Evil,*" Tyrone says. "Or maybe *Half Life.*"

Luka frowns. "Yeah. Not quite, but close."

"Big elevator. Two cars. Massive metal doors. Underground facility." Tyrone pauses, then says to Luka, "I'm the guy who's here to save the world."

Luka snorts. "I thought I was the good guy."

"No, no," Tyrone says. "You're on the team with the supersecret underground base. I'm the guy breaking into the base. That makes me the good guy."

"What are you talking about?" Lien snaps.

"*Splinter Cell: Chaos Theory,*" Luka says.

"A game?" Lien asks, incredulous. "You're quoting lines from a game?"

"Wait," I say, holding up my hand, palm forward. I turn my attention back to Tyrone. "You're saying you've seen this in a game? This exact place?"

"Not exactly this place but something like it. The elaborate underground base." He shrugs. "It's a common trope."

I try to figure out why it matters. It shouldn't. We're in a big elevator leading into the ground. Games have big elevators leading into the ground. So do movies and books and manga. It *is* a common trope. But the whole thing has a creepy vibe.

"Heads up, eyes open," I say. "If something's off about this place, at least we have a warning, right?"

"There's no *if*," Lien says.

"So what now, CL?" Tyrone asks, and he and Luka exchange one of those I'm-a-guy-and-that-makes-me-awesome looks.

I hold on to my patience by a thread. "CL?"

"Clan leader. That's you. We're the clan," Lien explains, her tone terse.

"Nice," Luka says, "and a little surprising."

She shoots him a passive look. "What? You're not the only person who's ever picked up a controller."

"I thought clans are teams that play other teams in FPS or MMO," I say. "You counting the Drau as a team?"

"Been reading up on first-person shooters and massive multiplayer online?"

"I checked out a couple of sites in case they might help me understand the layout of the game. Not that I've had much time to work on that yet. But I will, when we get back." I say that last sentence like it's a done deal.

"Task left unfinished," Lien says, then elaborates when I glance at her. "You left a task unfinished so you'll make it back to finish it." I notice that Kendra's hovering close beside her, saying nothing, staring at the ground.

"I thought that's why ghosts come back . . ." Luka says.

Lien shoots him a cool glare. "I modified the superstition. It's like we're ghosts here. So we go back to finish the unfinished."

"Oooookay," Tyrone says.

"Did *you* leave a task unfinished?" I ask Lien.

She runs her fingers through her still-damp hair. "Blow-dryer's still plugged in."

Kendra slams the side of her thigh with her fist. "How can you be so calm?" she explodes. "Talking about bullshit? Even joking around?" She glares at us, tears shimmering in her eyes, then she rounds on Lien. "How can you chat with them about superstitions and stupid gaming terms as if they matter?" Her words tumble out in a rush. "As if we aren't going to—"

"Get started on our mission," I cut her off before she can finish the thought. None of us needs a reminder of our mortality. We know. Each and every one of us knows.

"You're right, Kendra," Tyrone says, conciliatory, holding up his hands, palms out. "We should save the chatty-chat."

I nod. "Break time's over. Let's move." I'm channeling Jackson. I understand so much more about him now, about the way he acted and the things he did. I only hope

I get the chance to tell him that, to feel his strong arms close around me once more, to breathe the scent of his skin and rest my ear against his heart just to listen to the steady, solid beat.

"Move how?" Lien asks. "You got an idea to get us out of here? Or any idea of where *here* is?"

"We're in an elevator," I say as I examine the keypad by the door. I don't have an ID card and I don't know the code.

"Yeah, I guessed that much." Lien plants her fists on her hips. "Got any idea as to the code?"

I key in a few sequences: 1-2-3-4. 4-3-2-1. 1-3-2-4. 4-2-3-1. We could be here for a week at this rate. I glance at the LED number overhead, and try: 7-7-7-7.

Nothing happens.

"You mind?" Tyrone asks, stepping up beside me.

"Knock yourself out."

He enters 3-2-7-2. Luka snorts.

"Three-*A-R-C*," Lien says. "Add UNLOCK and it's a cheat code for *Call of Duty*."

When the door stays shut, I say, "Why *COD*? Why not *Halo*, or . . . I don't know . . . *Donkey Kong*? There are probably hundreds of cheat codes for every game. How do we pick just one?"

"Try *Resident Evil*," Lien says.

Tyrone tries some codes. The door stays firmly shut.

Kendra's pacing circles. I have a feeling that if we don't get out of here soon, I'm going to lose her to whatever black hole her inner dialogue is dragging her to. I study the keypad.

"We could try—"

"No more codes," I say, cutting Luka off as I signal Tyrone to make room for me. I trade places with him and trace my fingertips along the numbers, hoping the Committee will just feed me the knowledge in that freaky, crazy way of theirs. No such luck. I'm on my own.

"If I can't do this with finesse, I'll try force." Reaching back, I grasp the handle of my sword. I slip the tip of the black blade into the card reader, plant the heel of my palm against the end, layer my other hand on top, and ram it in with all my might. A shower of sparks erupts from the casing, followed by a crackling noise. But the massive metal door stays shut.

"That was effective," Lien says. There's an edge to her tone, and while it grates, I do understand. She's been at this longer than me, she's a transfer from a team that was wiped out, and despite the fact that we made it through the last mission, she has no real reason to have tons of faith in me.

Luka bristles and looks like he's about to lace into her. I give a tiny shake of my head. He frowns, but keeps quiet. Yay for small miracles.

"Patience, grasshopper," I say to Lien.

She narrows her eyes. "Condescending, much?"

And here I was thinking the whole hand-holding thing had rallied the old team spirit. Not so much.

"No. My grandfather used to say that to me as a joke. It

was from some old TV show. No condescension intended."

She looks like she's going to say something more, but in the end she keeps quiet.

I play with the settings on the side of my weapon cylinder, the way Jackson did to break into the cold room in the caves. When I fire, the black surge isn't greasy and oily; it's a thin, powerful stream that hits the control pad where it hurts.

A second geyser of sparks erupts, bigger and brighter than the first. The front of the keypad falls free, hanging on by a single, melted screw, and the wires within spark and flare. A horrible chemical smell rises from the mass of heated metal and melting plastic.

Lien smirks. "And that was equally—"

"Effective," Luka cuts her off as the door cracks open in the middle, letting in a narrow stripe of bright, white light.

CHAPTER**SEVEN**

LUKA AND TYRONE CURL THEIR FINGERS INTO THE NARROW crack and slowly, slowly drag the door open, revealing a patch of light and a sliver of white floor and white walls.

I signal for quiet, then point at Luka and Lien and cock my head to the right. I point at Tyrone and Kendra and cock my head to the left.

For an instant, Kendra hesitates and I think she's going to argue. But I can't pair her with Lien. Enough of this our-team-your-team crap. We are one team and she needs to get that right now. And Lien and Luka need to stop glaring at each other. Pairing them up seems like a good plan.

I stare Kendra down and she falls in beside Tyrone. She closes her eyes for a second and takes a deep breath before opening them again and offering a tiny nod. I guess it's her way of telling me she knows what I'm doing and she knows I'm right.

I hold up my thumb and two fingers, then just two fingers, and finally, one finger alone. We explode out the door, my team going right and left, me going straight.

"Clear," I call.

"Clear," Luka echoes back at me just before Kendra says, "Clear."

I take a second to evaluate our surroundings. The walls aren't white; they just looked that way in the initial burst of light. They're pale gray, polished concrete, smooth, a little shiny. The ceiling overhead appears to be made of corrugated metal—like the door we just burst through—with rows and rows of bright inset lights.

"Still weirdly familiar," Lien says softly.

Luka frowns. "Yeah, sort of like *Halo*, but not quite."

Tyrone shakes his head. "More like *Resident Evil*, I'd say."

"Creepy," Lien says.

"They're close," Kendra whispers. "I can feel them."

We can all feel them. My gut writhes with the certainty that the Drau are just around the next corner or maybe the one after that. Too close for comfort.

When we were in Vegas, Tyrone told me that when we get dropped in, it creates some sort of rift that alerts the Drau. In highly populated areas, we get dropped fairly close because the other people around can help mask our presence. If we enter the mission in a more isolated spot—like the caves—we respawn farther away to decrease the risk that the Drau will pinpoint our location right away. For an added layer of stealth, our cons scramble our signal once we're here, and that makes it even tougher for the Drau to find us.

Where we are now definitely doesn't feel like a populated area, so we ought to be far from the Drau nest, not right on top of it. But my whole body's on alert, every neuron pulsing the word: *enemy*. From the intensity of the urge to flee, I'm guessing we'll run into them within minutes.

"Clusterfrack of the first degree," Tyrone mutters.

Kendra and Lien exchange a veiled look, and Lien whispers, "You do what I told you."

Kendra nods.

I hope Lien gave her some advice on how to deal, because the possibility of her freaking out on a mission is terrifying. It could put all our lives at risk.

My con tells me which direction to go. I point and say, "Stay behind me. Stay paired up, no matter what. Follow my lead. From here out, stay quiet."

Luka looks like he wants to argue. I suspect some inner well of machismo makes him want to offer to take point, or makes him want to point out that I'm not partnered, that there's no one to watch my back. But he swallows any argument because my con's the one telling us where to go, which means everyone else gets to follow, like it or not.

The corridor's wide and cold. We move forward silently, except for this weird flapping noise . . . I turn and glare at Lien's flip-flops. They're pink with white cartoon kitties festooned with a bow on top. I stare at them, feeling very much like we're a bunch of kids and not at all like a group of soldiers who can save the world.

Lien steps out of the flip-flops, leaving them behind. I wonder if they'll materialize with her back in the real world when we're done here. Not ideal, her going barefoot, but the noise and the risks of trying to run in flip-flops aren't ideal, either. Barefoot on cold concrete's better than dead.

Still following my con, we go straight, then left, then left again. I feel like a mouse in a maze. This place is just a jumble of corridors. Every hundred feet or so, we get to a three-way split with hallways running at right angles to one another. We pass a few doors but not many. So why all the corridors? Where do they lead?

We round another corner and another. I stop dead.

Ahead of us is a huge group of Drau, glowing like hundred-watt bulbs. They're in neat rows, weapons drawn, aiming down the corridor.

Facing the wrong way.

All we see are their backs. I didn't just feel like we were walking in circles. We *were* walking in circles. The Committee brought us around behind the enemy.

I'm not a look-a-gift-horse-in-the-mouth kind of girl. I signal my team to fan out to the sides, backs to the walls, firing as we move.

The Drau barely realize we're here before we take

down the rear line. I'm guessing about a dozen of them get sucked into the oily, black, speed-of-light ooze that comes from our weapons. They're swallowed whole. My stomach turns as two get pulled in at once, limbs melting together, fusing them into one writhing, shrieking entity. Their comrades fire, raining pellets of light and pain down on us like a storm.

Chaos.

They move at impossible speeds.

We hit them hard with the element of surprise, but that's gone now. And there are way more than a dozen of them.

Luka and Tyrone work in unison, shooting, taking down anything that comes at them.

I aim. Shoot. My shot wings one of the Drau, but doesn't take it down. Lien's right beside me, but it's Kendra who fires, killing it before I can take a second shot. There's barely time to nod my thanks before I have to take down the next one and the next.

"Fall back," I order, staying in front and covering my team while they back up. Luka's right behind me, covering me. I want to give him hell. He isn't exactly following orders, but I'll save it for a moment that isn't quite so . . . hectic.

We back around a corner.

"Stay with Lien," I snarl at Luka. I'm surprised that he listens. He falls back a couple of steps so he's shoulder-to-shoulder with her, and I catch a glimpse of Tyrone and

Kendra a few steps behind them.

I do a quick assessment of our surroundings, trying to pick a direction. My con's no help. It's showing five green triangles clumped together, but no hint of the best route to take.

The Drau surge forward, almost on us.

My blood races, my heart jackhammering in my chest. I have to choose. Right now.

"That way." I pick a corridor at random. "Go!"

They go.

Taking down as many of the enemy as I can, I back away as I shoot and shoot, my kendo sword held at the ready.

There's a cry behind me. I don't dare look back.

"Luka?" I call.

"Lien took a hit to the thigh."

Damn. "How bad?"

"I'm still standing." And still sounding bitched out, which at this moment makes me very happy.

The Drau advance as we retreat.

We're all firing—us, them. Despite their speed, we hold them back, mostly because we've moved to a narrowed corridor that isn't wide enough for them to all come at us at once. But how long can we hold them off? What the hell was the Committee thinking, sending us in here alone?

They push toward us, a wedge driving us apart, me and Luka and Lien into one branching corridor, Tyrone and Kendra into another. We were a unit of five, and now we're a fractured five.

We don't stand a chance.

I stomp on that thought like the crawling slug it is. I can't think like that, not even for a second.

A Drau comes at me, so close I can see the jagged edges of its teeth. Its form is basically humanoid—arms, legs, head, face—but that's where any similarity to a human ends. It's a pure, eye-numbing white, the surface of its body polished and smooth, like opaque glass that flows and glides.

It's beautiful.

And deadly.

A predator that wants to make me its prey.

I almost make the mistake of looking in its eyes, drowning in them, dying in them. At the last second, I jerk my gaze away and hack with my sword at the same time as I fire.

I take it down, but not without a price. Pinpricks of pain erupt across my shoulders and upper chest. With a cry, I stumble back, shoot, retreat. I try to catch sight of Luka and Lien. But they're gone.

I'm alone, cut off from my team by the sheer number of Drau that fill the space as they surge into the gaps created by their downed comrades. I feel like they're herding me in the direction of their choice, and each time I try to veer aside, they force me back the opposite way.

There's no chance to assess or plan. All I can do is keep

moving, keep killing, because the option is to stand still and die here.

I stay close to the wall so they can't get behind me. My weapon cylinder hums, black sludge eating my enemies whole. I hack at sunlight-bright bodies with my sword, not even pretending to maintain proper stance or form. There's no honor in this. Only ugly, raw death.

My arms burn in all the places that their light droplets hit me, leaving scorched holes in the sleeves of my shirt and open wounds in my skin. Blood trickles down my arms, drips off my fingertips to the floor.

There's one of me and maybe ten of them. They could take me down anytime. They don't. They're toying with me. Playing with their prey.

Fear is like an avalanche, a heavy, crushing weight, tumbling and roaring until there's nothing but blinding, white terror.

A burst of pain explodes above my eye. My vision blurs as I fire again and again, aiming at nothing, reckless and desperate.

I won't die here. I can't.

Instinct takes over, honed by eight years of kendo training. Sofu's voice echoes in my thoughts. *Your opponent strikes and you do not merely defend. You counterattack. Oji waza. But better that you do not wait. You initiate. You attack. Shikake waza.*

With a *kiai* shout, I run directly at them instead of away, adrenaline pushing me to a place I never would have imagined. Pinpricks of light rain down on me, pain so bright it blurs my thoughts. It isn't like in the movies. I don't run up the wall or leap ten feet in the air and do aerial cartwheels. My soles slam against the floor; my heart slams against my ribs.

I fire, up close and personal, the lightning-fast black ooze eating my opponents while their screams flay ribbons from my psyche and the light from their weapons flays my skin. I don't look into their shimmering eyes—mercury gray, indescribably lovely, terrifying, and deadly. I don't give them the chance to suck out the electrical action potentials that power my nerves, my muscles, my brain. My life.

From the corner of my eye I catch a flash of movement. I spin, feeling like the whole world's slowed down and there's just me and the Drau standing an arm's length away, lowering its weapon to firing position. This close, the blast will blow me away.

I lift my sword so it's pointing back and up at a forty-five-degree angle; then I step forward and swing at the Drau's forehead. *Men-uchi*—the move is as familiar to me as breathing. The black blade sinks deep in the Drau's skull. With a cry I tighten my hold on the silk-wrapped handle, yanking the weapon free as I shoot black ooze to my left, annihilating yet another enemy.

Glowing forms fill my field of vision, too many of them, all firing at me. All wanting me dead.

I wish I had a shield. I wish—

A Drau comes at me, a blur of light. I feint left, right, surge forward, and duck.

I cry out in rage and desperation, forcing all my strength into a *tsuki* thrust, sending my sword through the Drau's chest, through its back, impaling it. I hold the squirming body before me as a shield, bracing my elbow against the arc of my hip bone to help me bear the weight. Adrenaline and terror make me strong.

Them or me.

My mantra.

Grunting and gasping under the weight of the Drau pinned at the end of my sword, I back up step by step. It stops struggling. The tops of its feet drag along the floor. The shots of the other Drau fall on their comrade, making his corpse jerk and twist as I shoot a stream of black death that swallows them whole.

My arm and shoulder are on fire, screaming under the weight. Nausea curls in my belly at the horror of what I've become. I push it down, lock it away.

There are fewer Drau now. I lower my sword and let the body slide off as I back into another corridor. They follow. I cut them down with my weapon cylinder, shooting anything that moves, sweat trickling down my spine.

I've lost any sense of orientation. I don't know where my team is or if they're okay. There's no chance to look at my con and see if there are still five green triangles in place.

Please, I whisper silently. *Please.*

Opportunity presents itself in the form of a door. I shove it open and slam it behind me, panting, shaking. A lock. I turn it, nearly sobbing with relief. They'll get through it. I know that. But at least I've bought myself some time.

Minutes.

Seconds.

I glance at my con. Two green triangles somewhere to the left of me, so close together they almost overlap. Two more triangles a bit to the left and behind, touching at a single vertex. My team's alive and still paired up. The frame of my screen's dark yellow edging to orange. My health bar's not looking so healthy.

Tears drip down my right cheek. I lift my hand to swipe at them and it comes away red. Not tears. Blood.

I jump as something slams against the door. It shakes on its frame, but holds. For how long? I hear a sizzling sound, like bacon in a hot pan, and I figure they're trying to fry the lock. I need to find a place to make a stand.

The room is massive. Rows of metal shelves stacked with black barrels run a grid with aisles in between. I run down the first, stop, turn left, keep running, turn right. My one thought is to get as far from the door and the Drau as I can. Is there another exit? I try to picture the corridor and fail. But I do remember that when we first left the elevator, I noticed that there weren't many doors along the hallways.

I'm almost at the far wall. The sound of Drau bodies

slamming against the door carries to me.

I dart right again.

Hide? Keep going?

Terror clouds my thoughts.

I keep running and at the last second veer left.

Good choice.

There's a door on the opposite wall, one with no Drau slamming against it. Chest heaving, I skid to a stop, press my ear to the metal. I don't hear anything on the other side.

I grab the handle . . . slowly . . . turning . . .

Sounds of battle carry to me, muffled, distant. I dart into the empty corridor and quietly shut the door behind me. No lock on this side, but maybe they won't find this exit right away.

Run, or hide?

I glance up. There's ductwork running along the ceiling, and vents. I can't reach them, and even if I could, they're too small for me to fit through. I try to remember which way I moved when I was cut off from the rest of my team, which corridors I took in the heat of the fight.

Two options: right or left. Only one will take me back to Luka, Tyrone, Kendra, and Lien. It should be an easy choice: pick the one that runs in the direction of the green triangles on my con. But it isn't that easy because all the corridors here branch and angle, so even if I run left now, I might end up running right in a few turns.

I'm alone. And I'm lost.

I'm no fricking leader. I don't even have eyes on my team.

"Pull it together, Miki," I mutter.

A crash echoes from behind me, the slam and rebound of the first door against the wall. They're through. They'll find me.

I run.

Straight into a Drau.

CHAPTER**EIGHT**

I SKID TO A STOP MAYBE THREE FEET FROM THE DRAU. INSTINCT
sends my head jerking back. Our gazes collide. Eyes of
endless, swirling gray. I'm drowning in a silvery lake, the
eternity of a storm, beads of mercury swelling and coalesc-
ing to swallow me, take me.

Pain.

My existence pulled out through my eyes.

My knees go weak, but I lock them, refusing to fall.

Don't. Look. Jackson's voice inside my head. But he's not
here. He's just a memory, and if I let go, just let go, let the
cool mercury glide over me, through me—

There's a thud against my abdomen, like I've been
kicked. I tear my gaze away. My breath rushes out. I gasp
for air, pressing my hand to the wound. My sword clatters

to the floor, falling not from my hand but from the Drau's.

How . . . ?

The Drau looks up, over my shoulder, somewhere behind me. I turn my head . . . except . . . I don't.

I can't.

My ears are ringing, my head buzzing with the drone of a thousand wasps. I feel like a pricked balloon, deflating, sagging.

I'm cold.

Shaking.

I look down and everything's red. My hand. My sleeve. The front of my shirt. Glossy red. The air smells of copper. Of blood. My blood.

I've been stabbed. I'm bleeding everywhere, my clothing soaked with it. But I don't really feel any pain. I don't feel anything at all.

Why doesn't it hurt?

I rest my shoulder against the wall, aim, fire, take out the Drau that's just killed me and another as it streaks up the hall.

Daddy, I'm sorry. I didn't mean to leave you all alone.

Jackson, I'm sorry. So sorry.

I hear a hiss, like someone exhaling through their teeth. A girl with light brown hair loose around her shoulders steps in front of me firing down the corridor, taking out two more Drau.

Her presence means there's another team here. We're not on our own like I thought. I slide the rest of the way down the wall, my legs like celery stalks forgotten in the back of the crisper. Then I lie there, too weak to move, my shoulders and head propped up against the wall, the rest of me a splay of limbs on the cold floor.

The girl fires and fires again, then drops to her knees beside me, reaching toward my wound.

She pushes aside the sliced edges of my shirt. Two more Drau, twelve o'clock. I lift my weapon and point it over her shoulder. Panting, I fire, take out the first one, but the second keeps coming. So fast. So bright. My hand shakes, so weak, and drops to my side.

Numb. Useless.

"Drau," I gasp. I expect her to leap up, turn, shoot. But she does none of those things.

"They've got my back," she says.

Then a shower of light hits the Drau I missed, and it goes down screaming. I turn my head looking for the girl's teammates, but they must have taken cover out of sight.

The floors and walls spin and dip. My lids drift shut. I feel a tug, like someone's pulling my shirt off. I drag my hand to my opposite shoulder and realize it's bare. I'm only wearing my sports tank.

"Why are you taking off my clothes?"

She doesn't answer. I force my eyes open again. Force myself to focus.

Nothing makes sense. A shower of *light* took down the Drau that I missed. The girl's teammate took out that Drau with light.

That's not right.

Our weapons shoot darkness.

Then I notice the weapon the girl has holstered. It isn't like mine. It's metallic and smooth, but it doesn't look solid. It's fluid and jellylike: a Drau gun. Confused, I ask, "Why . . . ?"

"Shh. Don't talk," she says. "Save your strength."

The floor moves beneath me, tipping away.

For a millisecond, her eyes meet mine. And they're not right, either. Everyone's eyes are blue in the game. *Everyone's*. Except Jackson's. His are always Drau gray, no matter what. But this girl's aren't blue.

They're green. Lizzie green.

I remember the pictures in the front hall of Jackson's house. I remember Lizzie's face when I shared Jackson's nightmare. This girl . . . she's Lizzie.

She reaches for my wound and I cry out from the pain.

This girl can't be Jackson's sister. Lizzie's dead.

I'm losing it. Hallucinating.

Drau appear to the left of us. I try to lift my hand, to aim, to shoot. My vision wavers and then clears. There are no Drau there now. Only a wall.

"I'm in trouble, aren't I?" I whisper.

"You'll be fine."

Right.

She's holding a T-shirt in her hands—my T-shirt—and she folds it into a thick square and presses it against my wound. At first I feel nothing. Then I do. I grit my teeth, but a groan leaks out.

"Press," she orders, laying my hand on the wadded shirt and pushing my fingers flat.

I press.

She grabs her weapon and another off the ground, one that a downed Drau must have dropped, and bounds to her feet. Only then do I realize that the battle kept going without us. That her team members are still warding off the Drau attack. I don't even have enough strength to turn my head and look for them again. She spins and fires, double-handed, over and over.

"Hang on," she calls to me over her shoulder. And then, ". . . Going to lose it if . . ." The rest of her words are lost as she moves to fight off another two Drau.

My blood leaks through the makeshift pad, leaving my fingers warm and slick. I have the crazy thought that this isn't like they show on TV where the guy with his gut ripped open leaps to his feet and battles the bad guy to the glorious end. I won't be doing any leaping anytime soon; I don't think my feet would hold me.

I have the bizarre urge to laugh and laugh.

I want to close my eyes and sleep.

So weak. So tired.

I force my eyes open and will myself to stay awake. I turn my wrist and look at my con. More red than orange. Not good.

Footsteps, moving fast. I turn my head to see Luka running toward me. Behind him are Lien and Kendra and Tyrone.

The girl who saved me turns around. A Drau steps out of a corridor behind her. She doesn't see it. She doesn't know it's there.

I scream, but the only sound that comes out is a gasp.

She can't die. Not like this. I *owe* her.

I lift my hand. The weapon cylinder feels like it weighs a thousand pounds.

I fire.

I miss, the Drau moving so fast I never stood a chance.

The girl never stood a chance.

But before it can take her down, a thousand droplets of light rain over it. The Drau falls, writhing, hurt but not dead, a speckling of dark spots marking the places it was hit.

I don't know who made that shot. I'm too slow turning my head, and by the time I do, there's no one there.

The girl sweeps my sword off the ground, lunges, and pins the Drau through the chest. It arches, shudders, lies still. She tosses my sword down beside me and takes off down the corridor, chasing after a blur of light—a fleeing Drau. She pours on speed. But the Drau are so fast. She shouldn't be able to catch it. . . .

They turn a corner and they're gone.

"Miki!" Luka drops and slides across the floor to my side. He jerks my fingers out of the way, and makes a low sound as he stares at my wound. Then he puts the wadded T-shirt back in place, layers his palms, right on left, and presses hard. I scream. Really scream.

"I'm sorry." His jaw clenches, but he doesn't ease up. "You're bleeding out. I need to put pressure. I need to keep you alive."

"Two Drau. Two o'clock," Tyrone snarls, his weapon belching black death.

Lien and Kendra zip forward. Lien's faster, her weapon aimed and steady, but she doesn't fire. It's Kendra who takes both Drau down.

"I had it, but thanks for the help," Tyrone says. He sounds angry, and the way he said *thanks* made it sound like he meant anything but.

I want to ask him why, but I can't find the strength. I'm tired. Weak. My side hurts. I pull at the edge of the pad Luka's pressing down on my wound. The whole thing is sticky, even the edge I'm tugging at.

My head falls back against the concrete floor. I stare at the corrugated metal ceiling, trying to breathe through the pain. My eyes drift shut. I exhale, but can't seem to find a way to inhale again.

Jackson's there. I feel his cheek against my lips, then his lips on mine, warm, smooth. His breath is my breath. My lungs fill.

I love you.

Did I say that, or did he?

"Breathe, Miki. Come on! Breathe!"

With a gasp I open my eyes. Luka's above me, his face inches away.

"Okay," he says, his voice ragged. "Okay, she's breathing."

My vision goes foggy. I hear Tyrone's voice from a million miles away. He's talking, but I can't figure out what he's saying.

Snap. Luka's face comes back into sharp focus.

"Miki, answer me! How long till we make the jump?"

"What? Why . . . ?" I stare at him. "Did you kiss me?"

"Yeah. Right. Kiss of life. You stopped breathing," he says, his voice is tight and strained. "Be happy that I know CPR. How long till we make the jump?" he repeats.

"Thirty," I whisper as the knowledge gets dropped in my head by the Committee. My gaze drifts away from Luka and I see Tyrone and Lien and Kendra watching me, faces pale, expressions drawn. I try for a reassuring smile, and from Tyrone's frown, figure I fail miserably. "The girl . . . ?" I ask Luka. "She okay?"

"What girl?"

How did he not see her? He was running toward me as she was running away.

"There's no girl," Kendra says, her voice gentle.

"There is . . . was," I whisper, weak, so weak. "From another team."

"She's not here now," Luka says, and I can tell he doesn't think she was ever here.

"She—"

A shout of agony reverberates in my brain, deep and guttural. I echo the sound, crying out, my whole body tensing, pressure building inside my head as though a vise is crushing my skull.

As the cry in my mind fades, another follows. I arch my back, heels pressed to the floor, screaming. Screaming.

"Miki!"

Hands on my shoulders, holding me down.

"Keep her still!" Lien's voice. "She's making the bleeding worse."

Pain in my gut. Pain in my brain. Something trying to get in.

I can't—

Get out of my head.

I know that voice.

Jackson.

I can hear him, cursing them, fighting them.

You've taken enough. You don't get to take this from me. He sounds angry, determined.

"Jackson," I scream.

"It's Luka, Miki. I'm right here. Hang on. Just a few more seconds."

I want to tell him I know that Jackson's not here, that he's somewhere else, somewhere terrible. I can feel what he feels. Someone's hurting him. On purpose. Tunneling into his brain.

"Drau . . ."

"We got them. We're going to jump. Any second now."

No. He doesn't understand. I think the Drau have Jackson. They're cutting open his skull, taking his brain, like they did to the girl in the cold room we found in the caves. They're going to use him to make an army of shells.

I thrash under the pressure of Luka's hand. He rests his palm against my chest, just like Jackson did the first time I woke up in the lobby.

"I need to get to him. I need to—"

Jump. The Committee's inside my head, the word shimmering through all my senses. I taste it. I see it dancing like a halo of light. I feel it skittering across my skin.

A familiar agonizing pain takes root at the base of my skull and pulses outward until it blows me apart.

CHAPTER**NINE**

MY BACK ARCHES AS I COME TO, MUSCLES CLENCHING, HEART racing.

"Jackson!" His name comes out as a howl. I try to jump to my feet, to fight my way to him, but my body's sluggish, refusing to obey my mental commands.

And there's no one to fight.

I'm alone, lying on a cold, hard floor, hands and feet prickly and numb, my stomach churning.

The Drau. The blood. The girl from the other team . . .

With a wince, I gingerly poke at the side of my abdomen. No pain. No wound. And the T-shirt that's wadded in my hand isn't drenched in blood. I've respawned fully healed. I made it through another mission.

For a second, I just lie there, breathing and feeling

grateful. Then I try to figure out where I am. Not home. Not the lobby.

I'm at the bottom of a massive oval amphitheater, tiers of seats rising all around me. They climb beyond the reach of the light and disappear into darkness. Every seat is occupied by a shadowy figure, forms and faces obscured.

I've been called to face the Committee. Good. If anyone can help me find Jackson, it's them.

I push to my feet, dragging my T-shirt over my head, not really into facing the Committee in my sports tank.

My thoughts scurry around like cockroaches at the flick of a light, zipping from the Drau to the Committee to the sensations that washed over me right before the jump. The pain, the rage—Jackson's emotions reaching across time and space to crawl inside my brain, making me a powerless witness to his torment.

I remember Jackson screaming. *Get out of my head.*

"They have Jackson," I say, not even sure the Committee's listening. "The Drau. They're hurting him." Killing him. What if they've already succeeded?

Fear for him slices me open and leaves me raw. I wrap my arms around myself, trying to hold it together.

When no one answers me I turn a full circle, searching for help, but the audience is dark and wraithlike. I feel like they're not seeing me at all. As I complete my turn, a raised platform appears directly in front of me, hovering in midair. It's empty.

"Show yourselves," I say, then add, "Please." It won't

hurt my cause to be polite. That whole catch-more-flies-with-honey thing.

The light dims, then brightens, revealing three figures sitting on the floating shelf, as shadowy and undefined as those who fill the amphitheater.

Last time I was here, they appeared to me as a trio of B-movie caricatures: a Cleopatra look-alike, a brawny guy modeled on a combo of Odin and Thor, a cowled grim reaper. Truth is, they look nothing like that. They manifested in the form I expected to see. I don't know what they really look like. When I asked, they said they look human. Which doesn't really tell me a whole lot of anything.

I have a name for the Drau and an idea of their home world from what Jackson told me in the cave. But I have no concept where my alien ancestors originated. I don't have a name for them or the planet they came from. The only knowledge of them I have is a combo of speculation and what they chose to show me last time I was here, when they implanted scenes in my mind like a video.

Devastation and ruin.

A world destroyed.

The heat of the flames seared me as they showed me their memories of my ancestors herded into pens. Cries rang in my ears as they were killed and cut into manageable-sized portions. Food for the Drau.

I'm a secondhand witness to the horrific destruction of an entire species, but clueless as to who—and what—they truly were before the Drau came. The Committee aren't exactly forthcoming, and I don't know if that's by intent or accident.

But I do know they're the ones holding the controllers and manipulating the consoles in this game.

And they're the ones who can help me find Jackson.

"They have him," I say. "I don't know where they're holding him, but I know he's in trouble. I need your help. I need weapons, a team. I need you to drop me wherever he is. I need—" I break off, certain my presentation's hurting my case rather than helping it.

"What is it you need, Miki Jones?" Their words tunnel deep, twitching my muscles, scraping my bones. They speak in one voice, if I can call it that. It's more an experience of sound that arouses every sense, amplifies touch and sight and taste until my entire body's a conduit for the thoughts they choose to share. It's similar to the way they communicate with team leaders in the game, but stronger, bigger.

The first time I was here, the experience was too intense. They've remembered to tone it down this time and I'm grateful.

"I'm babbling. Okay. I'll try again." I take a breath, slow things down. I hesitate, searching for the right words.

They misunderstand my hesitancy and say, "You may speak." The sound is metallic and a little bitter on my tongue, prickling my fingertips, dancing like fireflies across my field of vision. So weird.

"Jackson . . . is he still alive?"

96

Silence. How many seconds? Three? Four? An agonizing eternity.

Terror slicks my palms. My chest feels like a truck's pressing down on it. They're trying to find a gentle way of telling me he's gone, dead, killed by the Drau—

"He is alive."

I sag in relief. I can't speak, can barely breathe. I take a few seconds just to get myself together before asking in a rush, "So where is he? How do we find him? How do we get to him? Give me a team, or I'll go alone if you think that's best."

I wait, shifting my weight from one foot to the other, feeling like my skin's too tight.

"He is here."

I freeze. "What?" I look around, my head whipping side to side. "Where?"

"Here."

But he isn't. Not that I can see.

"Wait . . . he's here?" Hope bubbles like a shaken bottle of pop. "You already saved him from the Drau?"

"We did not. He has been with us since his last battle."

"His last . . . I don't understand. . . . But that means you were the ones—" *Hurting him, making him scream.* The bubbles of hope burst, decaying into horror. I almost run at the Committee, aching to tear them off that floating shelf, to look into their eyes, to demand explanations. But that's a plan doomed to failure. They aren't even really here; they're more of a memory bank than anything else. I have a feeling that if I reach out to touch them, there'll be nothing there.

I try to keep my tone even, to hide the fury and resentment I feel. I don't do a particularly good job of it. "Why would you do this?" I snarl.

The time between my question and their answer feels like a century. "It was necessary."

I take a long, slow breath. Straightforward questions. Straightforward answers. So why is it taking them so long to reply? Why are they weighing every word? Because there are things they don't want me to know, things they're unwilling to tell me. But my imagination is just as bad, if not worse than the truth.

"Is he unharmed?"

"He is alive."

I'm not reassured, but I try to hang on to the most important fact: he isn't dead.

"That isn't what I asked."

"No, it is not, but it is the answer we offer."

Which tells me a lot in and of itself.

"Why did you bring Jackson here after Detroit? Why didn't he respawn with the rest of us?"

"In war, discipline must be maintained. Order preserved. Independent action puts all at risk."

Or saves lives. But I decide against arguing the point. When I was thirteen, Mom and I suddenly started arguing a lot. Mostly about stupid things. What jacket I should wear. Which jeans I should buy. After a couple of months of that, she just stopped arguing back, no matter how hard I pushed. She'd get this serene sort of smile on her lips and she'd change the subject. When I'd try to keep the fight going, she'd tell me to choose my battles, to make them matter. I'm choosing mine now. "Why didn't he come back from Detroit?"

"He was detained."

"By you." I ball my fists at my sides and push the Committee for answers, because they matter. "Why? Why did you keep him here? Why did you hurt him?"

Again, a pause. Anxiety amps up my heart rate as I wait for them to speak.

"Jackson Tate was aware of the consequences."

"Consequences for doing what? You're not answering my questions."

"We answer with truth. We cannot alter your desire for a different reply."

I've heard the expression *seeing red* a million times. I never really got it until this second, as a haze of crimson films my vision and the thudding of my blood pounds in my ears. It's only the patience I learned doing endless, repetitive kendo exercises in Sofu's dojo that lets me keep the words I want to hurl at them locked away inside.

Deflect. Regroup. I have to come at this from a different angle, use what I already know to make them tell me what I don't.

"What rule did Jackson break?"

The air shifts against my skin. The silence is absolute. I

can almost feel the vibration of every atom, every molecule. And in that silence is confirmation of what I suspected: Luka and I were right. They *are* holding him prisoner for breaking some rule or law. What could he have done that was so terrible? I want to blurt out arguments and excuses, beg, plead, but I sink my teeth into my cheek and stay quiet.

"He is not Drau."

Thanks for the revelation. I press my fingertips to my temples. That answer means nothing, but it should. I know it should. He is not Drau. . . . No, that actually isn't true. He's not *fully* Drau, but there's a part of him that is.

"He did something a Drau would do," I say slowly, guessing. When they don't deny it, I keep going, working with what I know, adding layers. "And you said he was aware of the consequences, so . . . it isn't the first time he's broken this rule."

What did he do that enraged the Committee enough to hold him prisoner, to hurt him in order to get answers? He almost died doing their bidding, fighting the Drau in Detroit.

But Jackson traded me into the game as his way out. By the time we hit Detroit, I was already a team leader.

Which means the deal was complete; he shouldn't have been in Detroit at all. He should have been released from the game.

But he *was* there.

He took a hit meant for me.

He would have died if I hadn't—

"That's it, isn't it? He took the Drau hit. He was injured. Dying . . ." His con was full red, barely touched by orange. I stare at the Committee. "But it wasn't his almost *dying* that broke the rules. It was *living* that did. It was what he did in order to survive, wasn't it?"

"The method he employed is forbidden. Jackson Tate was aware of the stipulations and limitations. He chose to disobey."

I shiver, remembering that moment when I was hunched over Jackson's battered body, begging him to stay alive. I told him I didn't forgive him, that he had to live to grovel and earn my forgiveness for the way he trapped me in the game. Those were among my last words to him. Horrible, desperate words.

He looked at me, his eyes Drau gray, something dark and dangerous stirring in their depths.

Something predatory.

And then he took what I offered. He did what a Drau would do and pulled electric current from my body to charge his nerves, his muscles, his cells. Like recharging a battery. It kept him alive till we made the jump.

"He didn't want to," I whisper, then louder, "He didn't want to. It ate him alive, what he did to Lizzie." He used his Drau abilities once before, and it cost him. He didn't mean to kill her—maybe he didn't even realize he could—but his sister died so he could live. He's been living with that for five years. Hating himself for it. "He never wanted to do that again."

"He was warned."

"It's my fault. I forced him." My breath's coming too fast. The urge to run, to scream, pushes against the walls I've built. Anxiety in its purest form.

Focus. Breathe. Visualize.

Those techniques are useless against what I'm facing right now. "Listen to me. Please. I made him disobey. I couldn't let him die. I couldn't. And you should be glad I didn't. We need him. *You* need him. He has unique skills and attributes."

"He knew the penalty."

"But *I* didn't. And it's my fault."

"Ignorance of the law is not a defense."

I try to think, my mind skidding all over the place like bald tires on black ice. Jackson broke the law when his sister died, so he could live. He got a single reprieve. It wasn't until his second infraction that the Committee did . . . whatever they've done to him. That probably means I get a free pass, too. "Fine. If blame needs to be laid, if someone needs to pay, then let it be me."

The silence stretches and as the seconds ooze past, I have the sinking feeling that it isn't because they're processing their answer. It's because they don't plan to answer at all.

Indignation, rage, fear, and resentment combine, hot and sharp in my veins. "You weren't having any kind of civilized trial. You were torturing him. I felt it. I felt his pain, heard his screams." I stalk forward, my mouth dry, my pulse pounding so hard I can feel it in my temples. I want to hit something, break it, tear it to shreds. I can't. The only weapons that will help me in this battle are my words. "Is that what you do to soldiers who disobey? Never heard of the Geneva Convention and international humanitarian law?"

"Those are human rules."

Right. And they're aliens.

"You're on a human world. Your progeny are human. Including me. And Jackson. So the rules apply. How come you get to break them, but we're expected to adhere to a bunch of regulations you don't even spell out for us? What you're doing makes no sense."

My lungs feel tight and I can't get enough air, like I just ran a full marathon at top speed. I need to get myself under control.

"The Geneva Convention articles define treatment for prisoners."

I pounce on that and say, "Exactly. Jackson's a prisoner. And you can't just go around torturing people—" A sob chokes me as I remember the sound of his agony echoing in my mind.

"We do not torture. Any discomfort was incidental."

"Incidental? You hurt him. On purpose. When all he did was keep two of your soldiers alive. Himself and me. And probably a whole lot more than that during the course of the battle." A battle he shouldn't even have been part of because he should have been released from the game.

103

"We questioned him. That was our purpose. Pain was not the intent. It was a by-product of Jackson Tate's refusal to cooperate. He had only to allow us access and the pain would have disappeared."

"Blame the victim?" I feel like I'm listening to the villain in some really bad TV show, telling the hero that he's having his nails torn out because he isn't cooperating. But this is the Committee, the all-knowing consciousness that guides us through the game. The ones trying to save the world. "You aren't supposed to be the ones doing bad shit, especially not to your own soldiers. You're supposed to be the ones who have our backs." I seethe with impotent rage laced with a heavy dose of disillusionment. "You're supposed to be the good guys." God, could I sound any more pathetic?

"We allow Jackson Tate much latitude due to his unique makeup."

"You call making him scream in agony latitude?"

"You truly believe we tortured him?" There's actually emotion behind that question. Surprise, yeah, but mostly amusement, if I'm judging right.

I don't get the joke. But the sensation of their amusement dancing along my nerves is enough to give me pause.

"I heard him scream," I say. "If there's any other way for me to interpret that, I'm open to hearing it."

"He is stubborn. As are you. Jackson Tate needed only to open his thoughts. You are familiar with our method of communication."

"The way you convey what you want to say directly into all my senses?"

"Correct."

I reason that out. Try to see what it is they want me to know. They can convey their thoughts directly into my head, but— "You don't hear my thoughts in your heads. I have to actually speak words out loud. You can talk directly to my brain, but can't hear what I think."

"That would be inappropriate. We enter only with your permission."

"*Choose* to enter only with permission, or *can't* enter without permission?"

"You are astute to pinpoint the distinction. It depends on the individual. Some are stronger than others."

I wrap my arms around myself and take a reflexive step back. The thought of them climbing inside my head at will sickens me. "What about me? Am I strong?"

"Yes."

They didn't hesitate over that answer. Not even for a millisecond. I bite my lip, unconvinced. Is that the truth, or a version of the truth they want me to believe? I don't know anymore if I can trust them.

Then I think of all the minds they wipe when someone dies in the game, the knowledge they steal, the memories they take, and I realize this isn't some unexpected revelation. I knew all along that they could get inside human minds. I guess I just didn't want to acknowledge exactly what that meant. Kind of like every cheesy horror flick where the girl alone in the cabin in the woods doesn't want to acknowledge what it means when she hears the floorboards creak.

I'm usually the one yelling at that stupid, stupid girl.

"You can't get into Jackson's head unless he lets you."

"We requested access. He declined. We insisted."

"You forced your way in." I'm so angry I feel sick. "Against his will."

"For the greater good."

"That's—" I barely catch myself from screaming *bullshit*. I've never been a great believer in the "greater good" justification. "I want to see him. Talk to him. I want proof he's okay."

Seconds stretch into minutes and they don't say a thing. My shoulders tense. I want to lash out at them any way I can. I want to make them take me to Jackson.

And then they're gone. No shadowy figures lining the amphitheater. No forms sitting on the floating shelf.

Just me and my anger and my fear, alone in the vast, empty space, a little richer in knowledge about what the Committee can and can't do, more than a little disillusioned, and no closer to saving Jackson than I was when I first arrived.

CHAPTER**TEN**

WHEN THE COMMITTEE REAPPEARS ON THE FLOATING SHELF,
I'm sitting cross-legged on the floor, drenched in sweat. I
don't know how long they left me here. I lost count of the
number of oval laps I ran along the perimeter of the amphitheater. It barely took the edge off my anxiety.

They're alone. The rest of the amphitheater remains
empty. I want to ask them why, but I don't. I'll store my
questions up and only use the ones that really matter.

For a second, I consider the possibility that they don't
want any witnesses to what's about to go down. But the
Committee shares a consciousness. At least, that's what
they've led me to believe. So whether the other members
are here or not, they're aware of what happens.

"You are calmer, Miki Jones?"

"Yes," I lie.

"We offer a gift." The figure on the right gestures toward the far end of the amphitheater and I turn.

I gasp. My heart stutters to a stop, then thumps hard in my chest.

A boy's standing there, his back to me, his T-shirt stretched tight across wide shoulders, then falling loose to his narrow waist. His hair is light brown, shot with honey and gold. I can't see his face. I don't need to.

"Jackson!" The word's not even out before I'm running toward him. He doesn't turn, doesn't move. I call his name again, pile on speed. I'm almost there, almost close enough to touch him when I slam into a wall.

With a cry, I fall back, landing hard on my ass. I look up, shocked and confused.

There's no wall.

And now there's no Jackson.

He's gone.

I bound to my feet and whirl to face the Committee.

"Where is he?"

"We allowed you to see that Jackson Tate is alive and unharmed."

Rubbing my forehead where I slammed it against the unseen barrier, I stare at them, trying to figure out their angle. "I saw a boy's back. I don't know for certain it was Jackson. So that means I have no real proof he's alive." My voice cracks. I'm lying. I might not have seen his face, but it *was* Jackson. I could feel it.

"He just stood there," I say. "Didn't move. Didn't speak. Didn't respond when I yelled his name." I'm shaking, my forehead pounding. "You think this is a joke? A game?" As soon as I say the word, I suppress a shiver. "It isn't. It's my life. And his."

"Precisely. You may choose now. Your life, or his."

"What?"

"You claim responsibility for Jackson Tate's choices," the Committee says, "for his breach of the rules we set forth to protect all. And so, we offer a choice to you, Miki Jones. Your life, or his."

"That's crazy. Why would you do that? We're both valuable to the cause. You can't—" I swallow and try again. "You can't ask me to choose. That's either suicide or murder. And it makes no sense—"

"Choose, or we will choose for you."

"No." I back away, looking around, frantic to catch a glimpse of Jackson, desperate to see a way out. I'm trapped in a place I can't escape by beings that hold my life in their hands. All our lives in their hands. I feel the same horror and helplessness I felt back in the building in Detroit, Jackson dying in my arms, faced with the choice of letting him bleed out or risking my own life. An impossible choice. "Why are you doing this? You're supposed to be saving the world. You're supposed to—" *Be the good guys.*

"If our army cannot follow orders, if they cannot adhere to rules, then we have no hope of defeating the Drau. Choose. Now."

"This isn't just about me or him," I yell. "I have a dad. Friends. Jackson has a mom. A dad. And they've already buried one kid. This isn't just about one life lost. It's about all the lives touched, *ruined*, by loss when someone dies." Hearts broken. Souls shredded.

"Precisely. And how many will die if we fail to fight off the Drau? All, Miki Jones. All lives on the face of this planet. Think on that."

Sweat trickles along my spine. I need to think. I need to— "This is about saving the world? Then let's use that as our start point. We *need* Jackson. How does killing him benefit the cause? He can fight like no one else. He knows the Drau like no one else. Don't tell me that isn't true. I don't care how many teams there are, how good they are; we can't afford to lose Jackson Tate."

I'm breathing short and shallow, my thoughts tumbling, terror pushing me closer and closer to the edge. The Committee's had thousands of years to learn how to twist circumstances and arguments to their advantage. I've had sixteen. The scales aren't exactly even.

"So you choose to die?"

"No!" I stumble back, holding up both hands in front of me. "I didn't say that. This is all about enforcing rules? All about the greater good, the good of team human? Then let's talk about that. I wouldn't have been brought into the game if I wasn't important. I managed to lead my team through two rough missions with little training or knowledge." Not really. I didn't so much lead as survive by accident. "I'll only get better from here. You need me. The war needs me. How does killing me benefit anything or anyone?"

"Then you choose Jackson—"

"I'm not done," I cut them off as I stalk forward, going on the offensive. "A sacrifice needs to be made to satisfy your twisted reasoning? Fine, then it'll be made."

The Committee just sits there, three silent judges, waiting for me to get it wrong, waiting for an excuse to either kill me or cut out my heart by killing Jackson.

"The one responsible for the whole debacle gets cut from the team. One of *you* gets terminated," I say. "You're the all-knowing, all-seeing ones. *You* should have stepped in in Detroit. Should have pulled us before Jackson and I needed to make the choice we did. This is all about responsibility? All about laying blame? Then it's on *you*."

I talk faster, my arguments shaping themselves to a honed point. "You're the collective consciousness, right? That means everything you know is known by the others. So one of you is way more expendable than Jackson or me." I take a quick breath and shoot for the kill. "And if you could fight this war without us, you'd be doing exactly that. You'd have won it the first time, back on your own home world."

I'm being cruel. I don't care. They don't get to do this. I had no control, no say when I got pushed into this game, pushed into living this crazy double life. I had no choice when Sofu died. *If he makes it through the night, his chances improve.* He didn't. He died. I never got to say good-bye. I had no say when Mom died. *We'll know more after the biopsy.* Yeah, we knew more. We knew she had no chance.

But Jackson and I have a chance, and this time, I intend to have a say.

I stand before them, chest heaving like I've had the roughest workout of my life. I expect their rage. I'm ready for it.

What I get is their laughter, the sound of warmth and light rushing through my veins, dancing in my limbs.

"Well done, Miki Jones. Your arguments have merit."

I stare at them, incredulous. "This was some kind of test?" I don't even bother to try to keep the derision from my tone.

"Of a sort. We needed to assess essential leadership skills, your ability to think quickly, make rapid decisions in the face of imminent danger."

Like the decisions I've made in the game weren't rapid and tinged by danger.

"We needed to complete the puzzle."

The burn of resentment is powerful and fierce. I really thought they would kill me. Kill Jackson.

"The puzzle," I echo. An image of Sofu's collection of Japanese puzzle boxes flashes through my thoughts— boxes that could only be opened by an obscure series of manipulations. Sometimes the solution was as simple as a touch here and another there. Sometimes it was a complicated series of movements of tiny parts. With the right influence, the box would reveal its secrets. Kind of like the Committee, the game, the rules. The only way to get information is to touch the right spot, ask the right question in just the right way. But they aren't talking about themselves or the game or the rules; they're saying I'm the puzzle. So what secret was the Committee trying to get me to reveal?

"This was all an elaborate scenario to see how fast I think under pressure? To assess my leadership skills?" I pause, trying to follow the tangled threads of their logic. A horrible idea pops into my head. "Was this your way of confirming my suitability as Jackson's replacement before you release him from the game?"

"No."

I process that for a second. "You never meant to let him go, did you?" I don't even try to hide my bitterness. I'm starting to see the Committee in a glaring new light, and it's anything but flattering. "You used him to bring me in, then reneged on your promise."

"He could have chosen to leave. He had only to pay the price."

"He did. He brought me into the game. That was the price, the trade." Wasn't it? I remember Jackson's words echoing in my thoughts: *You've taken enough. You don't get to take this from me.* "What were you trying to take from him?"

"Memories."

"Of the game." That made sense. If he wasn't part of it anymore, they wouldn't want him to remember. "Why would Jackson fight so hard against you taking those memories? He hates the game. Why would he want to remember it?"

"Because in forfeiting his memories of the game, he would also forfeit his memories of you."

I gasp.

"He refused his freedom because of me?" I don't want that responsibility. But I also don't want to imagine him forgetting me, forgetting *us*, forgetting sharing lunch at the top of the bleachers, matching wits . . . kissing. I don't want him to forget loving me, even though remembering cost him his freedom. What kind of person does that make me?

"So what now? What happens to him? What happens to me?"

"We resume."

Resume the game. Resume our lives.

"This was all a setup." I shake my head, barely able to grasp that. "You kept Jackson here, made me think his life was in danger, made me think I had to choose between his life or mine, for a test?" I'm about to say that what they did wasn't *fair*, but even thinking the word makes me want to roll my eyes at myself. Life is unfair. Cliché of the first degree and oh-so-true. "That's twisted. It's sick."

"It is effective. And it was more than a test. Jackson Tate defied the rule. He must not do so again. It *will* mean his termination. We are confident he understands that now."

I shiver, the agony of his cries fresh in my thoughts. "So he's still part of the game?"

"Yes. In keeping his memories, he made that choice."

Which means my freedom was sacrificed for nothing. He didn't get what he wanted in the end. He didn't make it out.

"And what about me? If he's staying, do I get to leave?"

"The war continues. The Drau threat remains unchanged. But under the terms of our agreement with Jackson Tate, you are free to go because he chooses to stay."

I didn't expect that answer. I thought they'd say no. It takes me a second to readjust my thinking. I was Jackson's ticket out, and now he's mine.

I didn't think I'd be able to consign anyone to the game in order to win my freedom, and now I'm faced with exactly that choice. But not just *anyone*. Jackson.

Except I'm not consigning him to anything. He's already made his decision.

I'm the one who has to make mine.

I press my lips together. I feel like I'm a hamster on a wheel, running, running, getting nowhere. Running because I'm too foolish to stop, to make a choice other than the obvious one. "What happens if I take the free pass? Do I go back to the moment when the truck hit me? Do I die?"

"You return to your original life."

Because Jackson's still in the game, so I don't have to be. I get to leave.

Or do I? Can I trust the Committee? A day ago, I would have said yes. Now, I'm not so sure.

I run through everything that's been said since I first

got here, and my own words flicker neon bright in my thoughts: *I wouldn't have been brought into the game if I wasn't important. . . . The war needs me.*

This is about more than just me.

Everyone on this planet could die at the hands of the Drau.

From everything I've seen on the missions, from what the Committee's told me and what I've figured out on my own, every soldier matters. Every team leader matters. There are few of us and so many of them.

Where's my honor if I walk away from that? I can almost feel Sofu standing beside me right now. He used to talk about Bushido: the way of the warrior. Loyalty. Honor unto death. I know he would have stayed in the game and fought to the bitter end. He would have defended our world until the last Drau was either dead or chased off with its tail between its legs.

I stare at the Committee, torn. No matter how pissed I am at them, no matter how shaken my trust, I have to decide with a clear head.

A clear heart.

And the worst thing is, I sort of get them. Maybe I don't like all their methods, but in relative terms, they're still the good guys, the ones trying to save the world. I take a breath.

"I'm in," I say. In it until I see it through.

The form in the middle inclines its head in a spare nod and then without another word, they fade away like they'd never been here at all.

"Wait," I cry. "Did they all make it back okay from the latest mission? The kids on the other team? The girl that helped me?"

I stand there for so long that I think they've forgotten me. And then I feel their answer in my skull, in my bones. *We sent no other team. There was no girl. You saved yourself, Miki Jones.*

But I didn't.

CHAPTER**ELEVEN**

I WAKE UP TO LIGHT STREAMING THROUGH MY WINDOW, HIT-ting me in the face.

"Miki?" My door creaks as Dad pushes it open an inch. "Okay to come in?"

"Um . . ." I look down to find I'm lying on top of my covers, fully dressed. "Yeah. All clear."

He stands in the doorway, frowning as he studies me. "Everything okay? You were sleeping when I got home from work yesterday. I tried to wake you for dinner but you grabbed my sweater and threw an uppercut at my face."

I sit bolt upright. "I didn't."

He rubs his jaw. "Yeah, you did. See the bruise?" He drops his hand. "Must have been some dream, huh?"

"Must have been." I stand up and peer at his jaw. "Dad,

seriously, please tell me I didn't hit you."

"You didn't hit me." He smiles. A real smile that reaches his eyes, just like it used to when Mom was still here. I can't help but smile back. "Well . . . not too hard, anyway."

I grab a pillow and toss it at him. "Dad! That's not funny."

"You didn't hit me, Miki. You just mumbled something about some game and rolled over. You slept"—he glances at his watch—"for sixteen hours."

I scrub my hand over my face. "It's . . . Saturday?"

"Ten a.m. Saturday morning." Dad walks over and rests his hand on my forehead. Sometimes I think he just needs to touch me, sort of reassuring himself that I'm not gone, like Mom. "You don't feel warm."

"I'm not sick, Dad. I think I was just really tired." I respawned yesterday on my front porch in exactly the spot I was in when I got pulled. I didn't get to see Jackson. Didn't get to talk to him. My gaze slides to my phone. I want to check for a message from him, but I don't want to do it with Dad here.

"Still tired?" he asks.

I laugh. "Not even slightly. I'm a ball of energy." Then I crack my jaw on an enormous yawn.

"So I see." He pauses. "I'm going grocery shopping. Do you want to come along?"

There have been moments lately when I wished Dad would reach out, sit down with me, and just talk. This isn't one of them.

I make a vague gesture at my backpack. "Tons of home-work." Not a lie. I'm way behind on that English essay for Mr. Shomper.

Dad looks like he's going to say something more, but then he just nods and goes. I hear his footsteps on the stairs, and the sound of the front door closing.

I snatch my phone. A ton of texts. Three voice mails from Carly, one at 8:09 last night, another at 10:06, and a third from 9:30 this morning. One text from Dee. One from Luka. Nothing from Jackson. My heart sinks until I realize that there's a good chance he did the same thing I did—crashed for sixteen hours. He might even still be asleep.

I play the first message from Carly.

"Done with the family meal from hell. Where are you?"

My stomach clenches. I completely forgot I told her to come over after dinner last night. I exhale and press my forehead to my balled fist as I play her second message.

"'Kay. Guess you ditched me. Again. Whatever."

I don't want to play her final message, the one from this morning, but I do anyway because I need to know just how pissed she is before I call her back and grovel.

"Just came by and spoke to your dad. He told me you fell asleep as soon as you got in last night. I guess that panic attack yesterday really did a number. Don't worry, I didn't tell him about it. And sorry I got so mad. Hope you're feeling better. Oh, and I left a skinny latte with your dad. It's probably cold now but

you can nuke it. I'm at work from ten till two. Junior class then the private lesson for the trouble twins, then me and Kelley are lifeguarding a birthday party. Call you after."

I'm slammed by both relief and guilt. Relief that Carly's not mad and, if I'm honest, that I don't have to deal with her this morning.

What happened to the endless hours we used to share when we could do anything and everything and just be happy to be together?

That's where the guilt comes in. I hate feeling that way about my best friend. I hate knowing it's way more my fault than hers. Maybe I don't deserve her easy forgiveness. I should have remembered to call her before I crashed. If this is my life now, the two worlds I jump between, then I need to learn to balance them both.

It's on me, not Carly. I'm the one lying and hiding shit. I need to get my head together.

"Self-pity party, much?" I mutter, not very happy with myself right now.

I check my other messages. Nothing important. And nothing from Jackson.

I try Luka—first a text, then a call, but I can't reach him.

After a quick shower, I head down to the kitchen. There's a bowl on the table with about a quarter inch of milk at the bottom, a half-full mug of coffee, and an empty beer bottle.

I think back to that instant when Dad laid his hand on my forehead. Did I smell beer? I don't know.

I turn to the counter and see five more.

For a second, I'm blindingly furious at Dad. Then that anger turns on myself. The gray fog that's slunk after me like a shadow for the past two years creeps out from whatever hole it was hiding in. I feel like two hands that are ten times normal size are pressing on my ribs, stealing my breath. The voice of condemnation shrieks and roars, blaming me for things that were never my fault, demanding that I blame myself.

But I'm not the girl I was two years ago. I push through the fog, bury it, and snatch the bottle off the table.

It's time for me to stop feeling like I can fix whatever's wrong with him, time for me to stop taking his choices on my shoulders. He's an adult. He's choosing to drink; he's choosing not to get help and stop.

This isn't on me. I can only let him know how I feel about what he's doing—which I have. But it isn't my fault and I don't have to enable him or feed the problem.

This is Dad's problem. His choices. No matter how much I want to control this, I can't.

He's gone to get groceries. That means he's driving. Did he drink all these this morning or are they left from last night? I touch the rims of each bottle on the counter. Dry.

I'm hoping that means they're from last night. If they

aren't, it means he had six bottles before 10:00 a.m.

For the first time in recent memory, I don't put the empties away under the sink. I don't wipe the counter. I don't even clear Dad's dishes off the table. I put the bottle from the table back exactly where I found it, grab a Pop-Tart—it's Saturday, the one day I stray from my healthy-eating rule—microwave the coffee Carly brought me, and head back to my room.

I wonder what Dad will make of that.

I don't even know what *I* make of that.

All I know is that I can't keep hiding empty beer bottles under the sink, can't keep cleaning the kitchen till it sparkles, pretending that'll make everything okay.

I'm halfway to my room when I pause, sigh, clomp back down the stairs. I rinse Dad's bowl in the sink, dump his cold coffee, stack the washer, wipe the table without moving that lone empty bottle. And I leave the other empties where they are on the counter and call that a victory.

Baby steps.

Homework takes up a couple of hours. I check my phone every few minutes, wishing Jackson would call. I'm not trying to do the clingy, needy thing. I just want to hear his voice, know he's okay, know he made it back.

Which is in direct opposition to the part of me that's still angry with him for getting me dragged into the game in the first place. We never got to resolve the little issue of his betrayal, the way he tricked me and sold me into the game. Like I told him in Detroit, I don't forgive him.

I'm not exactly proud of that. But it is what it is.

And it leaves me tied up in knots.

He doesn't call. Which isn't all that surprising since I don't think he even has my number. I don't have his, which is why I haven't been the one to do the calling—something I plan to remedy as soon as I see him.

I help Dad unload the groceries when he gets back, organizing the tins, labels out, shifting the ones from the back of the cabinet to the front, according to expiration date.

Dad glances at the beer bottles, one on the table, the others still on the counter, and frowns.

"You didn't clear up the kitchen," he says.

"Yeah, I did." I look him straight in the eye. "I cleared away your breakfast dishes and wiped the table."

I wait to see if he'll bring up the bottles. He doesn't. We stare at each other, and for the first time in a long time, we communicate.

Silently.

Meaningfully.

I'm the one to break the stare.

As I head back upstairs, he steps out of the kitchen into the hall and watches me. I slow down, giving him the chance: if he says anything, anything at all, I'll stop, go back down, talk to him. But nothing has changed. He doesn't say anything and neither do I.

Once I get to my room I pick up where I left off with Mr. Shomper's *Lord of the Flies* essay. My concentration isn't exactly the best. I check my phone, then my page online to see if Jackson messaged me there. Nothing.

I'm anxious, edgy.

The urge to go for a run is nearly overwhelming. I get as far as laying out my running gear on the bed when Carly calls. We talk about how awesomely hawt Matt, her fellow lifeguard, is—well, she talks and I listen and make humming noises at appropriate times.

"So, you want to do Mark's Texas Hots on Monroe for dinner? Or Nick Tahou's?" I ask as she winds down.

"Can't," she says. "Like I told you, Kelley and Sarah are coming over to work on that group thing for Español. We haven't even started yet."

Did she tell me that? If she did, I don't remember.

"But you could come, too," she says. It comes out more as a question than a statement.

I hesitate, not sure what to say. Carly made plans on a Saturday night. Without me. The only other time she's done that is when she's had a date.

Finally, I ask, "And distract you from your work? What kind of a friend would I be?"

She laughs. It's a strained, uncomfortable sound. Or maybe I'm projecting the way I feel onto her.

When I end the call, it's almost three o'clock.

I close my laptop, put my running gear away. While a run might ease the tension, it won't get me answers.

I'm done waiting to hear from Jackson. I need to see him. I want to touch him and know he's real. I want to feel his arms around me. I want to see his trademark Jackson smile, white teeth, and that killer dimple in his cheek.

And then I want to give him a piece of my mind for what he did to me in the first place.

I press my lips together and stare out my window. I'm so tired of being angry with the people I love.

I unplug my phone from the charger and shove it, along with my textbooks, into my bag. I might not have Jackson's number, but I have his address. Nothing like showing up unexpectedly at someone's door to catch them at their best. But it isn't like he hasn't done the same to me the night he climbed through my bedroom window. I guess turnaround's fair play.

I pull my hair into a ponytail, change out my sweats for jeans and a cute top that's a silvery gray. It reminds me of Jackson's eyes. I don't usually wear much makeup, but I add a little mascara and lip gloss, then grab my jacket and my backpack and call *bye* to Dad as I head for the door.

"Wait." He comes out of his office, frowning. "Where are you going?"

"Heading over to a friend's. Then maybe the library." Truth—*maybe* isn't the same as *definitely*. There's always a chance I could go to the library.

That's how Dad and I get by: mostly honest but sometimes not.

"Which friend?"

Precisely the question I was hoping to avoid.

"A guy from my English class. We have an essay." Again, truth. Jackson is in my class and we do have an essay, just not one we need to work on together.

"That boy Luka?"

"No." I take a deep breath, remembering how Jackson told his mom all about me. "His name's Jackson," I say. "Jackson Tate."

Dad frowns even harder. "Why can't he come here?"

"Do you want to call his mom and ask?"

Dad rears back in surprise.

"Sorry," I say, meaning it. "Dad, seriously, I'm not doing anything sketchy. Have a little faith."

He mulls that over for a few seconds, then asks, "What about Carly?"

"Group project."

His expression lightens. "Oh, okay."

Uh-oh. I think he took that to mean we'll all be working together. I choose not to disabuse him of that idea.

"Keep your phone on. And call me to let me know if you'll be home for dinner."

"'Kay." I give him a quick kiss on the cheek. His arms close around me and he hugs me a little tighter and a little longer than usual. He smells like fabric softener and spicy shaving cream, just like he did when I was little. He doesn't smell like beer. I close my eyes and hug him tighter, too.

Then he lets me go.

I swallow, hesitate. After my pep talk to myself about letting Dad take ownership of the drinking thing, I know I ought to leave it alone, let him make his own choices. I shouldn't push. But there's this part of me that needs to be in control, and that's the part that says in a rush, "There's this meeting. Actually, meetings. Plural. They have them on the weekends and during the week after work. We could go tomorrow. I think there's one on Elmwood in the morning. And one at the church on Park in the afternoon. I'll go with you, if it's allowed. We could check online."

Does he know that I mean AA meetings? Will he take the hand I'm offering?

He stares at me for so long I think maybe he doesn't have a clue what I'm talking about. Then he scrapes his palm along his Saturday-stubbled cheek and says, "Not yet, Miki. I'm not ready yet."

Disappointment settles on my shoulders like a cloak. Then it kindles and flares to full-on anger. I fight the urge to snap at him, to ask if something terrible has to happen before he *is* ready. But then I remember what the website said: *If you want to drink, that's your business. If you want to stop, that's our business.*

I cool down a little, enough to recognize that he didn't shoot me down. He didn't admit that he has a problem, but he didn't pretend that he doesn't. This is progress.

He says he's not ready yet? Maybe tomorrow or the next day he will be. Dad has to want to make this someone's business other than his own or it won't work.

I have to keep the door open.

I want to say something else, but I have no idea what. So I just do this awkward smile-with-my-mouth-closed-and-nod thing as I heft my backpack and head out.

CHAPTER **TWELVE**

WHEN I GET TO JACKSON'S HOUSE, THE GARAGE DOOR'S OPEN and the garage is empty. Jackson's black Jeep sits on the drive exactly where Luka and I left it. Was that only yesterday?

I take a deep breath, fortifying my resolve, and stride up the walk to the front door. No one answers my knock. I ring the bell and wait. Ring it again.

Worry uncoils in my gut. Could the Committee have lied to me? Could this be another crazy test? Yes on both counts. My trust in them isn't exactly intact.

I frown. Wait . . . did they even promise they would send him back? Or did they just imply it?

What if he's still trapped there? Still being hurt—?

I need to know.

I jog around the side of the house. A quick check up and down the street ensures that there's no one in sight. I glance at the neighbor's house. The blinds are closed. No one's watching me. I don't even know why I'm worried that someone is. It's not like I'm going to break in or anything. I'm just going to scout things out.

The hairs at my nape prickle and I spin around, checking behind me. Nothing there. I'm freaking myself out.

I turn back around, unlatch the gate, and duck into the backyard.

I need to see Jackson. I need to know the Committee sent him back. Not just because I need Jackson to be okay, though that's the biggest part of it. I also need to know that despite the weird shit they did yesterday, the Committee's still the good guys.

Someone needs to be the good guys.

The backyard is bordered by flower beds, pink and purple impatiens giving their last gasp as the weather gets colder. There's an apple tree tall enough to get me to the second-story window on the left. Jackson's room? I have no clue.

Refusing to give what I'm about to do too much thought, I drop my backpack on the ground, leap for the lowest branch, and climb.

Disappointment punches me as I settle on a branch that's level with the window, and see that it's not Jackson's bedroom. It's a sewing room with a long table pushed against one wall and a smaller table with a sewing machine set at right angles to it. The door to the room's open and I can see the hallway beyond with its cappuccino walls and hardwood floor. I sit on the branch, deflated. What now? The tree isn't positioned in a way that I can get at either of the other two windows, and I think that sitting here yelling Jackson's name isn't the plan of the century.

Then it hits me. Jackson might not even be here. He's probably out somewhere with his parents. Would have been nice if I'd thought of that before I climbed the tree.

I'm about to climb down again when a boy walks along the hall, past the open sewing-room door. My heart stops, then hammers into double time. Jackson.

He's wearing black, wraparound sunglasses, a pair of dark blue plaid, flannel pajama bottoms that ride low on his hips, and nothing else. His skin is smooth over taut muscle, his abdomen ridged, his arms defined. I give myself a second to just appreciate the view.

He has a towel in one hand and he pauses in the hallway as he roughs his damp hair with it. Muscles shift beneath smooth skin. He turns, and I catch sight of the scars on his left upper arm and shoulder, a physical reminder of the Drau that somehow managed to escape the game and follow Jackson to the real world the day Lizzie died.

That's why I need the Committee to be the good guys.

Because the Drau are bad. Really, really bad. And if one of them escaped the confines of the game, circumvented the parameters the Committee has somehow created, then there's a chance all of them could get through.

That's the whole point of the game. To keep them from getting through.

Jackson rolls his shoulders and drops his arms so the end of the towel trails on the floor. He stands with head bowed, like the weight of the universe bears down on him.

I want to lay my hand between his shoulder blades, soothe him with a touch, remind him he isn't in this alone. I want to wrap my arms around him and hold him the way he held me when I needed it most.

I will him to turn. Maybe I make a sound.

Slowly, slowly, he pivots to face the window.

For endless seconds, he does nothing. Nothing at all. No expression. No movement. It's like the instant is frozen in time.

My breath rushes out. There's a ringing in my ears. My entire focus is on Jackson.

His lips shape my name.

My pulse trips and starts.

How many times have I dreamed that Mom isn't dead, that she's back, alive, here? How many times have I dreamed about Sofu and Gram?

This isn't just a dream. Jackson's here.

He came back.

He's alive.

It isn't until my lungs start screaming that I realize I'm holding my breath. I exhale in a rush.

In a second he's at the window, yanking it open, standing there with his fists curled so tight over the windowsill, his knuckles are white. He doesn't smile. He doesn't speak. His überdark shades hide his eyes, hide his thoughts. Nervousness writhes in my chest like a downed electrical wire.

"You're not supposed to be here." The words are a low rasp.

Not what I expected him to say. I can't read his tone. There *is* no tone. No inflection. I shake my head, icy doubt freezing my organs, stealing my words.

He isn't happy to see me. He doesn't want me here. Something's changed. Something's wrong.

Emotion overload. I can't deal with this after the roller coaster I've been riding since Detroit. I need to get away.

My instinct is to shimmy down the tree and run. Get away. Leave him far, far behind.

My hands won't obey my thoughts. Instead of letting go, they curl tighter around the branch.

He told me he loved me.

But he doesn't.

He's back to being the boy I can't read, the one who acts like an asshole, a wall ten feet thick between him and everyone else. Including me.

Jackson ducks through the window, clambering out onto another branch, the red and gold autumn leaves shaking free and fluttering down, down. I watch them go because I can't bear to watch him. Can't bear to look at his flat expression.

"What are you doing here?" he asks, sounding anything but welcoming.

"Sitting in a tree." My chin kicks up a notch. "I knocked and rang the bell. No one answered."

"So you climbed a tree?" His brows lift above the frame of his glasses. "I didn't hear your knock or the bell. I was in the shower. Answer the question."

"Yeah, I climbed a tree."

"Not that question," he says. One corner of his mouth quirks in the barest hint of the smile. He once told me, *There hasn't been much that makes me smile in a very long time. But you do. So thank you for that.*

Where's that boy now?

I look at the ground, wondering if I can make it in a single leap without breaking a bone. "Back to being an asshole, Jackson?"

"I never stopped. I told you, Miki. I'm not a good guy."

No shit. He's the guy who sold me into the game.

And saved my life.

And held me when I needed him.

My feelings for him are confused: I told him I love him, and at the moment I said it, it was the perfect truth.

But I'm not certain that loving him is good for me.

The branch I'm on dips as his weight adds to mine. I don't look at him but I know he's there, right in front of me, way too close. I smell a hint of citrus shaving cream and freshly showered, warm male skin. It makes me want to bury my face in his neck and just breathe. But we're as far from that as Rochester is from Australia.

He sits there, saying nothing, the inches between us stretching like miles.

This is not the reunion I imagined.

"Look at me." An order. Typical Jackson.

I raise my chin and glare at him, seeing little reflections of myself in the dark lenses that hide his eyes. He leans closer and the little reflections distort. I refuse to back away. I won't give him that.

"What did you do, Miki?" He sounds frustrated and torn. "What did you do?" A muscle in his jaw clenches as he reaches out and runs his thumb along my cheek. "You're crying."

Perfect. I'm crying. I rub away the tears with the heel of my palm. "I hate you," I whisper, wishing it were true.

"Do you now?" His smile is hard and dangerous, and I can feel something coiled tight between us. Anger? Yeah . . . but something else, too.

Then he shifts even closer, his palms cupping my cheeks. I should slap his hands away. I should scoot back on the branch. But I don't. I close my fingers around his wrists and just hold on.

Every cell in my body reacts to him. My lips part. My breath comes too fast.

He lowers his mouth to mine, his kiss both hard and soft, tasting like mint.

He drinks me in, a boy parched, and I am the deep, cool well. I'm falling, lost in him, lost in this, the wonder of his kiss, lips and tongue and the scrape of his teeth.

I want to lean in closer, tangle my fingers in his hair, and kiss him deeper, harder.

Then I remember that he's kissing me after telling me I shouldn't be here.

He doesn't want me here.

I'm about to bite him when he pulls away.

"My being here is so terrible that you just had to kiss me?" Glaring at him, I drag the back of my hand across my mouth. I don't get it. Don't get him. His touch, his kiss, tell me I'm the most important thing in his world. His words tell me I don't matter at all.

Seconds tick past before he clips out, "Yes."

His answer releases a flood of anger and resentment and, yeah, embarrassment, icy and razor bright. I scoot away, ready to swing down. "Fine. I'll leave."

"No, you won't." Last word. Some things don't change.

He catches my wrists and pulls my hands from the branch, sandwiching them between his larger ones. "You were supposed to forget," he says, sounding like every word is ripped from him, all the emotion that was missing from his voice earlier there now.

I freeze. "Forget what?"

"Me. You aren't supposed to be here because you're supposed to have no memories of me." His lips thin. "I was trying to be the good guy. Not exactly my forte, Miki."

"Why would I have no memories of . . . ?" I don't understand. *Trying to be the good . . .* "No," I whisper, finally getting it. "What did you do, Jackson?"

"Wasn't that just my line?" He tips his head back, face to the sky. "What did I do? I think I got played." He faces me once more. "And here I thought I was being so smart. Not to mention the whole self-sacrificing, nobility thing I was aiming for. I didn't even give in to the urge to stand up the street and watch your window last night. Didn't want to jeopardize the Committee's good will."

"Watch my window? You were going to do that?"

"Nothing I haven't done before."

"Stalker much?" I ask without heat.

"Funny accusation from the girl who climbed a tree to peek in my window."

His answers are flip, but there's an undercurrent to every word.

"Why would standing on my street jeopardize the Committee's good will?"

I reach for his glasses. He catches my wrist, but doesn't stop me as I push them up onto his forehead.

We stare at each other. His eyes are Drau gray, foreign and beautiful, framed by long, incongruously dark, spiky lashes—Carly would say girl lashes. They're the only remotely girly thing about him.

"Do you know how I felt when I looked up and saw you sitting out here?" he rasps, ignoring my question.

"Tell me," I whisper. My chest is tight. I can't draw a full breath.

His lashes sweep down, hiding his eyes. "It was one of the best and worst seconds of my life."

"Best?"

His lashes sweep up and he stares into my eyes. "Because there you were, right outside my window."

My heart does this crazy little dance in my chest. These were the words I wanted, the ones I was hoping for when I came here.

"Worst?"

He takes a long time to answer, then finally says, "Because there you were, right outside my window." He turns my hand palm up, traces the tip of his index finger along my lifeline. "You were supposed to forget. But you didn't. You remember me. And you remember the game."

"Why wouldn't I remember?"

Why am I asking? I know the answer even before he says, "When you're out of the game, you don't remember the game." He turns his face away and stares off into the distance. "But you aren't out of the game, are you, Miki? It was all for nothing."

He sounds so bleak. I remember him screaming inside my head, his pain and anguish. A chill crawls up my spine.

"I think you have this backward." I start to pull my hand from his, but he tightens his fingers, refusing to let me sever the connection. "You're supposed to be the one who's out of the game, Jackson. That's why you brought me into it. So you could be free."

I can't help the tinge of venom that colors those last words. Now that he's here, in front of me, safe and healthy and whole, the recollection that he betrayed me in the first place resurfaces. And it hurts.

In that second, I'm furious with myself for fixating on that, holding on to the hurt. How many times has Dr. Andrews told me that one of the roads to happiness is letting go of grudges? Forgiving. Moving on.

"That was the plan."

"What went wrong?"

His face jerks toward me. "Plans change. Why do you think something went wrong?"

"Because you were in Detroit. And I was already team leader by that point. You should have been out."

"I asked to go on one last run."

"Why would you—"

The way he looks at me stops my question cold. He asked to go because of me. To protect me.

"You almost died," I whisper.

"I knew the risks going in."

"Just like you knew the rules? You know . . . the ones you broke?"

"Which rule would that be?"

"Drawing my life force."

"It was either break the rules or die." His smile is self-deprecating. "Regrets, Miki?"

"No." I shudder at the thought that he might have died there.

"Then why are you so pissed?"

He's goading me. I can feel it. I won't give him the win. I force my tone to stay calm and even as I say, "I'm angry with you for bringing me into the game and then not getting out, not being safe, away from all of this. For wasting your chance. And I'm angry with you for not telling me the truth, for not warning me about the consequences of what we did." I would still have made the exact same choice, but I wouldn't have gone in blind. "You knew you're not allowed. They told you that after . . ." My words trail away. I don't need to remind him how his sister died.

But he says it for me, repeating a fragment of the story he told me once before, his tone hard and liquid-nitrogen cold. "You can say it, Miki. After I killed my sister. After I made like a Drau and sucked the life out of her, changing my con from red to yellow and hers from yellow to red. I traded her life for mine."

There's the Jackson I know: moody, bossy, cocky, a little scary, and chock-full of self-hate. And even though I haven't forgiven him for what he did to me, I can't bear to see him suffering.

It's one thing for me to be pissed at him, something else entirely for him to be so angry with himself.

"You were twelve years old, Jackson. It was your first mission. You were dying, terrified. She told you to do it, that it would be okay. She was your big sister. You were used to believing her, to doing what she said. Why would that time be any different?"

"You think that excuses me? Cuz I sure don't. I killed my sister and then I got hauled in front of the Committee, warned that if I ever did the Drau thing again it would be game over. Then next chance I get, I do the same damn thing and almost kill you."

"But you didn't do it willingly. I made you. I forced you. I—"

"You offered it, Miki. Dangled the hope of survival in front of me, but I'm the one who grabbed hold and hung on. None of this is your fault. It's on me. It's all on me. And the worst thing? I fed off you like fricking Dracula, knowing that you might end up just like Lizzie." He snaps a half-rotten apple off the tree and lobs it hard against the patio. It splatters, leaving bits of white and brown and red dotting the stones. "I keep telling you I'm far from good, and you keep ignoring the message."

"I think my therapist would say you have a really bad case of survivor's guilt," I say.

Jackson barks a laugh, then stares at me, shaking his head. "How do you do that? Make me laugh even when I feel like total shit?" He skims the back of his knuckles along my cheek. "You're like my personal dose of happy."

CHAPTER**THIRTEEN**

WE SIT ON THE BRANCH FACING EACH OTHER, QUIET. THE leaves rustle in the breeze.

"I heard you screaming," I say. I can't interpret the look Jackson shoots me. "Tell me what happened when you didn't respawn at the pizza place with me and Luka."

He reaches over to tuck a stray wisp of my hair back behind my ear. "After Detroit, the Committee pulled me directly to meet with them. They said I was done with the game. Finished. Out."

"Happy news."

"Yeah, for all of about a second. But with the Committee, there's always a catch. Turned out, the catch was that if I go free of the game, the price is you." He holds up a hand when I start to point out that he knew that already; he knew all along he was trading me for his free-dom. That was the whole point. "I don't mean that you'd have to take my place as leader," he says. "I mean I'd have to give you up entirely. I wouldn't get to remember any-thing about you."

"Oh . . ." The Committee already told me that, but the fierce expression on his face as he says it puts a different spin on things.

He strokes the backs of his fingers along my cheek, my jaw, my lips, like he needs to touch me. "And if that didn't suck hard enough," he continues softly, "they were going to arrange it so my family would move again. You'd be excised from my mind and I'd just . . . disappear from your life." He huffs a dark laugh. "Guess they didn't want to risk me seeing you, maybe triggering some memory. . . ."

"You think that would be possible? That you could recover memories they took?"

He lifts his brows and turns his hands palms-up in a who-can-say gesture.

"But even if they took you out of my life, I would have remembered you," I say slowly.

I would have missed him and mourned his loss.

Would my world have gone gray again, or am I stron-ger than that now?

My gaze locks on his and I get the feeling he knows everything I'm thinking.

"I told them it wasn't a trade I was willing to make." His mouth shapes a tight, close-lipped smile. "They told me I didn't get a choice. Consequences of breaking the rules. Their decision, not mine."

"That must have gone over well. You being such a complacent, easygoing kind of guy." I pause. "Then what?"

"Then they pushed into my head. I went a little crazy. Pushed them back out. I think that freaked them out. They pushed harder. I pushed back. It wasn't pretty."

"I felt it." A shiver chases through me as I remember his screams.

His eyes widen. "I didn't know that would happen. I would never want you to go through that, not even secondhand." He pauses. "I was thinking about you, holding on to an image of you with everything I am, refusing to let them take that away. That must have made me project my thoughts without intending to."

Thoughts. Emotions. Agony.

He'd done that before when he dreamed of the car accident that he was in with Lizzie, the one that brought him into the game. He somehow projected it to me so I dreamed it right along with him.

I almost tell him about my hallucination, about thinking I saw Lizzie in the game, then decide not to. Later. This moment is about him and me. "You wouldn't let them take your memories of me, but then in typical Jackson fashion, you decided it would be okay if I sacrificed my memories of you. You didn't think I might want to have a say?"

"You weren't available to have that discussion."

He did what he thought was best. He's been part of the

game, a leader, for so long, it's become intrinsic to who he is now.

"And I wanted you out of the game," he continues. "Out, and safe."

As if any of us will ever be safe until the Drau are gone.

He leans so close I feel his lips against my ear as he whispers, "I would do anything to keep you safe, Miki. Anything. Remember that."

I do remember. He almost died taking a Drau hit meant for me.

"So you were going to win my freedom by sacrificing yourself and having them make *me* forget. That wasn't your call to make, Jackson." I reach for him, pull back, clench and unclench my fingers. Finally, I lay my palm against his chest, close my eyes, and just let myself feel the steady beat of his heart, the warmth of his skin. "So what happened after you pushed them out of your head?"

"The Committee tried a different tack. Went all reasonable on me. Tried to coax their way into my brain. Explained that I'm dangerous if I don't obey the rules, that maybe it's better for everyone if I'm out. What's to stop me from draining any one of my teammates to stay alive if my con goes red?"

My breath comes out in a sharp whoosh. "You wouldn't."

"Wouldn't I?" He bares his teeth in a savage smile. "What do you call what I did to you?"

"You didn't force me. I offered. I gave it to you. And

you didn't drain me. You took just enough to stay alive."

"If I hadn't taken it, then all your offering wouldn't have been worth a damn. And as for taking just enough . . . is that because I was strong enough to stop or because the Committee happened to pull us before I killed you?" he asks in a hard tone. "Face it, Miki. No one on the team would stand a chance against me if I chose to go Drau on them. That's the Committee's fear, and it's justifiable. I'm a potential killer."

I laugh then, because it's all so absurd. "A *potential* killer? Are you kidding? You *are* a killer."

His expression goes blank. "Yeah," he says, and I know he's thinking of Lizzie. But that's not what I mean at all.

"You don't get it, Jackson. We're *all* killers. How many Drau have we taken down? And since we've all taken down Drau, what's to say we couldn't take you down if you decide to drain a teammate?" Before he can answer, I hold up my hand. "It doesn't matter. You wouldn't. It's not even a question."

"So much faith in me, Miki, despite all you know?"

"Because of all I know."

"Not smart," he says, very soft, but the way he's looking at me takes the sting out of his words.

"Probably not," I agree, and mean it. But it doesn't change the way I feel about him. I take a deep breath. "So . . . the Committee tried to get inside your brain, wipe it clean, send you away. Yet here you are. Still in Rochester. Still in the game."

"Yeah. I reenlisted."

"Because you thought they'd let me go? After all the effort you went to so I'd be in the game and you'd get to go free?"

"Yeah."

What a convoluted mess.

"I want you safe, Miki. Alive and safe. And out of the game."

"We don't always get what we want."

He rakes his fingers back through his hair in a completely un-Jacksonlike gesture. "Am I supposed to be happy that I did this to you? That I found you and told the Committee about you? Am I supposed to be happy that your life's still at risk? Because of me. The choices I made."

"Am I supposed to be happy that *your* life's at risk?" I ask.

I glare at him, angry on many levels, for many reasons: His reaction to me being here. The things he's saying. The way that he's so angry with himself that he's putting me in the position of defending him rather than blaming him. The ugly suspicion that this is just him manipulating my emotions, turning my thoughts inside out so that I forgive him. The anger at myself for suspecting him.

I am so screwed up.

And I don't put anything past him. Jackson's been playing the game for five years, dealing with the Committee, steering his team. He's a master. And the things he's learned, he's brought into his real life. I saw the way he handled Mr. Shomper the day he challenged Jackson about wearing his sunglasses in class. I've seen the way he can sit down with any group of kids in the caf and make them feel like he belongs there. I think Jackson doesn't just twist events to his advantage; I think he knows how to get inside people's heads.

My head.

And even knowing that, knowing he isn't lying when he says he isn't a good guy, I'm still here. Still want to be here. Still want him.

Because he's the boy who loves me enough to throw himself between me and a Drau weapon, then sign back on to the game so I could go free.

Not his fault things ended up such a mess, with both of us still exactly where the Committee wants us.

"If the Committee's so worried about the danger you pose, why would they let you stay in the game?"

He shrugs. "Guess they love me more than they hate me."

Sounds familiar.

"And why would you reenlist when all you ever wanted was to get out? Why would you do that?"

He shifts toward me on the branch until he can't get any closer unless I climb into his lap. "You know why, Miki."

I do. For me. Our gazes meet and lock. "Say it," I whisper.

His lips shape a smile, edgy and darkly playful. "Enough about me. Let's talk about you. I paid their price.

149

You should be free. But you aren't. I want to know why."

I narrow my eyes at him, just so he'll know I'm on to his evasion. "They played me, too. Guess you could say I reenlisted, just like you." And because I'd done it of my own free will, their deal with Jackson was made null and void. "We're both still stuck in the game."

"It seems nobility doesn't pay," Jackson says. Now his smile is just a quick flash of white teeth. "You wanted me to say it, so I am. You, Miki. I did it for you."

I inhale sharply.

He brushes the pad of his thumb along the crease of my wrist. I remember when he kissed me there, his lips warm against my skin. "I sacrificed to save you. You sacrificed to save me—"

"And we both end up screwed."

He laughs, a real laugh. I guess the only other option is to cry, and Jackson's not the crying type.

I take a deep breath. "So what do we do now?"

"We steer the nightmare."

"I don't think I'm very good at it."

"You're still alive, aren't you?"

I am, even though I almost died again on the last mission. Given the expression on Jackson's face, I decide not to mention that little factoid.

I look down and rub my fingertips back and forth along the rough bark. "I feel like an idiot. I let them play me."

"What makes you think we had a choice?"

My head jerks up and I stare at him.

The smile he offers is pure Jackson, dark and ironic, carving that long, sexy dimple in his cheek. My breath catches. I wet my suddenly too-dry lips. His gaze tracks the movement of my tongue, then slowly lifts to mine. Heat uncoils inside me.

"Aren't we just a pair of suckers?" I whisper.

I lean forward. Jackson meets me halfway, our foreheads resting against each other, our breathing synchronized.

I close my eyes, trembling as the tip of his nose traces the path his fingers took a moment past, along my cheek, my jaw. I part my lips on a gasp as he pulls back, longing and expectation making me feel like my nerves are on fire.

"They'll always be a step ahead. And I guess that's a good thing because maybe it means they'll always be a step ahead of the Drau, too." His palms cup my cheeks. "And I'm definitely not complaining about getting to hold you"—he nips my bottom lip lightly—"kiss you"—he drags my hand around his waist; I splay my fingers along the warm skin of his lower back—"touch you."

"There's a part of me that's still angry with you, Jackson."

He scoots even closer on the branch, his thighs slipping under my knees, one arm going around my waist. "I have that effect on people."

"I'm serious. How am I supposed to trust you? How can I know you won't lie to me again? Trick me?"

"I won't lie to you again."

I stare at him. "You didn't even try to sound like you mean that."

"I'll try not to lie to you again."

That, he means.

"It's a start, but not enough."

He nods. "We'll work on it."

He didn't dismiss me. Didn't wave aside my words. Didn't act like I have nothing to be angry about. *We'll work on it.*

My turn to nod, even though I'm not fully satisfied.

His fingertips skim along the V of my neckline just below my collarbone, under the strap of my bra, to the eagle tattooed over my heart.

"Did I tell you I like your ink?"

I can barely think with him touching me like that. I shake my head.

"I like what it represents," he says. "Courage."

That's it exactly. That's why I had it done. To represent Mom's courage as she faced the horror of her disease, and mine as I try to figure out how to live, and how to forgive her for dying.

"Not to mention how much I like the placement." He slowly slides his fingertips back and forth, just below my collarbone. "Wouldn't mind checking it out up close, with nothing obscuring the art."

"You mean, without clothes?"

He cocks a brow.

His fingers are warm on my skin. He's tempting, but I

slap his hand. "Not happening anytime soon."

He laughs, low and rough. "No rush, Miki. I'll wait."

His hands slide to my waist, safer territory. I lift my face to his, my mouth to his. He takes what I offer, his lips on mine, his tongue teasing, then slipping away. My lids drift shut. I'm adrift in sensation, in the warm liquid heat he builds in my veins.

He shifts closer.

The branch creaks. The leaves shake.

His fingers ease under the hem of my T-shirt, flattening against my bare skin above the waistband of my jeans.

My world shakes, heat coiling in the pit of my stomach, my breath stolen.

The branch creaks again.

Jackson draws back just enough that the tips of our noses still touch. "It's going to break," he says. Then he leans away and bounces up and down.

I wrap both hands around the branch and let out a sound somewhere between a squeak and a yell.

He grins at me as he swings to the next branch over. The cool air touches my skin. I already miss him.

"Jackson and Miki, sitting in a tree," he says in a sing-song voice. "*K-I-S-S-I-N-G.*"

I laugh. He never says or does what I expect. Maybe that's part of his appeal.

The wind rustles the leaves again, stronger now. I shiver despite my jacket. And Jackson's wearing nothing but flannel pajama pants. "You must be freezing."

"Hot-blooded. And you just make me hotter."

"Oh God," I moan, and roll my eyes.

He looks down at himself and sighs. "I need some clothes."

"You think?"

"Wait for me," he says, and clambers through the open window.

Forever.

CHAPTER**FOURTEEN**

AT 5:45 I CALL MY DAD TO TELL HIM I WON'T BE HOME FOR
dinner.

At 5:46 I lean over the gearshift console between us
and kiss Jackson, careful not to squish the white cardboard
cupcake box on my lap. His fingers thread through my
hair, and he kisses me longer and deeper than I expected.
I'm not complaining.

"You taste like vanilla," I say.

"Want another taste?"

Yes. But then I might never make it out of the Jeep
because one kiss will lead to the next. . . .

He runs his thumb along my lower lip, his dark glasses
hiding his eyes. But I know he's staring at my mouth and
that makes me shiver.

"No. Behave." I heft the box. "Thanks for taking me to pick these up."

"Glad to be of service."

I push open the door. It swings out and back. All I need to do is grab my backpack and hop out. But I'm tempted to stay exactly where I am, to keep hold of the hours we just spent together. They felt so . . . normal.

No Drau. No battles. No game. Just Jackson and me, driving around, listening to music, talking. Laughing. Picking out cupcakes. Just a boy and a girl on a date. A real date. Our first.

"Have fun at Luka's." I reach into the backseat for my backpack, but the box on my lap makes it awkward.

"You sure I can't tempt you to come with? Shoot zombies?" he asks.

I am tempted—to stay with him, not to shoot zombies—but I have something else I need to do tonight. Plus I have no intention of becoming one of those girls, one whose name gets combined with her boyfriend's. If I can even call Jackson my boyfriend. Which I guess he is. Sort of. Or maybe not. Does he think he's my boyfriend?

Could I be any more ridiculous?

I shake my head. "Not coming with you, for a bunch of reasons."

He wraps a strand of my hair around his finger, slides it free, then wraps it again. "Yeah? Tell me one."

"Because if I go with you, I might never want to leave your side. Because if I go with you, I run the risk of becoming your shadow, doing what you're doing just because you're doing it. Because if I go with you, it will be so easy to stop trying, to just float along in your wake, letting you make the plans and decisions, letting you choose where we go and who we see. I need to be me. Miki Jones. Not just Jackson Tate's girl."

"Wow," he says. "Not sure how I should take that."

I realize how harsh I sound and add, "Not that I think you want to make me into that girl, but because you're you"—I spread my hands—"the way you are . . . I need to be even stronger. I need to have my own life."

He tips his glasses up and stares at me.

Oh my God, did I just say all those things? They weren't for him to hear. They were just for me to know. And they weren't even really fair of me to say because despite how autocratic he is, he's never made me feel like he wants me to be anyone but who I am.

He's quiet for so long that I think I've seriously offended him. Then he grins and asks, "So . . . what you're saying is that you want people to call us Mikison instead of Jamiki?"

I bury my face in my hands.

"I can't believe I said all that. I'm so embarrassed."

"Don't be. I know who and what I am, Miki."

"Overbearing?"

"Putting it politely? Yeah. Besides, I like knowing what you think." I can hear the smile in his voice. "Even if what you think is really weird." He peels one of my hands away from my face and ducks his head to look at me. "Still embarrassed? Okay, let's pretend I just asked the question and you haven't answered yet. Give me an answer that you're comfortable with."

I hesitate, then play along. "Fine. I'm not going with you to Luka's because I don't get how you can go there and spend the evening shooting things when we already do so much of that."

"Zombies aren't aliens." When I don't answer he says, "Maybe I like FPS games *because* we do so much of that. Playing one in real life sort of lessens the importance of . . . the game we play in our other life."

Strangely, I understand what he means. But I'm not sure I feel the same way. I don't want to lessen the impact of the game. It's life or death. I'm not sure I ought to forget that, even for a minute.

He leans in for another kiss, his lips lingering on mine, his tongue teasing the corners of my mouth.

"Stop," I say with a laugh. "I am getting out. Now." I nudge the door wider with my foot.

"One thing," he says, taking the cardboard box off my lap. "We need to discuss costumes."

"Costumes?"

"For the Halloween dance."

My heart does a little dance of its own. Is he asking me to the dance? Or just asking *about* the dance. Flustered, I stammer, "Carly, Kelley, and Dee are going as condiments."

His brows shoot up. "I don't even want to know." He pauses. "In case I wasn't clear, we're going together."

"*We* being you and Carly and Kelley and Dee?"

"Funny." He pauses. "You and me."

"That's how you ask me out?" I ask, breathless.

"I wasn't asking."

Typical Jackson. "Last word?"

He gives me that dark, sexy smile, the one that carves the dimple in his cheek and carves a doorway into my soul. "Last word."

My insides melt, but I try not to show it. "Not this time. You have to ask. And that smile doesn't win you any points."

He slides a finger under the taped edge of the box in his hand.

"What are you doing?" I lunge for it, but he moves it out of my reach. Then he slides his finger under the tape holding down the opposite side. "Those are not for you, Jackson."

"I love it when you're bossy. And I'm holding these hostage. Answer, or I eat them all."

I drop my backpack out the open door onto the ground and crawl across the seat, which leaves me half-sprawled across Jackson's chest as I reach for the box.

"Go to the dance with me," he whispers, nuzzling my neck.

"Fine. Now give me the box."

"Fine? That's how you answer?"

I close my eyes as he traces his nose along my jaw and inhales against my skin. "I'd love to go to the Halloween dance with you. Better?"

"Much."

I open my eyes. "Good. Now give me the box."

"If I can't have a taste of these, I get to take a taste of you." He sinks his teeth gently into the spot where my neck and shoulder meet.

I elbow him in the stomach. And hit rock-hard muscle.

"You tightened up," I accuse.

"Gotta protect myself. You're a force to be reckoned with." He kisses me one last time and says, "Go, while I can still make myself let you."

He calls after me through the window as I head up the walk, "Hey, Miki . . ."

I stop and turn.

"You'll never be that girl. And I'll never try to turn you into her."

He presses two fingers to his lips, and then holds them out toward me. Then he puts the Jeep in gear and pulls away. Last word. Typical Jackson.

I stand there watching until his taillights disappear, then I head up the walk and ring the doorbell, my homework-laden backpack slung over my shoulder, the white cardboard box held in front like an offering. The two curved pieces on the sides flap up and down because

Jackson slit open the tape and left it that way. There's a cry of, "I'll get it," from beyond the door and then the click of the lock being turned.

The door swings open and Carly stands there, her hair in a high ponytail, her brother's sweats swallowing her, loose and comfy. For a second, her expression's completely unguarded, and there's no mistaking her unbridled happiness when she sees me.

I grin back at her, feeling like we're just Carly and Miki, exactly as we've always been.

Then the balloon pops. Used to be I could head over to Carly's anytime and it would be like she was expecting me, even if she wasn't. Now, as Kelley and Sarah step up behind her, I feel like an outsider. It only gets worse when Dee wanders up the hall. She's not in their Spanish class, so she's just here to hang with them, not to work on their project. I take a deep breath. The only way to fix this is to stop acting like I'm separate and apart.

"Hey," I say.

"Hey," Carly says. Her gaze dips to the box and the distinctive Sugar Hill logo. "You're kidding," she breathes. "You are kidding."

"Not kidding." I ease the box toward her, the smell of cupcakes wafting up. "You gonna let me in? Cuz that's the only way these cupcakes are crossing the threshold."

"A bribe?"

"Totally."

"Depends on the flavors," Carly says with a grin and a wink.

"S'mores, banana cream pie, chocolate raspberry, vanilla éclair, Roc City crunch, and lemon cheesecake. Two of each."

"A dozen cupcakes?" Kelley moans. She presses her palms together and holds her fingers to her lips.

"That's three for each of us," Dee says. "Because twelve divided by four is three. I mean, there's five of us, I guess, but Miki doesn't count." Everyone turns to look at her.

"Foot in mouth, much?" Sarah asks.

Dee narrows her eyes at her. "I mean, Miki never eats cupcakes, so I'm not counting her among the cupcake eaters."

She's right. I never join them for treats. My one exception is a single weekly Pop-Tart. I control every bite that goes into my mouth, making sure it's healthy, a holdover from when Mom was sick. She tried every medical option the doctors offered, and every alternative option she could find. That included healthy eating to up her antioxidants and bioflavonoids and stuff.

The healthy eating stuck with me. Which isn't a bad thing. But what Dee just said about me not being a cupcake eater *is* a bad thing, not because she said it, but because it's how she sees me. How they all see me. How, maybe, I need to start seeing myself. I'm so rigid that I snap at my friends if they even offer me a cookie. And that definitely isn't a good thing.

162

I'm starting to think that maybe trying so hard to always be in control is making me feel out of control.

So tonight I'm going to eat a cupcake and laugh with my friends and let the evening turn into whatever it is. Tonight, I loosen the reins enough to just *be*.

I take a deep breath and a leap of faith. "Actually," I say, "there are five of us. I'm planning on scarfing down one of these puppies." They all stare at me. "Just one. The rest of you get to split the other nine."

Carly steps outside and hugs me. She knows me better than anyone. She knows what this is costing me.

"Wait . . . nine? How does a dozen minus one equal nine?" Sarah asks.

"Oh, um, there are only ten cupcakes in the box. I bought a dozen, but Jackson ate one of the banana ones and one of the vanilla ones . . . payment for driving me to pick them up."

"Oh. My. Gawd." Dee's eyes widen, and she claps her palms together. "Jackson drove you? As in, you were with Jackson Tate? The two of you? Alone? Like a date? With Jackson?" She rushes out the door and scoots around me, then spins back, looking disappointed when she finds the street empty. "You could have brought him in."

"No, she could not," Kelley says. "Because then she couldn't spill deets." Carly takes the box. Kelley grabs my arm. "Talk. Now."

And just like that, I'm one of them again. Maybe I always was.

"Can I come inside first?"

"Always," Carly says, her smile so bright I think I need to borrow a pair of Jackson's shades. Her eyes meet mine. "And while I won't complain about the cupcakes, you will never, ever need a bribe to come inside."

CHAPTER FIFTEEN

THINGS ARE PRETTY CALM OVER THE NEXT COUPLE OF WEEKS. Jackson and I hang out. Carly and I hang out. Sometimes the extended group hangs out after school under the giant oak at the end of the field, but usually it's just me and Carly and Kelley and Dee meeting there for our after-school recap.

Despite the sun and clear, blue sky, the air's cold. I zip my hoodie, then my jacket, but the chill remains. I shiver and glance around, waiting for Kelley and Dee to catch up, trying to convince myself that the goose bumps on my skin are just from the cold and not from the feeling that . . . something's out there.

Which is kind of silly because something *is* out there: the Drau.

But this feeling is more immediate, more personal.

I push the thought aside and watch as Kelley pulls a checkered blanket from her backpack, snaps it open, and spreads it on the ground. She catches me watching her and says, "The ground's too cold. It makes my butt ache."

Carly flops down and gets comfortable. "If you'd put on a couple of pounds, it wouldn't be so much of a problem," she teases. "Or maybe start running, like Miki. She has a little muscle padding." She reaches up to slap my butt. I dance out of her reach just in time.

"Jealous?"

"Insanely. I could bounce a quarter off your butt." She grins slyly. "Or Jackson could."

"So start running with me."

She does the Carly eyebrow thing. "Not that jealous. I value the extra hours in bed." Her gaze slides past me to where a group of girls clusters around one of the picnic tables near the side door of the school. "Queen Bee and her drones," she says. "Again."

The Queen Bee being Marcy Kern with her head lady-in-waiting, Kathy Wynn, by her side.

"Weird," Dee says. "I wonder why they started hanging out after school. Seems like lately they're here every time we are."

"Weird," Carly agrees, then glances over at the track, where Jackson, Luka, and Aaron are doing laps. "Maybe they like the scenery."

Dee laughs.

I study Marcy's group a moment longer, trying to shake off the impression that they aren't watching the guys, they're watching us.

"So did you hear about Aaron and Shareese?" Kelley asks. "They broke up."

"What?" I ask, my attention snared by the news.

"Oh my gawd." Dee's eyes widen. "They've been together forever. They *can't* break up. They're, like, the perfect couple."

"Are they?" Kelley asks. "They've been together for, what, two years? And Aaron's parents still didn't know they were dating. He snuck around behind their backs because he knew they wouldn't approve. Supposedly, he even went on a date with some girl who's the daughter of his father's friend just to placate them."

"Seriously?" Dee asks. "That's horrible. Poor Shareese."

"I know, right?" Kelley shakes her head. "Perfect couples are also perfect friends, and perfect friends don't lie and hide things."

"In a perfect world, no they don't," Carly says, shooting me an unreadable look. Guilt scampers onto my shoulders. I'm still lying to her about the game, or if not exactly lying, evading. Then she surprises me by continuing, "But sometimes people can't share everything. They just . . . can't."

And if the guilt doesn't exactly go away, it shrinks to a more manageable weight.

My shoes are pink with green laces. They look nothing like my sneakers, nothing like any shoes I would ever own, but I know they're mine. Just like I know they have to be tied exactly right before I can take a single step. I stare at the shoes and tip my head. It's the pink-and-green combo that makes me think I'm dreaming, one of those dreams where you know it's a dream but don't try to wake up, just go along for the ride to see where it leads.

I do up the laces, undo them, try again and again and again until finally the bows are perfectly even, the knot dead center, the feel just right. It matters that everything be just right, lined up and perfect and . . . just right.

I straighten and bounce on the balls of my feet. The ground feels spongy, like I'm standing on memory foam. Each bounce pushes me deeper, until I can't see my feet anymore. I'm sinking, the ground swallowing me, confining me. I shift and sway, certain that if I move just right, I'll get myself free.

But I only make it worse. I lose my ankles, my shins, my knees, parts of me disappearing. How long until there's nothing left?

My grandfather reaches down and takes my hand. That's another clue that this is a dream, because Sofu's dead. Gone. He can't be here.

"Do you miss them?" I ask, touching the yellowed picture of my grandfather's parents in its simple wooden frame. My fingers are small, my hand plump, my voice that of a little girl.

Sofu smiles down at me, his hair more black than gray, his face less lined than I remember. "I miss them, but their spirit is never far from me. They watch over me." He touches the tip of my nose. "And you."

His hand grows cold in mine. His features fade and begin to disappear.

"Sofu!"

"I am here, Miki. Right here. Always here."

Icy fingers touch my skin. Gray. Gray. Gray. Then Sofu's hand is back in mine, warm and comforting and familiar, like he never left at all.

"Hey," Jackson says.

I look up to see him standing at the edge of my driveway wearing black-on-black shades and black running gear that hugs the long lines of his muscles. I don't know why, but I toss my head back and twirl in circles, laughing and laughing until I collapse on the ground.

But I'm not on the ground. I'm running, the air bright and cold, the sky blue and clear, and Jackson's running beside me. He turns his head. He smiles. Not just with his mouth, his beautiful mouth, but with his eyes. His mercury eyes.

They change, growing darker, brighter, grass and leaves and Mom's little emerald earrings.

Not Jackson's eyes.

Lizzie green, like they've always been.

"Run," he says. "Faster. You can get there. You can find it. Faster, Miki. Come on." But it isn't Jackson's voice. And it isn't Jackson running beside me. It's a girl, her honey-brown hair streaming out behind her.

"What are you doing here?" I ask.

"Running."

Typical Jackson answer. I roll my eyes at him.

No, not him. Her. I recognize her face and her smile, just like in the pictures. "I'm trying to help," *Lizzie says, looking sad.*

"I know." *I do. I feel it inside. She wants me to know something.* "Are you dead?" *I swallow.* "Is my mom there with you? She left me."

"She didn't. She'll never leave you."

I shake my head. "Can you find her? Can you tell her to come home?"

"We aren't in the same place."

"What does that mean?"

She doesn't answer. I'm alone, running and running, my legs pumping, but I'm going nowhere. If I could just run faster, harder, I'd get there. I'd see what I need to see. Find it. Fix it.

I run until I hit the wall, the point of exhaustion, the point of I-can't-take-another-step.

I push through.

"I'm here for you, Miki," *Jackson says.* "To help you figure things out." *Jackson who isn't Jackson. Jackson who is Lizzie.* "It's important. You need to understand. They're watching. You have to hurry."

Marcy tosses her hair and laughs, her mouth growing bigger and bigger, the sound growing louder until it's all I can hear. Beside her Kathy shrinks to the size of a thimble. It's funny, but Kathy, tiny Kathy, is the one I watch even though Marcy swells to fill my field of vision.

"You don't get it!" *Lizzie says, looking at me, wanting me to get it. But I don't. I don't get it. I run faster, harder. I need to make it to the end.*

I'm not running for the run.

I'm running for the finish line. And that's so unlike me that I stop. Just stop.

"Don't trust them. They're poison. Do you understand?"

The world tips and tilts. Time slows. I can hear the rush of my blood in my ears, drawn out so it takes a thousand years for a single beat of my heart.

I respawn in a place that's blinding and bright, so white it tears at my eyes. This feels different. Real. Not like part of the dream. I blink. Blink again. There's no floor, no walls, just a gaping black square straight ahead of me. I don't want to walk through it, even though I know I should. I don't want to see what's on the other side. I'm afraid. It's something terrible. Something I can't bear to know.

I walk through, heart pounding, and there she is, Lizzie, watching me with Drau eyes.

She lets out a little laugh of relief. "You're here."

"Where's here?"

She's holding something metallic and smooth. Fluid. Jelly-like.

Her mouth tightens. Her eyes flick to a point above my shoulder as she raises her hand and shoots, sending a thousand pinpoints of bright agony speeding toward me, burning my left shoulder as they overshoot the mark.

I jerk awake, disoriented, afraid, heart slamming against my ribs like a caged bird. It's dark. I'm cold. Shivering, I reach for my comforter.

There's a tap at my door. "Miki?" I glance at my bed-side clock. It's just after midnight. "You okay?" Dad pushes the door open and light from the hall spills in, leaving him a dark silhouette in a dark frame, surrounding by a soft, yellow glow.

"Nightmare," I croak.

He frowns and takes a step into my room. "The usual?" The usual is the one where I dream I'm being buried, clumps of earth hitting the lid of the coffin that holds me.

I shake my head.

"The car accident?" he asks, taking another step into the room. The car accident is the one where I shared Jackson's dream about Lizzie and the night Jackson first got pulled into the game.

I shake my head again. "Neither. Just a regular, run-of-the-mill nightmare." But that's a lie. There was nothing regular or run-of-the-mill about it. That last part where I respawned in the white room—it felt real.

Dad starts to back out of the room, pulling my door shut as he goes.

"Wait . . ."

He ducks his head back inside.

"Just . . . um . . . leave the door open, 'kay?"

He nods, and I'm grateful that he doesn't comment.

Once the door to his room is closed behind him, I ease the neckline of my pj top over to one side, baring my left shoulder and the healing burns that mark my skin.

CHAPTER**SIXTEEN**

I BEAT JACKSON ON OUR *LORD OF THE FLIES* ESSAY FOR MR. Shomper, an *A* to his *A-*. He takes it in stride, vowing to beat me next time.

"Seriously? I worked on mine for weeks, outlining my arguments, planning every paragraph," I say. "You banged yours out the night before it was due."

"You have a problem with that?" he asks, his arms crossed over his chest, his shoulder propped against the doorframe of our English class, his black-on-black Oakleys hiding his eyes.

"No problem. I'm still the one with the better grade." I sashay past him, my grand exit ruined when he lets out a low whistle and catches up to me to whisper, "I love watching you walk away."

"Me? Or a certain part of my anatomy?"

"Anatomy," he says and, when I shoot him a look, continues, "Hey, I'm all about education." Then he slides his fingers into my back pocket, grabs my hand, and guides my fingers into his back pocket, and we walk down the hall, appreciating each other's . . . anatomy.

I haven't told him about the nightmare or the now-healed burns I woke up with. Maybe I think it's too weird or crazy or strange. Maybe I don't want to tell him I'm dreaming about his dead sister. I don't know how it would make him feel and I don't want to hurt him. I do know the marks are gone now, as if they had never been, and there are a million ways I could have hurt my shoulder without realizing it, ways that don't involve Drau weapons and the game.

At least, that's what I keep telling myself.

A couple of days later, I'm heading to the caf when I see Jackson, fingers curled over the door of an open locker, head bent as he talks to Kathy Wynn. She hands him a folded slip of paper, closes her locker, and scurries up the hall to where the Queen Bee and her friends are waiting. Marcy smiles at one of them and nods, her gaze locked on Jackson as Kathy says something to her.

Guess I know why they've been hanging out at the picnic table after school whenever Jackson decides to run laps with Luka.

Marcy tosses her hair back over her shoulder, taking

her time, running her fingers through the shiny strands. Her teeth catch her lower lip. Her eyes never leave Jackson's face.

In health class last year we had to break into groups and discuss self-esteem and the media. Marcy was pretty frank in her self-assessment, saying that she isn't exactly pretty. She claimed her eyes are too small and too close set, her nose pointed, her lips thin. She wasn't fishing for compliments; it was more of an explanation of why she didn't try for the career in modeling her friends were always saying she should go for.

Pretty or not, between hair and makeup and clothes, she knows how to work it, and she does—not too much skin, not too much makeup. Just enough.

And Marcy's a girl who knows what she wants and never fails to get it. She does as she pleases, especially where boys are concerned.

In the past, I've actually been a little awed by her single-minded determination and the way she carries herself, like she's the most confident girl in the world.

The way she steamrolls over anything, or anyone, in her way, not so much.

But I have a philosophy about relationships based on something Mom told me when I went steady with Sam Pitt in eighth grade: no one can break up a couple unless that couple's already got some problems, whether they recognize them or not.

Marcy's group starts whispering and giggling as Jackson unfolds the note and reads it—all except Marcy. She just watches him, confident and poised and expectant. I stay where I am, curious. And if I'm honest, just a little wary. I know what she wants. I'm almost a hundred percent certain that Jackson won't give it to her.

But there's this very tiny ridiculous part of me that worries he might. Because Jackson and I do have a problem or two. Having him in my life comes with a hefty price—the game—and he's the one who set that price. Our relationship is predicated on the way he betrayed me for his own gain. No matter how many times I remind myself that he couldn't follow through in the end, that he stayed in the game so I could go free. I can't quite forgive him, can't quite let go of the possibility that he might betray me again, no matter how hard I try. Stupid. I know.

I suck at forgiveness. Dr. Andrews has told me a million times that I need to work on letting go, but there's a part of me that holds a grudge like it's superglued.

I'm not proud of that part, but it is what it is.

All of which suggest that I'd be the one doing the leaving, not Jackson.

Jackson refolds the note and saunters over to Marcy, his back to me.

He holds out his index and middle fingers, the note sandwiched between them. I think he says something.

Marcy's face flushes red and her cat-got-the-cream smile disappears. She snatches the note and, with a flip of her hair, she turns and marches off, her ladies-in-waiting skittering in her wake.

Jackson turns, catches me watching, and heads in my direction. I duck my head, embarrassed.

I want to ask what that was all about, but I don't, because Jackson really could go out with pretty much any girl he wants.

I have to believe that the fact he's with me means I'm that girl.

If we don't have trust, we don't have much.

Ugh. Moments like this, when my own insecurities rear their ugly heads and test me, when I'm the girl who was mourning while everyone else was learning the dating dance . . . these moments make trust the hardest. But is it Jackson I don't have enough faith in, or me?

"Checking up on me?" Jackson asks as he plants his palm flat against the wall just above my left shoulder.

I cut him a look through my lashes, go up on my toes, and whisper in his ear, "If she can get you, she can have you."

He laughs. As he draws back, I know he's studying my face from behind his opaque lenses. "She can't get me, Miki. You know that. It's been you all along, ever since Atlantic Beach."

I hear the crash of the waves, feel the water on my skin as a memory comes alive. Mine? Jackson's? He has this weird ability to talk inside my head, and a couple of times he's even pushed one of his memories to blend with mine.

I taste salt on my tongue, feel it stinging my eyes. There's a boy on the beach, his hair flashing gold in the sun. Then I'm not seeing him, I'm seeing *me*, seeing what he sees. I dive, the water closing over me, my hair trailing behind me sleek and dark. I come up, blinking water from my lashes. There's the tattoo of an eagle over my heart, only partially covered by my bathing suit. I turn and look at him, my eyes blue. Indigo blue. And I feel his shock, his interest.

He's torn. He doesn't want to do this. He doesn't want to drag someone else into the game. But here I am, a gift dropped right in front of him, a way out. He wants me even as he plans to betray me.

Then his emotions undulate and shift, different now. The catch of awareness. Attraction.

His.

Mine.

Powerful.

He wants to kiss me, touch me. . . .

Snap. I'm back in the hallway, the noise from the caf pouring through the open double doors.

I aim for a cocky expression. He laughs again, soft and low.

My skin tingles. For a second, I think it's from the way the sound of that laugh winds around my heart.

But the tingle grows stronger, sharper. It isn't pleasant. The hairs at my nape prickle and rise. A shudder crawls up my spine.

"What?" Jackson asks, suddenly alert.

"Creepy feeling," I say. "Like someone watching me, or walking over my grave."

"I hate that expression," Jackson says. Then he juts his chin to my left. "That someone?"

I turn to look, and there's Marcy, the expression on her face as sour as month-old milk in the back of the fridge. Kathy stands beside her. And, yeah, they're both watching us. I remember the nightmare, Marcy growing and growing and Kathy shrinking. I almost tell him about it, but I can just imagine the smug look he'd give me and the way he'd ask if I'm jealous.

"Not them," I say, careful with my words. Not any of the kids walking along the hall. After my first mission, Luka told me that we don't talk about the game outside the game. I didn't get it at first. Then I found out it's because the Drau can watch us anywhere, using human satellite technology. And they create armies of shells—human forms that house Drau consciousness. I've only ever seen their failed attempts at those, but what if they've succeeded? The shells could be anywhere. Anyone. Any kid walking past.

Marcy.

Kathy.

Mrs. Tilson, carrying her mug of steaming tea. Any one of the lacrosse guys shoving one another and laughing as they walk.

"Not them," I say again, but I'm not so sure anymore.

"Someone else?" Jackson asks.

"Some*thing* else."

It's as if Jackson dons a different persona. Gone is the teasing and the flirtation. His posture changes, not a lot, but enough that I notice. He scans the perimeter, watching, weighing.

"You still feel it?" he asks.

I think about that for a second, then shake my head. "Not now. And I'm not even a hundred percent certain I felt it to begin with. It was just for a second." I pause. "You didn't sense anything?"

"No."

If the Drau were here, I think Jackson would have noticed. I glance over at Marcy. She's still staring at us.

"Oh, give it a rest," I mutter, then to Jackson I whisper, "Maybe it was her all along. Maybe I'm just edgy."

He smiles a little and leans in to whisper against my ear, "Maybe we should find a way to work off that edge."

"We are in school," I point out.

He grins in reply.

Carly and Dee come up the hall, heading for the caf. Carly does a quick assessment of the situation and gives Marcy an are-you-kidding-me-back-off-now look. That's Carly, always the peacemaker except when someone goes up against a friend. Then she's Carly-the-poison-tree-frog— gorgeous but deadly.

"I'll save seats," she says as she walks past us.

Marcy stalks off, but I can't help looking around one last time, feeling like something's still not quite right.

"Aren't you dying to know what was in that note?" Jackson snags my backpack, slings it over his shoulder, and starts walking down the hall. I take four steps to his two and catch up.

"No."

"Liar," he says, then after a pause, "Her phone number and a time."

Pretty much what I expected. The phone number part, anyway. The time? Not so much. I can't imagine assigning Jackson a time to call me, as if he'd take orders from anyone.

"Dying to know what I said to her?"

"No."

It isn't until I'm tucked in front of him in the cafeteria line that he leans in and says, "I told her I already have what I need. And that any little girl who has to send her friend to pass me a note instead of walking up to me herself isn't the girl for me."

"Harsh," I say, feeling a little sorry for Marcy.

I'm in the kitchen trimming Brussels sprouts when I notice the counter's completely clear. No bottles. Not even one.

As I pop the Brussels sprouts and cubed squash in the oven to roast, I think back to the past few days and realize that Dad's started putting his own empties away.

We've reached a new understanding, it seems. Ever since the day I told Dad about the AA meetings, I've stopped counting the cold ones in the fridge and the empties under the sink. At least, I try to stop. Sometimes I slip and when I realize he's had five or six or nine, I wish I could go back and unslip.

I'm still working on the whole chillax, go-with-the-flow thing.

When we're done with dinner, Dad helps me clean up, then grabs his keys.

"Going out?" I ask, trying to sound casual. He's been going out almost every night, leaving after dinner, coming back after I'm asleep.

"Yep." He kisses my cheek.

I almost ask where he's going, and if he wants me to come.

Then I don't, partly because I can't be the parent here, can't control his actions or his choices, and partly because if he's going to meetings he might not want me there. I don't want to do anything to make him stop going.

I'm in my pj's before he gets home—showered, teeth brushed, homework complete, ready for bed but not for sleep. I lie in the dark, waiting for the sound of his car in the drive, his key in the lock, knowing that what I'm doing isn't good for me. Not knowing how to fix that.

Sometimes, when I'm alone late at night, tossing and turning, my thoughts start to spiral to places I don't want them to go. To places I inhabited for nearly two years. To the negative self-talk. To the creeping fingers of gray fog that want back in.

Tonight's one of those nights.

I'm tempted to call Jackson, to let him shoulder the weight of my mood. And that's exactly why I don't.

I will not let anyone be my crutch.

At least, that's what I tell myself.

But then that little voice, the one that's sibilant and cruel, reminds me everyone leaves.

The only person you can rely on is you.

Better not to fully let down my defenses.

Tonight, like every one of those nights, I cry in my sleep. I know that because I wake up in the morning with tracks along my cheeks.

CHAPTER**SEVENTEEN**

"I CAN'T HELP FEELING THIS NIGGLING SENSE OF EXPECTA-tion, like something bad is waiting in the wings. Like the other shoe's about to drop," I tell Jackson later that day, trying to explain it.

"Wings . . . shoes . . . that's quite the mix of metaphors," he says, taking a bite of his sandwich.

I roll my eyes.

Despite the cold weather, we're sitting at the top of the bleachers, sharing the lunch I made for both of us. I shiver, partly because talking about this makes me nervous, mostly because I didn't dress warmly enough for the weather. Jackson shrugs out of his jacket—the brown leather worn and faded to beige in spots—and drapes it around my shoulders.

"You'll be cold," I say.

"I have my hoodie." Last word.

His jacket's still warm from his body and I hug it close, watching Luka and Carly and Dee race one another up and down the stairs. We haven't been pulled since the time I almost died—the time I thought Jackson's dead sister saved my life—and that's freaking me out.

Jackson bites off half a sandwich, chews, swallows. "I've gone up to three months without getting pulled," he says. "A few weeks isn't unusual. Be happy for the break."

"How do you handle the not knowing?"

He shrugs. "I can't control it. I know that, so I don't even try. When it happens, it happens. I'm not going to waste my good moments by obsessing about the bad. *The Beast in the Jungle*, right?"

"What's that?"

He finishes his sandwich and eyes the half of mine I haven't gotten to yet. "You going to eat that?" he asks, reaching for it.

I shift the container out of his reach. "Yes." Then I dig through my pack and pull out another container. "But I made extra." I hand him his second sandwich.

"You are a goddess," he says around a mouthful.

"Your turn to make lunch tomorrow," I remind him. "And no cheating by buying crap in the caf like you did last time. So . . . *The Beast in the Jungle*?"

The wind catches my hair, blowing it all around. I

reach back and gather it in my fist, then tuck the length under my collar, down the back of my—Jackson's—jacket.

"It's a story by Henry James." Jackson catches a stray strand and tucks it in with the others. "It's about a guy who's obsessed with the belief that something catastrophic is going to happen to him, like a beast waiting to pounce, so he wastes his whole life, afraid to do anything that'll encourage it. Terrified. Waiting for it to happen."

"So what happens? What's the catastrophic thing?"

"Nothing. That's the point. Nothing terrible happens. The catastrophe that gets him in the end is the fact that he didn't really live. He was too afraid."

"Sounds like an uplifting read." And it sort of sounds like my panic attacks.

I put my empty container back in my pack, watching Carly run down the stairs shrieking and laughing, with Luka a step behind.

"Sometimes everything feels too big," I say. "The Drau. The threat. Knowing that they've already destroyed at least one entire species and now they're after us. The future of the whole world weighing on our shoulders." Carly shrieks as Luka catches her, then breaks away and darts off. I gesture at them. "Regular high-school life just doesn't seem important."

"It's the most important," Jackson says. He shifts us both around so we're straddling the metal bench, my back against his chest, his arms wrapped around me from behind. He rests his chin on my shoulder. "When we beat the Drau, this is the life we'll still have, Miki. This is what matters most. Our families. Our friends. This is exactly what we're fighting for. This moment, and a thousand others just like it."

I twist my head to look back at him over my shoulder. "*When* we beat the Drau? You say that like you have insider knowledge of the exact day and time. You know something I don't?"

Jackson looks away, like he's avoiding an answer, and for a second a chill grabs hold of me, turning my blood to ice. What isn't he telling me?

Then I look where he's looking to see Dee sprint past Luka and tackle Carly to the ground. Luka trips over them and all three land in a heap, laughing, caught up in their game. Luka lifts his head, catches my eye, and for a second he looks almost guilty. For what? For having fun?

His gaze shifts to Jackson and it's like the three of us are connected, thinking about another game where it isn't about fun.

"Two against one. Unfair advantage. Take 'em down," Jackson yells, and Luka grabs Dee's ankle just as she gets to her feet. She's back on the ground, laughing.

Her joy is infectious, pushing past my barriers and doubts and fear, trickling through me like sunshine.

"You're right," I say. "This is what we're fighting for. This moment. That's what matters."

I jump to my feet and toss Jackson's jacket in his lap.

"Race you!"

And then I leap from bench to bench, tearing down toward the field with Jackson hot on my heels.

The ringing of the phone wakes me. I roll over, the last vestiges of a great dream about me and Jackson and a dog and a beach still clinging to my thoughts. I check the time—1:00 a.m.—then check the number. Carly.

Worry uncoils, rattling and baring venomous fangs.

"Hey," I say.

She doesn't answer right away.

I sit bolt upright, tightening my grip on my phone as I flick on my bedside lamp. "Carly?"

A gasp followed by a shaky exhalation.

Images flash through my thoughts of blood and death and the Drau darting through Carly's house like bright reapers.

"Carly, what's wrong?" I throw back the covers and jump to my feet, ready to wake Dad, to head over there. I reach for my jeans, dragging them on one-handed. I'm struggling to get my second leg all the way in when she lets out a gasping sob.

"Miki."

"I'm here, Carly. What's wrong?" I demand, my voice hard and tight with fear. I get my jeans the rest of the way on and pace the length of my room, waiting for her answer.

"Grammy B," she whispers.

Grammy B is Carly's mom's mom. She's funny and fun, and I have great memories of her from before she moved to

Florida to help Carly's aunt Melanie through her divorce. That was three years ago. She stayed on to help watch Carly's little cousins while Mel works. She says she likes feeling needed and she was here to help Carly's mom with her brood when they were small, so it's Mel's turn now.

I know Carly misses Grammy B even though they talk on the phone all the time. On the phone isn't the same as in person, and Christmas visits and a week in the summer just aren't enough.

"Is she okay?" I whisper back, a reflex even though it isn't the brightest question. If she were okay, Carly wouldn't be calling me.

Everyone leaves.

I press the back of my hand to my mouth. Carly stood beside me at Mom's funeral—Dad on one side of me, Carly on the other. She held my hand. She held me up when my knees went weak. She slept in a sleeping bag on my floor beside my bed for a week afterward, waking up with me every time the nightmares ripped me open, sitting on one side of my bed while Dad sat on the other.

I'll do the same for her. I'll go to Florida, go to the funeral, unless they're bringing Grammy B's body back here—

"She's in the hospital," Carly chokes out. "CICU. They said it's acute myocardial infarction."

Hospital. Not dead.

Myocardial infarction is a heart attack. That's bad.

But people can recover from that. I know they can. Mr.

Shomper had a mild heart attack a couple of years ago and he's still here—still teaching, even.

"That's good," I say, fighting my own tears. "That's great."

"What?" Carly chokes out.

I shake my head, then realize she can't see me and my words aren't making much sense to her.

"It's great that she's alive," I say, all the hope in my heart coming through in my tone. "She's alive, Carly."

"You're right," Carly says after a few seconds. "She's alive. She has a chance."

"A good chance, right?" *Please let her have a good chance.*

She sniffles. "They say that if she makes it through the night, that it's a good sign."

I close my eyes and silently hope that she makes it through the night. That she doesn't pass in her sleep without ever waking up like Sofu did.

"They'll take care of her. They'll make her better," I say even though I'm not convinced of the last part. I don't exactly have the best track record with hospital outcomes. But I want Carly to have hope. And I desperately want my words to prove true.

"What do you need?" I ask. "What can I do to help?"

"We're heading to the airport in a couple of hours. We're all going. The whole family. Just in case." She pauses. I can hear her crying—big, snuffling sobs. Tears prick my lids and I blink against them. "I don't know how long we'll be there."

You'll be there till she's well enough to go home. Or until she can never go home. . . . The thought rips me up inside.

"I'll get your homework," I say, needing to be able to do *something.* "And I'll tell your teachers."

"And Kelley and Dee. Sarah. Amy. I didn't call anyone. Just you."

"I'll tell them." I feel so sad for her.

"And can you watch my Daimon?"

Daimon. Her fish. It's a betta—a Siamese fighting fish. She swears he's brilliant. That he does tricks. Personally, I think that he comes to the surface when she dips her finger because he's genetically programmed to attack.

"You know where Mom hides the spare key. Can you come get his bowl and keep him till I get back?"

"I'll get him first thing in the morning."

"You need to feed him once a day. I do it right before I leave for school. Don't overfeed him," she says, her words rushing together. "Just give him what he can eat in two minutes. No more. Or bacteria will get in the water and that's not good."

"Got it. His food's in the freezer on the door, right?"

"Yes. Take care of him. Promise."

"I promise."

A promise I'm destined to break.

Four days later, Carly calls with the awesome news that Grammy B's going to be okay.

"She has to take aspirin every day and beta-blockers

and something else that's a blood thinner . . . it starts with a *P*. She was only in CICU one night; then they moved her to a regular room, and then they let her out of the hospital today. We're flying home tonight," she says, sounding happy and relieved. "Can you bring Daimon by? I miss his wavy blue fins."

I glance at the bowl on the end table. "Sure."

"How's he doing?"

"Good." Sort of a white lie. He didn't eat yesterday. I ended up having to scoop all the food out after a few minutes so it didn't taint the water. He didn't eat this morning, either. I take a step closer to the end table. "He's good."

"Did you do the little trick where you put your finger in the water and he bumps up against it?"

I'm standing over the bowl now, looking at the fish. He's not moving at all. Not even the flick of a fin. I dip my finger in the water and bump it against the little blue body with its fins sagging toward the bottom.

Oh crap, oh crap, oh crap.

"Yep. Bumped the fish in the water. Doing it right now. As we speak." Truth. Sort of.

She laughs. "Gotta go. The taxi's here to take us to the airport. See you soon."

I stare at the fish, willing it to move. "You're sleeping, right?"

Right. Sleep of the dead.

With a sigh, I text Luka. Twenty minutes later, he's at my door. "What's up?"

"I need you to look at something."

"Okay." He steps into the hall as I pull the door open. "How come you called me instead of Jackson?"

"Two reasons," I say. "First, I just think you have this relationship with Carly." A few weeks ago, Luka acted all territorial a couple of times in the game. It made me wonder if he was into me. But lately, I've had the feeling he's into Carly. Hard to tell.

His eyebrows shoot up.

"I mean, a friendship . . . that you're friends with her—"

"So's Jackson." He gives me a weird look.

"Second," I continue as if he hadn't interrupted, "Jackson took his mom grocery shopping because her car's in the sho—" I break off as Luka laughs. "What?" I ask.

"When you met him, did you ever picture him taking his mom shopping?"

"Honestly? I never pictured him having a family."

"You thought he just sort of arrived in the world preformed. Spawned."

My turn to laugh. "Pretty much."

Luka's expression turns serious. "So what's going on with Carly? Did you hear from her? She okay?"

"She's okay." Until she finds out about the fish. "Shoes," I remind him.

He toes off his sneakers. House rules. Mom never let anyone wear shoes in the house, so I don't, either. Just like Sofu never let anyone wear shoes in the dojo. It just isn't something you do.

I lead him into the den. "Well?"

"Well what?" he spreads his hands.

"Is it dead?"

He looks at me. Looks around again. Finally spots the bowl sitting on the end table.

"Uh . . ." He stares at the bowl, reaches in, stirs the water in circles, stares at the fish, then pulls his hand out and looks for something to wipe it on. He's reaching for the afghan that's draped over the back of the sofa, the one my mom made when she was pregnant with me. I lunge for it and get it out of harm's way.

"Use your jeans," I say.

"It's either dead, or"—he wipes first the front then the back of his hand on his jeans—"There's no 'or.' It's dead."

"Oh God." I bury my face in my hands. "I killed Carly's fish."

"Are you sure you killed it? If this is the same one she had before I went to Seattle, it's, like . . . what . . . more than two years old? Maybe it just died of natural causes."

"It's still dead. After I promised I'd take care of it. What do we do?"

"We?" Luka's brows shoot up. "You just tell her you're sorry. I don't know. Offer to hold a fish funeral?"

The front door slams. "Miki?"

"I killed Carly's fish," I wail.

Dad wanders into the den. Luka offers his hand.

"Don't shake that," I warn Dad. "He just had it in the water with the dead fish."

"Right. Because it isn't like I haul fish out of the lake all the time," Dad says with a grin. Which is true, him being a fishing fanatic and all.

Still, he does this sort of half-wave-half-salute thing instead of shaking Luka's hand.

Luka scrubs his hand on his thigh, then shoves it in his pocket.

Dad peers at the fish. "Buy her a new one. Make sure you look for one that has the same red tinge on the front fins."

"You mean, like, don't tell her the old one died?" Luka asks. "Just get her a replacement and try to pass it off?"

Dad shrugs. "That's what I did with Miki's turtle when she was six."

"What?" I gasp. "Yurtle? You tricked me? What kind of thing is that to do to a six-year-old?"

"Better than having you freak out over the dead turtle. You never knew a thing. Yurtle one, two, and three kicked off within a couple of months of one another. Four stuck around for a while."

I stare at his back as he wanders to the kitchen.

I remember my parents telling me Yurtle got out of his tank, that we might not find him. And I remember freaking out. Next morning, there was Yurtle, back in the tank. Was that version two, three, or four?

Was it better to let me blithely believe it was the same turtle all along? Or should my parents have told me the truth?

I agonize over the fish thing for hours. Actually, Luka and I rent a movie and I agonize intermittently during the slow parts.

As the final credits roll, I shift on the couch so I'm facing Luka with my legs crossed. A quick check reveals Dad to be nowhere in the near vicinity; he wandered upstairs about an hour ago and hasn't come back down yet. Still, I lower my voice to a whisper. "Can I ask you some stuff?"

Luka narrows his eyes at me. "Depends on what sort of stuff."

"Have you ever had nightmares about the game?"

"Not lately, but in the beginning, yeah. I was pretty freaked when I first got pulled." He's told me that before, when we finally talked after Richelle got killed. He studies my face for a few seconds, then asks, "Are you having nightmares?"

I nod. "Some. Not a lot. One that was different, though. It was weird. I know you said you didn't see the girl who helped me when I got hurt last time"—and the Committee had claimed the same: that they hadn't sent any other teams on that mission, that I was alone—"but I dreamed about her. She looked like Lizzie."

Luka just stares at me blankly.

"Lizzie," I repeat. "Jackson's sister."

"Jackson doesn't—whoa," Luka says after a pause. "You're seeing the ghost of your boyfriend's dead sister. That's—" He looks at me incredulously and he shakes his head.

"She's trying to tell me something, Luka. Something

about the game. I saw Marcy and Kathy, and Marcy was laughing and Kathy was really small, like, smaller than my baby finger and—" I break off and stare at Luka as he starts laughing. "What?"

"You sure the nightmare was about the game? I mean, Marcy's obviously . . . her and Jackson . . ." He holds up his hands as he realizes what he's saying. "I don't mean that the way it sounds. I know there is no *her and Jackson*. It's just, she watches him all the time. She's not exactly subtle. Actually, she watches both of you."

"I know. I feel like every time I turn around she's there with her posse, and it's creepy."

Luka stares at me, the laughter fading from his expression. "You don't mean stalker creepy, do you?"

I shake my head and whisper, "Drau creepy."

"You think Marcy Kern's a shell?"

"No. Yes. Maybe. I don't know." I exhale in a rush.

"Her eyes are blue," Luka says. "Light blue. Kind of icy. Not Drau gray."

"Do shells have Drau eyes?" I ask.

Luka holds my gaze. I could ask him if he knows about Jackson's eyes, if he's seen them. We've never actually talked about that. It's something Jackson and I keep between ourselves. At least, I think it is.

"Drau eyes?" He frowns, shrugs. "I have no clue. But I still think that if you're having nightmares about Marcy it's because she's trying to get into Jackson's pants—" At my chilly look, he finishes, "Just saying."

I uncross my legs and cross them in the opposite direction, so my right foot's now on top of my left. "Let's forget about Marcy for a second. There's something else. Near the end of the nightmare, I got pulled, and it felt real. Not like the rest of the dream. Real and . . . important." I try to line up the details in my thoughts. "Have you ever been pulled somewhere other than the lobby?"

"All the time. So have you."

"No, I'm not asking this right. I don't mean pulled on missions. I mean pulled somewhere like the lobby but totally different. White and cold and . . . cold," I finish lamely.

He shakes his head.

"Have you ever . . . brought your injuries back with you?"

"What? No. If we come back, we come back healed. What's going on with you, Miki? What aren't you telling me?"

"Nothing. Seriously, nothing." I rub my left shoulder even though it doesn't hurt, even though the marks that were there are gone. "Nothing," I say again, and cover my unease by stacking our empty glasses and offering Luka the last piece of sliced apple on the plate.

A little while later, Carly calls from the airport to tell me they've landed.

The pet store will be open for another half hour. I could make it. I could buy Daimon 2.0.

In the end, I decide the hard truth's better than the easy lie.

I get in the Explorer and drive Daimon's corpse—which is no longer floating and has sunk to the gravel at the bottom and started to turn white at the edges—over to Carly's.

"I'm sorry," I say, holding the bowl out toward her, barely able to get the words out because I'm crying so hard. Over a fish.

Or maybe it isn't over the fish at all.

And maybe she's just so grateful that Grammy B's going to be okay or maybe she's the greatest friend ever, or maybe it's a combination of the two. Whatever the reason, Carly wraps her arms around me and we cry together.

And then she forgives me.

CHAPTER**EIGHTEEN**

THE NIGHT OF THE HALLOWEEN DANCE I PULL ON A PAIR OF black jeans and a black turtleneck. I add a black military-looking vest that I found online, and finish running a brush through my hair just as the doorbell rings.

Dad's out again. He called a few minutes ago to check on me.

"Yes, my phone's charged, Dad. Yes, I'll be in by midnight." I find it odd that he didn't ask who I'm going to the dance with or how I'm getting there. It's like he's going through the motions of being the concerned parent without actually participating in anything but the most superficial level.

The hope that surged inside me the day I told him about the AA meetings has faded to a dull shade of pale.

Last week, when I was vacuuming his office, I found an empty clear glass bottle with blue block letters on the floor under his desk. I picked it up and stood it beside the waste-paper bin. He never said a word about it. Neither did I.

But that night, when I tried to open a conversation with an oblique reference to AA, Dad shut me down like a steel trap. He's graduated from beer to something stronger. Or maybe he's been drinking both all along.

The doorbell chimes a second time.

I push aside the negative thoughts.

I choose to focus on the moment, this moment, the first time a boy's taking me to a dance. And not just any boy. Jackson.

I tear down the stairs to pull open the door. He's lean-ing against the porch rail, arms crossed over his chest. He's dressed all in black, like me, but he's wearing a V-neck, long-sleeved pullover, and his vest's bigger and bulkier with these round things on it. Very *Gears of War*.

Two black paintball masks dangle from his fingers. We were going to wear paintball guns as accessories, but that didn't quite pan out as hoped. Ms. Smith made an end-less announcement that made it clear there were to be no weapons of any kind at the dance, not even cardboard cut-outs. Definitely not unloaded paintball guns.

So we're going as weaponless warriors. Which is fine with me. I have my fill of weapons in the game.

Jackson pushes off the rail and walks past me into the house, snagging my belt loop as he passes and dragging me inside. He drops the paintball masks, pushes the door shut, and backs me against it, his arms caging me, his thighs against mine.

"Trick or treat," he says.

"Treat." I give him a peck on the cheek, duck under his arm, and lift the nearly empty bowl of mini chocolate bars sitting on the kitchen chair I dragged to the front door. "Happy Halloween." I hold the bowl out to him.

"I was hoping for something sweeter. Say . . . your lips on mine . . ."

"You'll have to settle for chocolate. Luka's waiting. Are we picking him up?"

"He's meeting us there. He's picking up Sarah and Amy on his way." Jackson pokes through the bars and chooses one. "All the peanut-butter ones are gone?"

"I don't do peanut butter. Too many kids have allergies."

There's a crinkle of paper and he downs the candy in a single bite. He tosses the wrapper back in the bowl. I hold out my hand, palm up. With a faint smile, he fishes out the wrapper, deposits it in my hand, and helps himself to another bar.

"Planning to hand out any more candy?"

"I think all the little kids came through earlier." I reach across him to turn off the outside light. "It's pretty late for them now."

"Then I can eat the rest." He takes another chocolate bar.

I surreptitiously check him out while I put the bowl back on the chair. "I'm a little surprised you're so into this whole Halloween thing."

He turns to me and tips his glasses up, his silvery eyes preternaturally bright against his dark, spiky lashes. "You're into it, so I'm into it." Leaning in, he whispers against my ear, "I want it to be good for you, Miki."

I do a fair imitation of Carly's arched-brow thing. "Behave."

"Not gonna happen."

I know. And I kind of like that. And I definitely like the fact that he never pushes too far.

"So what's with you and the love of Halloween?" he asks.

"I loved dressing up as a kid. Mom used to make a big deal out of it every year. We'd carve pumpkins together and plan my costume for weeks and she'd buy tons of candy. Give it out by the handful instead of just one or two at a time."

I remember the Halloween after Mom died. I didn't dress up. I didn't even give out candy. And just a few weeks ago, I was standing by the giant oak, listening to my friends talk about the dance. I felt flat and broken, wishing I could feel as excited as they did. But I didn't.

And now I do.

I'm not sure what that means.

Jackson tugs at one of the buckles on my vest. "You okay with this now? Our costumes?"

When he and Luka first came up with the idea of the three of us dressing like characters in a game, I balked. Jackson pointed out that it was pretty much the only way he was going to wear anything close to a costume. I still wasn't convinced. Then Amy and Sarah joined in, and it actually started to sound like it might be fun.

"Yeah. I'm okay with it. And it'd be kind of late to back out if I wasn't." I nudge him with my shoulder. "You look good." Better than good. "Where did you get those boots?" They're black, knee high, with a bunch of buckles and snaps.

"Made 'em." He opens the front door, bends to grab something from the porch, and holds it—them—out to me. I gasp. He has another pair of boots just like his, and they appear suspiciously close to my size.

"You made these for me?"

"Better than chocolate or roses, right?"

"Hey, I gave you chocolate."

"That doesn't count. I had to scavenge the remnants. And I'm giving you boots."

I laugh, then throw my arms around him and hug him because, yeah, thinking of the hours he must have put into creating these, they are way better than chocolate or roses.

"How did you know what size . . . ?" I take the boots from him and take a closer look. My jaw drops as I notice the color of the lining and the logo stamped inside. "These are my red rain boots."

"They're black now."

"How?"

"Automotive spray paint. Made the buckles from belts I found at the secondhand store."

I shake my head, not sure whether I'm supposed to feel awed or annoyed.

"Did you have to use my rain boots?"

"How else would I be sure they'd fit?" He has a point.

"Did you make some for Luka?"

"He made his own. Mine are better."

Of course they are.

I slip my feet into the boots and Jackson hands me one of the paintball visors. I pull it on and glance at myself in the hallway mirror, Jackson's reflected image a little behind and to my left. He looks good in black. I can't see his eyes, but I know he's studying me in the mirror, and the faint curve of his lips tells me he likes what he sees.

"You look badass," he says. "Let's go."

We climb into the Jeep. I'm snapping my seat belt in place when color explodes, hurting my eyes, the candles in the jack-o'-lanterns next door too bright, the streetlamps singeing my retinas. The cool air on my skin feels like a thousand needles.

The whole world tips and tilts around me, under me, the seat falling away.

No, no, no. Not now.

"Jackson!" My cry's distorted and slow, like I'm caught in a slo-mo movie. I reach for him, the movement taking forever. My hand passes right through where he used to be. He's gone. He made the jump.

My fingers fumble at my seat belt, numb and clumsy.

The thrum of my pulse beats in my ears. My head pounds.

The world drops out from under me, leaving me spinning end over end.

I respawn flat on my ass.

Trees.

Grass.

The two familiar boulders.

The lobby. I can see other teams gearing up.

"Jackson?"

"Right here." My heart does a little flip when I hear his voice. I didn't know if the Committee would put us back on the same team. I thought they might, given my inexperience. At the same time, I thought they might not, since putting two leaders on one team doesn't immediately appear to be the best plan of action.

I hear the crunch of boots on grass; then he holds out a hand to me. I grab it and he pulls me to my feet. He's wearing his sunglasses, and his paintball visor is clipped to his vest. Only then do I realize I'm still wearing mine. I pull it off.

"Should we take these off? The vests? Leave them here?" I'm not sure how we're going to wear our harnesses over them, or if the vests will be a risk in the game.

Jackson shakes his head. "Can't leave anything here. They go in with us."

I almost reach out and touch him, then hesitate at the last second. He's not the Jackson who backed me up against my front door to steal a kiss. This Jackson is alert and focused, watching every corner, every shadow.

This is game Jackson. Untouchable. Unchallengeable.

That's okay. It's this Jackson who knows how to keep us alive.

"Incoming," he says.

It takes me a second to catch on. He heard them—the Committee—and I didn't.

"You're team leader again."

"Disappointed?"

"Relieved. Glad I'm not going into yet another mission with my team's lives on my shoulders." I shake my head. "I don't know how you ever get used to being responsible for someone else's life."

"*You* don't." His expression is savage, his tone controlled. The combination makes me shiver. "Every man for himself."

"I'm not a man."

"No, you're not. You're a girl, my kick-ass warrior girl. I want you to watch your own back and no one else's. Tonight's going to be—"

I tense. What? What does he know? What doesn't he want to tell me?

His mouth turns down at the corners. "Like I told you

the first time you got pulled, you make it through this, Miki Jones."

The first time I got pulled he had to make a horrible choice: me or Richelle. He couldn't save us both. And while he's telling me not to care about anyone else, he's the one who'll watch out for everyone on the team.

"I'm sorry," I whisper. "Sorry that you have to be responsible. Sorry that—"

"Don't apologize. I've been doing this a long time, Miki."

Long enough that he was desperate to find a way out. *I* was that way out, his exit strategy, and now thanks to me, he's stuck here for good.

"It's just . . . Richelle . . . you couldn't save us both. What happens if it's Luka this time?" He stiffens. "Or Tyrone?" Or Lien or Kendra? I feel sick even thinking about it.

With a snarl, he pushes his glasses up and steps close enough that I can see every individual lash, see his pupils, dark and dilated, surrounded by a thin rim of mercury gray.

"I know what you're thinking. It's all over your face," he says, low and hard. "Don't you think it. Don't you start second-guessing your choices or mine." He pulls me to him and gives me a short, hard kiss. "You know the drill. Stay close enough that I can hear you breathe."

"Conversation over? Just like that?"

"Conversation over."

Except, it's not. "Jackson, it isn't just that. It's the

Committee. They tricked you. Tricked me. I just don't—" I throw my hands up, frustrated, not even sure what I want to say, never mind how to say it. I think of that crazy nightmare, the one where Lizzie warned me, *Don't trust them. They're poison.* She was talking about the Drau—at least, I assume she was. But what if she meant the Committee? I know it's really out-there to think like that, but for a second, it seems possible.

"What if they aren't the good guys?" I whisper.

"No 'what if' about it. They aren't. Not the way you mean." He brushes the pad of his thumb along my cheek. "Miki, they might not be all kittens and ponies," Jackson says, "but they're on the right side of the line. It's the Drau we need to worry about."

"I know. It's just . . . the last time I saw them, they were threatening to kill you. Or me." I sigh and lay my hand on his arm. "I'm sorry, Jackson. Sorry your way out ended up"—I make a vague gesture at the lobby—"like this."

An odd expression flits across his features. Regret? Maybe.

"What?" I ask. "What has you frowning like that? What are you not telling me?" As soon as I ask the question, an eerie chill crawls over me. "Tell me."

He scrubs his palm over the faint stubble that shades his jaw. "I knew exactly what I was doing when I told the Committee I'd stay," he says. "You want the truth, Miki? I'll give it to you, plain as porridge, so there's no more question in your mind. I knew what I was reupping for. And there's a part of me that wants it. Bad." His fingers tangle in my hair and he says, very low, "There's a part of me that likes this."

The way he says it makes me shiver. Because he's telling me the truth. I feel it in my gut. He likes the fight, the adrenaline rush. Maybe even loves it. But there's another truth, one he's keeping hidden, and I don't know what or why. So I push a little harder for answers. "And?"

He lets me go, steps back. "And just for clarity, I'll spell out a few points. One: I signed on, eyes wide open. Two: if I'm in the game, I will lead, not follow." The silver in his eyes swirls and deepens to stormy gray. "Three, and the most important point: if you're in the game, Miki, then that's where I'll be, watching your back. End of discussion. We don't talk about this again."

I believe every word he's saying. But I know there's something he isn't saying. He's doing it again. Hiding things. "There's the Jackson I know and love. Moody, bossy, cocky—"

"Asshole," he finishes for me.

My chin comes up. I hold his gaze and inch even closer. We're almost nose-to-nose. Tension thrums in the air between us.

"You. Are not. The boss. Of me," I say, holding up my index finger and making a wavy line in the air, throwing as much attitude as I can into both the words and the action.

He stares at me. Blinks. Bares his white, white teeth. Not a nice smile; not warm, not friendly. Dark. Feral.

Appealing.

"Sometimes," he says, very soft, "I think you're the boss of me."

My insides melt. How did Miki, the girl who would never in a million years fall for a boy like Jackson Tate, end up falling for a boy like Jackson Tate?

Maybe because there are no other boys like him. There's just him.

"As if," I say back, equally soft.

The sound of a muted cough makes me turn. Luka's on the far side of the clearing, hands shoved in his pants pockets. I don't know how long he's been standing there. I don't know how much he heard. And I don't think I want to know.

Jackson flips his glasses down, covering his eyes.

Did Luka see them when he first arrived? I try to picture exactly how we were all standing, what his sight lines were. If he did notice anything, he isn't saying.

"Seriously?" he asks as he saunters over. He's wearing an outfit very similar to what Jackson and I have on. His paintball visor's pushed up on top of his head. "Are we seriously doing this tonight? When I have not one but two attractive and slightly tipsy ladies sitting in my car right now?"

"Slightly tipsy?" I ask.

He shrugs. "Seems that Sarah's brother supplied a few bottles of beer for her and Amy."

I study his face, worried that he's going into the game

at a disadvantage. "Are you slightly tipsy?"

All humor fades from his expression. "I don't drink and drive."

I nod. "Sorry."

He bumps me with his shoulder.

"We're due for a mission," Jackson says. "It's been weeks since we've been pulled. Might as well be tonight."

Or any other night. Or how about no night? Ever.

"Let's get this done," Luka says, looking first at Jackson, then me, before pulling off his paintball visor and hooking it to his vest. "Not the ideal getup for alien hunting."

"Deal with it," Jackson says, and tosses me a harness.

Tyrone shows up a few seconds later.

Jackson nods at him. "Hey," he says.

Tyrone nods at Jackson. "'Sup," he says.

"You good?" Jackson asks.

"Good." Tyrone juts his chin in Jackson's direction. "You?"

"Yeah."

And that verbose conversation somehow leaves me with the impression that they're happy to see each other. Gotta love guys.

But I remember Tyrone before Richelle was killed. She teased him about talking too much and slowing the team down.

He's changed.

I guess we all have.

Tyrone takes a quick look around the lobby. "Before

they get here, I need to give you the heads-up," he says to Jackson. "We've got one, maybe two."

"Two what?" I ask.

"Problem players," Tyrone says.

I think about that. "Kendra's pretty freaked out," I agree. "She's definitely scared. I don't know if I'd say she's a problem, though. She did her share the last couple of times."

"More than her share," Tyrone agrees.

So why do I feel like he's saying something really horrible about her? Like whatever it is, he'll trust Jackson with the information but not me?

"Tyrone, do you have a problem with me?"

His expression softens. "Never, Miki. Got nothing but respect. You kept a level head through some pretty rough shit. I'm just a little concerned about them."

"Them being Kendra and Lien?" When he doesn't saying anything more, I turn to Luka. "What about you? Are you worried about them?"

"Not worried. I actually think Lien's interesting. But I'm not convinced I'd trust either of them with my life."

CHAPTER**NINETEEN**

"INCOMING," JACKSON SAYS, HIS POSTURE WATCHFUL, VIGI-
lant. Makes sense. He doesn't know the new team
members yet, and he's not exactly the type to trust anyone sight unseen. Especially not after Tyrone and Luka
expressed their concerns.

Kendra shows up in red sneakers, denim shorts, yellow
T-shirt, and red suspenders. Her blond hair's been colored
a bright orange, straightened, and pulled into a one-sided
ponytail. Lien's wearing jeans and blue sneakers, a black
T-shirt, a blue bowling shirt with short white sleeves and
a white collar, a red ball cap, and green fingerless gloves.
There's a black mesh bag hanging from her belt loop with
a red-and-white ball banded in black inside.

"Awesome costumes. Misty and Ash?" I ask Lien.

"Pokémon rules." She offers one of her rare smiles.

"We're cosplayers," Kendra adds. "We made these for Anime Expo last year."

"You went together?"

"Uh-huh."

That surprises me. Not that it's impossible for people to know each other from outside the game—Jackson and Luka and I do. But I'm a little surprised that I'm only just figuring this out now about Lien and Kendra, on our third mission together.

My gaze collides with Kendra's. She's watching me watching them. I can't quite read her expression.

"Did you meet in the game? Or did you know each other before and both get pulled?" I ask at the same time Luka says, "Pikachu, I choose you," and winks at Lien as he mimes an overhand throw.

"Pikachu? I'm all about Charizard," Lien says with a sniff, choosing to ignore my questions.

"Makes sense. Fire-breathing lizard with a bad attitude?" Luka lifts his brows. "Suits you to a T."

Lien sends him a dark look.

And Luka looks back at her like he's . . . interested. Wow. Obtuse much? He and I have to have a little talk.

"We're really gonna have a conversation about Pokémon?" Tyrone asks, sounding disgusted.

"We're not having any conversation," Jackson says. "This isn't social time. We aren't here to make friends."

"Have you practiced that speech?" I ask. "Because it

sounds a lot like the one you gave me the first time I got pulled."

"Who the hell are you?" Lien asks. From the expressions on her and Kendra's faces, this is about to get interesting.

In typical Jackson fashion, he's about as friendly as a post. "Jackson Tate," he says by way of introduction.

"Lien. That's Kendra." She's barely civil as she says it.

"I know."

Luka's brows shoot up. I'll tell him later about the Committee dropping info into Jackson's head. I've had enough of the whole we-don't-talk-about-the-game-outside-the-game. I'm more certain than ever that knowledge is power, and the more we know, the better we'll be able to do this job.

"Gear up," Jackson says.

I wince at the militant expression on Lien's face. This is not going to go well.

Kendra crosses her arms over her chest and cocks a hip out to the side. "What makes you—"

Jackson's right in front of her and I barely even saw him move. Lien tries to get between them, but Jackson sidesteps her easily.

"My team. My rules," he clips out. "This is not a democracy. You follow my lead. Do what I say when I say it and I will get you both out of this alive."

Lien glances at the knife strapped to Jackson's thigh. Her expression's mutinous, but it's Kendra who answers back.

"Who died and made you king? Miki's still alive, still in the game. That means she's still leader. You're the new guy. You don't get to just waltz in here and take over with all your macho shit." Then she stomps over and stands beside me, shoulder-to-shoulder.

Tyrone lets out a low whistle. "Mutiny." He crosses his arms over his chest and leans back so his butt and the sole of one boot rest against the larger of the two boulders. "Let the show begin."

Lien shoots him an ugly look. "I don't think I like you," she says to Jackson as she flanks my other side. I'm a little stunned by the show of solidarity. She and Kendra haven't exactly been fan one and fan two up to this point.

"You don't need to like me," Jackson says. "You just need to take orders."

Beside me, Lien tenses.

Was there ever a boy who was more adept at pushing people's buttons?

"Actually," I interject before this degrades any closer to nuclear meltdown, "Jackson's the leader of our merry little band. I was just filling in for the last couple of missions. But he's back. And trust me, he has way more experience than I do."

"Yeah?" Lien gets too close, right in his face. Jackson doesn't move a muscle. "How much experience?"

"Five years."

Lien's jaw drops and Kendra gasps. "I've never . . ." Lien

snaps her mouth shut and shakes her head. "Five years? Longest I've ever heard anyone being in is two. Five years and you still haven't hit the thousand? You must suck."

The thousand. The magical number of points that's supposed to guarantee an exit from the game. According to the scores that came up last time we got pulled, none of us is anywhere close. And none of us has actually met someone who hit the thousand and got out. When I asked the Committee about the thousand-points-and-you-get-to-go-free rumor, they didn't really give me a straight answer. They danced around it, saying that no one on the planet would ever really be free until the Drau threat was neutralized.

I cut a glance at Jackson. For team leaders, the thousand points really is just a rumor. The only way out for a leader is to find a replacement, and neither Jackson nor I even have that option open anymore. We're in the game for life, married to it, till death do us part—as in, either the Drau are dead or we are.

"Save it," Jackson says to Lien, his tone harder than I've ever heard it. "Save that anger for the Drau." He waits a beat, then continues, "Here's my philosophy. Adopt it, and you'll make it out alive. Every man for himself. You watch your own ass. Your con goes orange? You fall back to defensive position. No heroics. And no stupidity. Got it?"

"That makes no sense. We're a team," Kendra says with a wary look in my direction as she and Lien grab their harnesses and gear up. "What do you mean, every man for himself?" at the same time as Lien says, "You are some kind of asshole."

Tyrone snorts a laugh. "Not *some kind* of asshole. The consummate asshole."

Luka cuffs Jackson on the shoulder. "Nice way to make friends, Jack."

This all feels so familiar. Jackson said a lot of these things to me the first time I got pulled. I didn't understand any of it then. I didn't understand *him*. But now I do. He'll tell each of us to be selfish, to watch our own backs and no one else's, but *he'll* be wholly unselfish, watching out for all of us, expecting no one to watch out for him.

I consider explaining that to Lien and Kendra, then decide against it. Even if they believe me, which I'm not certain they will, Jackson will deny it. So why waste my breath? They'll see soon enough.

Instead, I clarify his philosophy because I figure understanding it might mean they follow it. And that actually might help them at some point. "In Jackson's opinion, if you're trying to keep an eye on someone else, it splits your focus. That could get both of you killed."

"It's not just an opinion," Tyrone says, his eyes locked on mine in a frozen instant of mutual understanding.

Richelle was killed because she was watching Tyrone's back. At least, that's what Tyrone believes. He thinks it was his fault.

"Scores," Jackson says.

Kendra catches my eye and jerks her head in Jackson's

direction. "What's with the shades?"

I smile a little, despite my nerves. "He likes to think he's cool."

Tyrone and Luka laugh.

"I don't get the joke," Lien says, snippy and pissy and dripping attitude.

"You will. Patience, grasshopper," Luka says with a teasing grin.

Lien punches him in the shoulder. Hard.

She steps closer to Kendra and takes her hand. They exchange a look I can't read and when Lien glances up and catches me watching them, her expression closes.

Then we all turn to face the screen hovering in the center of the clearing. The 3-D digitized rendering of Jackson appears, making him look like a character in a video game. He's wearing the clothes he had on in Detroit. It's like a snapshot of the last time he was in the game, the last seconds of that mission. I wince as I study the image. He's lying on his back, his face chalk pale. His eyes are closed.

The emotions I felt in that second—hopeless, desperate, half-deranged—bite at me now. I tamp them down, refusing to set them free of their chains. I need to stay calm. I need to focus. One mistake could cost lives, and despite Jackson's mantra, I'm not all about me. I'll keep an eye on everyone on this team. We are all coming back.

The picture of Jackson flips end over end, then shoots to the top left corner of the screen.

Luka's next. He has on the clothes he was wearing

during our last mission. He's down on one knee, leaning over something, his hands stained with blood. I'm guessing that's my blood because there's a clear view of my arm and my con, almost fully red.

"Something you forgot to tell me?" Jackson asks against my ear, his tone low and rigidly controlled. A sure sign he's majorly pissed.

"I'm fine," I mutter.

"But you almost weren't."

What am I supposed to say to that?

Luka's picture flips over and over and zooms to the top left corner, knocking Jackson's down a notch.

Tyrone's next. He's running, his expression intent, his focus complete. Up and over he goes, then zips into place above Jackson, below Luka.

The next picture's Kendra. The black frame forms and her picture shimmers into place. Her eyes are squeezed shut, her mouth twisted, her arms raised before her, the black ooze from her weapon obscuring half the screen.

It's a weird angle to have captured. Not for the first time, I wonder exactly where these pictures come from and how the Committee creates them.

Lien's picture comes next. She's pulling back, like she was about to take a shot and then didn't.

My picture's enough to make Jackson hiss through his teeth. I'm on the ground, wearing my sports tank, blood everywhere. Great. I tip my head back and stare at the sky for a second before looking back at the screen.

The two columns of numbers appear.

"What's with your score?" Lien asks. "I know you lost points to injury penalty, but . . ."

My gaze skids down the list to the bottom.

My picture's second last. Jackson's is last. Our scores are set to zero.

"We got reset," Jackson says.

"Never seen that before," Luka says at the same time Lien demands, "What does that mean?"

"Leadership snafu," Jackson says, his tone making it clear that the subject's closed.

Tyrone squeezes my shoulder. Kendra shifts her weight from her right foot to her left, arms wrapped around herself, palms rubbing up and down, up and down until Lien reaches over and stills her. But no one says anything more. How does Jackson do that?

"We jump in thirty," Jackson clips out.

"If he's the leader, how come you get a sword?" Kendra asks, pointing.

I follow the direction of her finger and see my kendo sword placed neatly beside the weapons box. I cut a glance at Jackson. He shrugs.

My sword shouldn't be there. Only the leader carries an extra weapon. Jackson's is the long-bladed black knife strapped to his thigh. He did combat application technique training when he lived in Fort Worth, and he brings that knowledge into the game.

"Bring it," Jackson says as he picks up my scabbard and

tosses it to me. I snatch it out of midair, mentally counting down seconds to the jump. Tyrone reaches over and helps me get the sword strapped to my back, the handle between my shoulder blades, perfectly positioned so I can reach back and grab it.

As I turn, the screen catches my eye. I stare at it, stare at the scores. Kendra's second from the top. That means her cumulative score is second highest. I frown, thinking back to what the scores looked like before the last mission, before we respawned in the elevator. I was so focused on Jackson, finding him, saving him, that I really didn't pay attention. Was Kendra that close to the top last time? For some reason I think it was Tyrone, then Luka, then Lien, then Kendra. So either I'm wrong or she's gained a ton of points in a single mission.

Luka makes an odd sound. I glance at him. He's staring at Kendra, his expression closed.

My stomach twists. Something's off. Something's wrong.

And then the jump takes hold and turns me inside out.

CHAPTER**TWENTY**

WE RESPAWN IN A WIDE HALLWAY. BEIGE LOCKERS LINE ONE
wall. A large, glass-fronted case full of pictures and tro-
phies and plaques takes up the opposite wall. Sports stuff.
We're in a high school. I glance at the name and don't recognize it.

I wait for the feeling of urgency, the sense that the
Drau are near, and get nothing. Looks like they're late to
the party.

A pounding bass beat carries from a distance. There's a
dance going on here, somewhere not too far away. I glance
at Jackson. "This is not good. There are civilians nearby."

"Civilians?" Luka asks, his brows shooting up. "What
are we? Special Forces?"

Lien snorts.

"Vegas," Jackson answers me, typically verbose, reminding me that we've been in a position like this before. When we went after the Drau in Vegas, they were in a warehouse in a populated area. I remember jogging along a crowded street, groups parting to let us through, sensing us but not seeing us, as if we weren't there.

The reminder settles my nerves a little.

"So if we run into anyone, they won't see us, right?"

"Never have before," Tyrone says.

Not wholly reassuring, but the best I'm going to get. I'm more than curious about how this all works. Different dimension? Different plane of reality? Maybe I'll try to get answers out of the Committee next time I see them.

Good luck with that.

I glance at Jackson, waiting for his confirmation. He doesn't say anything more, which isn't unusual for him on a mission. So why does his silence leave me uneasy?

Lien and Kendra hang back, close enough that their shoulders touch, hands resting on their weapon cylinders. The whole we're-one-big-happy-team thing I was aiming for last mission has definitely fizzled.

Suddenly Jackson holds a finger to his lips, then draws his right hand palm down across his throat in a slicing motion. I don't need to know anything about military-style games to read the message: *danger.* The Drau are near. He can feel them.

So can I.

I sense their presence, some primitive part of my soul

reacting to the threat. My pulse ramps up.

Enemy.

We all feel it. Genetic memory. Instinct. The urge to flee the Drau is blueprinted into our DNA.

But we don't flee. We're going to head straight for them, swallowing the horror and fear that bubbles inside. It creeps me out that the battleground's going to be a high school with a bunch of oblivious kids dancing in a gym somewhere close. The selfish part of me is grateful it isn't *my* high school.

Jackson taps his con. I hold mine up. All green. So is everyone else's. His con's got the live feed and the map and the moving triangles. That means the Committee wants us to stick together and follow Jackson's lead.

Weapon cylinders drawn, we proceed down the hall in a column. Jackson gives the halt signal and he and Luka check a door. Locked. We keep moving. Something's off. It isn't just the Drau alarm clanging in my gut. It's something else. Something I haven't felt before.

I catch Tyrone's eye. He frowns and offers a half shrug, and I get the feeling that he's getting the same weird vibe I am.

I focus on it. Dissect it. Can't quite put my finger on what it is that's bothering me. I just feel off, like I didn't respawn here quite right, like my molecules aren't totally in sync. It makes me think of a transporter failure in an old Star Trek episode. *Beam me up, Scotty!* The thought sparks a really inappropriate urge to laugh. My nerves are wound so tight that one more turn of the screw will make them pop.

Jackson and Luka check another door. Same result. We move down the hallway, Lien and Kendra bringing up the rear. Every door we try is locked. The rooms beyond the doors are dark. And with each step, the music gets a little louder.

We turn a corner and a wave of vertigo nearly knocks me to my knees. I slap my hand against the wall and close my eyes. Doesn't help. Everything still feels like it's spinning, or maybe I'm the thing that's moving. I press harder against the wall, using it as my anchor, focusing on the rough texture of painted brick beneath my fingers. When I open my eyes, I see that whatever hit me hit us all. Except maybe Jackson. Hard to tell with him. He always looks like a hard-ass.

I take a step forward, keeping my palm flat to the wall for balance, sliding it from brick to the cool metal of a bank of lockers.

Wait . . . the lockers are a different color. They were beige. Now they're dark blue.

A color shift shouldn't bother me, but it does.

My stomach gives this weird little flip.

I shoot another look at Jackson. His jaw is set, his attention focused. Even though I can't see his eyes behind his mirrored lenses, I can sense him scanning the perimeter, always vigilant. Whatever's setting me off, he feels it, too.

Or . . . maybe he already knows what it is. Did the

Committee warn him, give him a heads-up about what to expect? I suspect they did, and he's choosing not to share.

Jackson points at Luka and Tyrone. They move ahead, check the next few doors, and we follow behind.

The music's louder, closer. I can hear voices and laughter.

People. The dance. The auditorium.

It's just along this corridor and to the left.

How do I know that?

I close my eyes for a second, not wanting to admit what I've already figured out: I know where the dance is because I've been in that auditorium hundreds of times, because I walk these halls almost every day.

We're not at the high school we respawned at.

We're at Glenbrook.

The Drau are at Glenbrook.

At my dance. With my friends. People I love.

But they can't be here. That's the whole point of the game. To keep them away.

My skin crawls and I turn to look behind me, certain I'll find a Drau, a dozen Drau, a hundred. But there's only Kendra and Lien.

I shake my head and spin back, muscles tightening, ready to sprint. Jackson grabs my upper arm, stopping me as I take a step forward.

I gasp. I don't even know what I was thinking. That I'd run into the dance, weapon cylinder drawn and blazing, kendo sword at the ready? I get myself under control, holding tight to the knowledge that while my school may be offering the backdrop, my friends and teachers are safe. We're here but not here. Same with the Drau. We'll pass through the throngs of people, but they won't see us. And they won't see the Drau, won't be subject to their attack. Just like the people we passed in Vegas. The tension knotting my muscles eases a little.

"Luka," Jackson says, no longer bothering to stay silent. "Scout the dance."

"They know we're here?"

"Just like we know they're here." Jackson snags Luka's paintball visor off his vest. "Leave this."

Luka turns his hand palm up in a what's-up gesture.

Jackson cocks his head in Tyrone's direction and says, "Tyrone might need it. Student-only rule."

The rule Ms. Smith made says only Glenbrook students are allowed at the dance. Kendra and Lien will probably be able to sneak through thanks to their costumes. It's kids at the ticket table, not teachers. Usually no one checks ID.

But Tyrone's wearing regular clothes and he looks older than high school. He'll definitely get stopped at the door.

He takes the visor and slips it on, leaving it on top of his head for now. Not much of a costume, but better than nothing.

"He doesn't need a costume," I point out. "It's like Vegas, right? No one can see him. No one can see any of us. We'll sail through the crowd." Unseen. Unnoticed. In an alternate version of Glenbrook High. "He doesn't need a costume," I repeat, the words tense and low.

Jackson's lips thin as he reaches over and moves Luka's weapon cylinder from his holster to one of the big, baggy pockets at the front of the vest he's wearing.

"Go," Jackson says. Then to me, "Yeah, he does."

We hang back and watch as Luka strides toward the auditorium doors.

Maylene George is sitting behind the ticket table, along with Kathy and Marcy. I stare at them, at Marcy, wondering if she knows, if she's one of *them*.

I expect Luka to walk past, unseen. Like Vegas.

But this isn't like that at all.

Actually, I don't expect it to be. Not anymore. Something's different. Something's very, very wrong.

Maylene tips her head and smiles as he approaches. "Hey, Luka. I thought you were bringing Sarah and Amy."

Maylene can see Luka. She knows he's here. Which means he's in the same reality as she is.

And so are the Drau.

They're not in a parallel place that doesn't touch anyone who isn't part of the game. They're here.

Really here.

Right now.

My fingers dig into Jackson's forearm. I feel dizzy, sick, my anger and fear and confusion swamping my thoughts until I think I might throw up.

I look at the walls, so familiar, the top third painted white, the bottom two-thirds beige. I look at the rectangular fluorescent lights. The ceiling tiles. The banks of lockers lining the walls.

This is my school, and they are here.

In my world. My real world.

The boundaries have failed.

The Drau have pushed through.

Horror tastes like ashes, dry and desiccated.

I step forward. Jackson snags my hand, holding me back. I tug. He tugs back. The rational part of me rears its head and he wins.

Luka says something to Maylene about Sarah and Amy being on their way. He hands over some cash and Kathy hands him a ticket, her fingers grazing his as she looks up at him through her lashes. Either he doesn't notice the way she looks at him or he chooses not to notice. He heads into the dance.

Seconds ooze past. Ten. Thirty. Ninety.

Then Luka appears at the auditorium doors and signals us. No Drau inside. Not yet.

My heart's pounding so hard that it's all I can hear. It takes me a second to realize that Jackson's talking to Tyrone.

". . . rule about students only. Don't want to take a chance on drawing attention. You three head outside. Go around back. Find the rear doors. I'll crack them open from the inside. Be careful, take your time, and don't take any risks."

"Take our time? Guess that's gonna cost us the time bonus," Lien quips.

The time bonus for getting the mission done at warp speed. It starts out as triple points and decays by increments of point five. There are a ton of options to score bonus points in the game. Stealth-hit bonus points. Multi-hit. Head-shot bonus points. Tyrone explained it all to me the very first time I was pulled. But I rarely think about points and scores, and in the heat of battle, I *never* think of my score. I just think of staying alive.

"Are you serious?" I ask, my whole body vibrating tension. "I get that you want to earn your thousand, that you want out. But you're talking about scoring bonus points when these are people, real people, my friends—" She looks at me, her eyes wide, surprised. She doesn't understand. She doesn't know.

And then she does. I see the change in her the second that it hits her. She holds up both hands in front of her like she's warding me off. Her expression reflects all the worry and distress I feel. She might not know my friends, but she knows what this means: If the Drau can come into my real world, they can come into hers.

"Sorry. We good?" she asks.

"Yeah." I nod, recognizing how close to the edge I really am.

Kendra's strangely quiet, hanging back a couple of feet,

pale, shaking, sort of huddled into herself. Not good. I'm worried she's going to freak out again, like she did before the last mission.

Holding Lien's gaze, I cock my head in Kendra's direction. Lien sinks her teeth into her lower lip and shakes her head as she falls back to talk quietly in Kendra's ear.

I glance at Tyrone. He's watching them, narrow-eyed, and then he looks over at Jackson. He mouths a word, but I'm at the wrong angle to catch what it is.

Some silent agreement passes between them, but I have no idea what.

I walk over to Kendra and Lien and take both their hands in mine so we're a little circle. "We are all coming back. Remember?"

Kendra lifts her eyes and whispers, "I remember." But her expression's vacant.

"Jackson," I say, wanting to tell him I don't think she's all here. And I think that in her current state, she just might get herself—or someone else—killed.

I'm on it.

I gasp. I'd forgotten what it was like to have him push his thoughts inside my head, his voice right there, part of me.

"Go. Get them outside. Back doors," Jackson says to Tyrone.

Lien shoots him a glare, but doesn't argue and I have a feeling that's for Kendra's sake.

As the three of them jog down the hall, back the way

we came, I realize Jackson knew before I did that Kendra was in trouble. That's what this whole rear-door thing is about. He sent Tyrone to babysit. Which means it's me and Jackson and Luka. Three of us against who-knows-how-many Drau.

Awesome.

CHAPTER**TWENTY-ONE**

I GRAB JACKSON'S ARM. "HAVE YOU EVER BEEN IN A SITUA-tion like this before?"

"Like what?"

"The game pushing into the real world."

He bares his teeth in a smile that isn't a smile. "You ever seen my left shoulder?"

I swallow. Of course he's seen the Drau in the real world. One attacked him. Scarred him for life.

Incongruously, I wonder what he told his parents about that scar, about how he got it. I wonder if the Committee just planted some bogus knowledge in their heads. Can they do that? I know they can take memories away. Can they add them, too?

The possibility is horrific.

Then another thought hits me. Did Jackson know? Did he know we were coming to Glenbrook? Did he know the walls between our two realities would fail?

Did he choose not to tell me?

Jackson snaps his fingers.

My gaze jumps from his shoulder to his face.

"Stay with me, Miki. Wherever you just went inside your head, don't go there again. Not till we're out." He unstraps his knife from his thigh and shoves it into one of his vest's many pockets, then does the same with his weapon cylinder.

I follow his lead and tuck my weapon cylinder into the pocket of my vest. The pocket isn't as big and loose as Jackson's and Luka's, and the outline is still clearly visible through the cloth. I poke at it, trying to make the shape less obvious.

"I'm not worried about that," he says. "I'm more worried about your sword."

"Crap. Forgot about that. What do we do?"

He walks around behind me and I feel him undoing the sheath; then I feel the weight lift off me.

"Don't turn around," he says.

I hear a swoosh, like a belt pulled quickly through a loop. I turn around. Jackson's standing there with his pants undone, hanging way low on his hips, revealing most of his dark-gray boxers. He slides the sheath of my sword down his pant leg. He's holding the bottom of his T-shirt up, baring smooth, gold skin and ridged muscle and the thin line of light-brown hair that trails down his belly. With a gasp, I turn away.

"Told you not to turn around," he says, and I can hear the smile. There are faint sounds as he finishes what he's doing—I'm guessing buckling the sword to his thigh—then, "I'm decent. Shirt safely in place."

Echoes of what he said to me the night he climbed in my bedroom window to prove to me he wasn't a shell. Weeks ago. A million years ago.

I feel like I've known him my whole life.

"We're lucky Glenbrook isn't a school with a metal detector or we'd be screwed," Jackson says.

"If we get caught with weapons, Ms. Smith is going to be pissed. We could get suspended. Expelled."

"That's your biggest worry right now?" Jackson asks with a short laugh.

"No," I whisper, thinking of all the things that could go wrong. But they're too big, too terrible to think about, so I focus on the small, the less important.

"Steer the nightmare, Miki. Clear your mind. Think of this like a kendo competition. We go in. We fight. We win. Doesn't matter that you're a girl and they're boys, faster, stronger. Doesn't matter that some of them look at you like you shouldn't be there, like you don't have a right. You fight. You win."

He's right. Doesn't matter that the Drau are faster, brutal, deadly. What matters is that I'm deadly, too. The fact that I'm still alive proves it. So I do what he says. I take a couple of deep breaths. Focus. Visualize.

"So what now?" I ask. "You said we go in . . . but Luka gave us the all-clear sign. There are no Drau inside the dance."

"Not yet." His expression is ruthlessly neutral. And his answer makes my stomach churn.

"Maybe they'll go somewhere else. The science room. The roof. The weight room. The—"

"They won't," he says. "You know that. You feel it here"—he splays his fingers over my abdomen—"and here." He shifts his hand to my chest, over my heart, over the tattoo of the eagle. "Courage," he whispers. "You have enough of it to fill an ocean, Miki."

"Why here? Why are the Drau *here* at Glenbrook?"

Jackson shrugs. "Maybe coincidence. Maybe they're going for something that matters to us."

I swallow and force the words past my too-dry lips. "Maybe the Committee chose this battleground. Maybe they're trying to make a point. Keep us in line."

I desperately want him to shoot down that possibility, but he only tips his head toward the open double doors to the dance. "We'll keep them safe."

My next exhalation is a shuddering sigh, but the one after that is smoother. I nod.

We stop at the ticket table and Jackson somehow manages to smile at Maylene like the world isn't about to come apart, like the Drau aren't about to ramp up their game. Like my heart isn't slamming against my ribs, my palms damp. He chats with her. Gets our tickets.

And despite the mission jitters, I can't help but notice the way Marcy's looking at him. I glance at Jackson. His head's turned toward her. His expression gives nothing away. I can't tell what he's thinking. And it doesn't matter. Marcy ogling Jackson is so far down my list of issues right now, it barely ranks high enough to scrape mud off my boots.

So why is it giving me the creeps?

My gaze slides to Kathy, sitting at Marcy's side. Her head's down as she counts bills from the cashbox, then slips a paper clip on to hold a small stack of them. She's a shadow eclipsed by Marcy's light.

I stare at them both, considering impossible things. That Marcy's a shell. That she scouted the school in advance for her Drau masters.

No time to tell Jackson what I'm thinking as we head into the dance. I'm not even sure I would tell him if we weren't overwhelmed by sound and the crush of bodies. The whole idea's so out-there. So crazy. And right now, we need to be dealing with facts and tangible threats rather than wild suspicions.

The music's loud. The dance floor's packed. People are clumped in groups, the space limited not just by bodies, but by costumes.

I see faces I recognize and some I don't because they're hidden behind makeup or masks. We push our way through the throng, searching for Luka. When we find him, Jackson points to a relatively uncrowded corner. He takes my hand, tucks me behind him, and starts pushing his way through the mass of bodies. I let him take point mostly because he's bigger and broader and something about him makes people move aside.

I hear a familiar laugh and turn. There's Carly with Kelley and Dee. They're dressed in identical skintight bodysuits and coordinating wigs—Carly's in yellow, Dee's in red, and Kelley's in green. They each have a hand-drawn label stuck on their stomachs: Carly's is Dijon mustard, Dee's is ketchup, and Kelley's is sweet relish. When they told me what they planned to wear, I thought colored spandex didn't exactly scream *condiments*. I was right. They look like three girls in spandex bodysuits with cardboard cutouts stuck on their bellies. But they seem happy.

I'm about to lift a hand and wave when I realize I don't want to get their attention. I don't want any of them anywhere near me when the Drau attack goes down. I want to tell them to get out, go home, be safe. But I can't.

The rules.

I don't know what the Committee will do if I break them. I can't risk telling my friends information they aren't allowed to have—as if they'd even believe me—and I can't imagine they'll leave just because I tell them to, if I don't provide one hell of an incentive. All I can do is lead the Drau away, defeat them, win the battle. That will keep the people I love safe.

I turn away and follow Jackson deeper onto the dance floor. There's a cry that carries above the music, awe and wonder and excitement. Jackson stops dead in front of me.

People turn and shift, the crowd moving like a wave.

Through the spaces between bodies, I catch a glimpse of a streak of light, impossibly bright, tearing through the dance floor.

In my mind, the whole world slows down, like I'm watching separate frames in a stop-motion movie.

The single streak of light is beautiful and terrifying, a lone Drau, a portent of the attack to come.

Three girls, obviously tipsy, squeal in delight. From their gestures, I can tell they think the glowing shape in humanoid form is someone dressed in a fabulous costume. They reach for the Drau, miss, stumble. One girl falls to her knees. They all laugh, and even though I can't hear the sound over the music, I can see their faces, lips curving, teeth flashing, eyes crinkling up at the corners. With the strobe lights of the dance highlighting their expressions, altering shadows and nuance, they could be caught either in an instant of hilarity, or terror.

Another Drau darts between the dancers. And a third. They zigzag through the crowd: right, left, right. One person stops dancing, looks at the light, frowning. Then another and another.

I reach for my weapon cylinder. Jackson stills my hand. He's right. There are too many people, too much potential for collateral damage. We need to figure out a way to draw the Drau off.

The crowd surges, a tide of bodies, pushing everyone as close as packed sardines.

Jackson pulls his knife from the pocket of his vest and, under the cover of the crowd, gets the Drau in the gut. It stumbles but doesn't go down; then it breaks away and streaks off, the tide parting to let it through. Jackson holds his knife flat against his thigh, the black blade barely visible against his black pants.

Another Drau zips among them, not even trying to avoid the crush of bodies. Someone cries out, but I can't see who, or why. People step back, clearing a path, sensing now that there's a threat here, that the streak of light isn't a cool show or an amazeballs costume.

It's something else. Something frightening.

"They're heading for the back," Jackson says against my ear.

I nod and follow as he starts to move, our way blocked by bodies, some dancing, some frozen as they start to clue in that something's terribly wrong.

A few people yell as another Drau tears through, cutting the crowd in two. It lifts its hand, its jellylike weapon smooth and sleek. A spray of bright droplets arcs down like fireworks on everyone in a five-foot radius.

I try to push through, to get to the Drau. Too many bodies block my way.

The Drau fires again.

Mouth rounding in shock, a girl stumbles, hands pressed to her chest. She pulls her hands away and stares at her palms, blood from her wounds dark against her pale skin. She screams, pulls in a breath, screams again.

I can hear her over the music.

She needs to get out of here. They all do.

Jackson's a step ahead of me. He pockets his knife. He points to the left, the direction the Drau went, indicating that I should follow.

There are doors at the back of the auditorium that open to the hallway that leads to the gym. That's where they seem to be heading. I have no idea why, and no chance to ask.

Jackson turns and pushes back the way we came, through the crowd to the double doors. He anchors them open with the little rubber wedges. Then he grabs the closest girl and yells something at her that I'm too far away to hear, but whatever it is, she listens and grabs a couple of other girls. Jackson shoves them through the open doors and moves to the next group. He's organizing, leading. Of course. That's what he does.

I'm torn between going after the Drau and helping get people out. I decide to do both, guiding people toward the doors as I move in the direction Jackson sent me. If we don't get these people out, there's going to be a massacre.

I grab a boy's arm, yelling to make myself heard. I don't even know what I say, but he gets the general message and heads for the doors.

People are pushing and stumbling, some trying to get to the doors, some in the far corners still dancing, oblivious to the danger.

The music turns off and there's a second of comparative

silence before Ms. Smith comes on the loudspeaker and tells everyone to leave, stay calm, fire drill–style. Then voices fill the void, footsteps, cries, shouts. The teachers start guiding people out, funneling students toward the exits.

I clamber up on a table that's against the wall, searching for the Drau. They're gone. Vanished. Then . . . there . . . a flash of light near another set of exit doors, the ones that lead to the corridor that leads to the gym, exactly the direction Jackson pointed me in.

Carly, Dee, and Kelley are on the far side of the room, near the exit. I can't focus on them for long. I'm just grateful they're getting out.

I scan the crowd, looking for Luka. I spot him after a few anxious seconds, and catch his eye as he turns.

He works upstream, against the crowd, until he's next to me. I hop down from the table, grab his hand, and we move, sticking close to the wall, avoiding the main flow of bodies that stream toward us.

"Jackson?" Luka asks, his voice pitched to carry over the noise.

"He'll find us. He knows where we're heading."

"Which is?"

"Wherever the Drau are heading," I yell back.

"What about Tyrone?"

We pass a set of back doors just as a couple of kids shove them open and run outside. More follow, and there's a mass exodus. No way anyone's getting in through those doors. If we'd been one step slower, we'd have been carried out with the flow.

I gesture at the next set and Luka gets the message. We push through the crowd faster now, trying to get the doors open and get the rest of our team inside. Someone slams my shoulder and I hit the wall, my breath forced out in a whoosh. I stagger, get my balance, still holding tight to Luka's hand.

We keep going. Too late. By the time we get there, the doors are open and kids are pushing their way outside. Tyrone and Lien and Kendra aren't getting in this way.

I get pushed and shoved. My hand tears from Luka's. I can't see him. I'm being dragged toward the doors by the sheer momentum of the group. It's all I can do to stay on my feet and not get dragged under. As I near the door, I grab the metal bar and hold on as tight as I can. Inch by inch I drag myself from the swarm toward the edge. My arms scream. My hands slip on the metal.

One hand slides free.

I tighten my grip with the other, struggling to hang on. If I get dragged out, I don't know how I'll get back in. I can't leave Jackson and Luka in there, alone against an army.

My knuckles ache as my fingers are pulled . . . pulled . . . I can't hang on.

I cry out as my hand tears free.

Luka grabs my wrist and hauls me to the side.

"Close," he says.

"Too close," I say, panting like I've run ten miles.

Luka turns his head and meets my gaze and by silent

agreement, we push on, aiming for the spot I last saw the Drau. We grasp each other's wrists to decrease the chance that we'll be pulled apart again.

People are screaming, pushing. The orderly evacuation has devolved to a mob, spurred by flashes of light that erupt in different spots. The Drau, creating mass pandemonium on purpose.

I think of the girl caught in the spray of light, her chest scored open, her hands bloody. I know what it feels like to be hit by a Drau weapon. Is she okay? Did she make it out? Have the Drau killed anyone yet, sucked their energy out through their eyes, leaving them a dried-out husk?

Please let Carly be safe. And Kelley and Dee and Maylene. Everyone.

There's Ms. Smith trying to keep people calm. And Mr. Shomper, shuffling along, directing students. I'm afraid for him. He's so old and fragile. But despite his rumpled, stooped form, he maintains an air of calm, and kids listen when he points them to the exits. He's like an island in a storm.

A blare of sound joins the general cacophony. Someone's pulled a fire alarm. Great.

Flashes of light catch my eye. I turn, only to have another flash appear. I turn again and realize the Drau are running circles around us at impossible speeds. Like we're cattle and they're herding us.

Horror claws at me. I can't let it slow me down.

Luka and I slam through the double doors on the far side of the auditorium.

246

With a clang, they shut behind us.

We pause, breathing hard. The doors bang open. Jackson strides through, favoring his right leg.

"Are you hit?" I ask.

"No. Luka, give me a hand," he says, and reaches for his fly. I get it then. My sword is hampering his gait.

"What the hell, bro?" Luka asks as Jackson drops his pants, then he sees my sword and gets with the plan, helping Jackson get it unbuckled. Luka and I settle the sheath between my shoulder blades while Jackson rebuttons his pants.

"Weapons," Jackson says, knife in one hand, weapon cylinder in the other.

I grasp my weapon cylinder, feeling it warp and shape itself to my hand, but leave the sword in its sheath for now.

"What about Tyrone?" Luka asks.

Jackson checks his con. It shows three triangles—us—and another three triangles somewhere southwest of us, moving along the edge of the building.

"They're looking for a way in. Any thoughts on how we can connect with him?" Jackson asks, not sarcastic—serious.

Luka shakes his head. "In that pandemonium? Not hardly. What do we do?"

"We can't wait," I say, the Drau's presence squirming inside me, almost painful in its intensity.

"Agreed," Jackson says.

Luka takes a breath. "I'll miss having Tyrone at my back, but I'm not sure going in without Kendra and Lien is a loss. I don't trust them. Well, one of them. Kendra. She's a griefer."

Gaming term. Luka explained it to me before. A griefer steals points, lets other players wear down the target, then takes the kill. I shake my head. It's hard to believe that of Kendra. But her score . . . I remember thinking that it was freakishly high. And I remember other things. Fleeting expressions I caught on Luka's face or Tyrone's. And Tyrone saying something to Jackson right before he took Kendra and Lien outside. They must have suspected this for a while.

Luka glances at me. "I think Lien's helping her." He pauses. "Out of love. I think she wants Kendra out of the game before one of her freak-outs gets her—or someone else—killed. I've noticed that she's giving Kendra her kills, not just helping her steal ours."

"It's a problem we'll have to deal with after we deal with the Drau," Jackson says. "If Kendra and Lien do catch up with us, watch your backs."

He and Luka exchange a look, and I know it's because they've dealt with a griefer before—the boy I replaced.

"Let's go." Jackson heads down the hall, through the double doors at the far end, then through a second set of doors to the stairs. Luka and I follow.

"What about the Drau in the auditorium?" I ask.

"They'll be coming for us. We're the ones they want." Jackson barely gets the words out before the doors slam open, streaks of light coming at us.

I raise my hand, hold my ground, and fire until every one of those lights goes dark.

CHAPTER TWENTY-TWO

MY SENSES ARE HEIGHTENED, THE FEEL OF THE BANISTER under my palm sharp and clear, the sensation of my feet pounding the stairs jarring and stark. My heart rate's amped. My breathing's fast and shallow. Adrenaline rush.

Deep inside me the writhing awareness of the Drau ramps up, like a nest of snakes. They're somewhere ahead of us. I can't see them, but they're here. I feel it in every cell of my body.

And it's me, Luka, and Jackson against an army. I'm not liking the odds.

We follow Jackson to a door, then down more stairs to the basement. I've been down here once before, last year, when the drama teacher had me and Carly help go through some boxes to find costumes.

The walls on either side are painted white, the stairs here narrow and steep. At the bottom is a long corridor, dim and empty, with shadowy doorways marking the walls.

The Drau could be anywhere, in any one of these basement rooms.

"Trap?" I whisper.

"Maybe," Luka answers.

"What do we do?"

"We go in," Jackson says.

I open my mouth, then close it. I already know what he'll say: *What makes you think you get a choice?*

He's right. My gut's telling me this is a bad idea, that the Drau are playing us, leading us into a trap. Why run through the dance like that? Why create pandemonium only to hide here?

And why be here at all? Why Glenbrook High?

Again, the ugly possibility that the Committee planned it this way, that they're sending a message to me, to Jackson, worms through my thoughts.

Doesn't matter. I have to keep going. We have to keep going. And not just because that's the instruction the Committee's feeding Jackson.

It's because the Drau pushed into my world, my real world. They are threatening my friends. I have to stop them.

Jackson holds a hand up to signal a halt when we come up on the first door. It's open. The room beyond is dim but not dark, a single naked bulb hanging from the ceiling. It's more a large closet than a room, and it's empty.

We move to the next door. He signals Luka, then me. We flank the two sides of the door, weapons ready.

I hold Luka's gaze, feel eerily calm despite the thud of my own pulse and the energy pushing me to move.

Jackson gives the signal.

Luka and I round the doorjamb into a crouch, weapons aimed. And there it is: the kick of my heart, the depth of my breathing, the singular focus, my eyes taking in every detail, my ears straining for sounds. I'm in it now. Scared. Agitated. Exhilarated. In it with everything I am.

Game on.

There's nothing here. No movement. No threat.

But they could be hiding.

We go in, me right, Luka left, Jackson straight ahead. The concrete floor's gray and discolored. The far wall has four thick, black pipes sticking out of it. There's a pile of stained and frayed cream-colored cushions tied together with rope in the middle of the room. But there are no Drau.

Jackson gives the thumbs-up: clear.

We continue along the hall, clearing rooms, tension drawing tighter as we go.

Another door opens to a huge room with two black metal boilers and tons of thick pipes sticking out of the walls, the floor, spanning the ceiling. Lots of places the Drau could lie in wait.

We fan out exactly the way we've done every other room so far. Luka left. Me right. Jackson straight ahead.

I check behind the boilers, behind three thick pipes. Nothing.

Jackson gives the thumbs-up again.

We turn to go.

A wave of fear and bone-deep revulsion hits me, violent, shocking, like ice in my veins. It comes out of nowhere, intense and powerful.

Drau.

Here.

I spin. Spin again.

Where are they?

Trap! Move! I hear Jackson's voice inside my head as we sprint for the door.

Light comes at us from both ends of the hallway. The Drau are everywhere.

My weapon cylinder hums to life, obeying my will, the dark, deadly stream catching a Drau in the chest. I switch it to my left hand, the shape changing subtly to account for the differences. I shoot. Shoot again. Not even taking time to aim.

I throw my weight forward onto my left foot, kick back with my right, my heel connecting with the bottom of the sheath hanging between my shoulder blades.

The handle of my sword flies up and I grab it and clear the scabbard, bringing the blade into position. I crack it down on a Drau's forehead, yank it back, and slam it down a second time.

Hiraki-ashi: pivot.

I take out two Drau that come at me from the side.

My skin burns where their weapons hit me, droplets of pain that sink into every part of me.

I fire. Fire again. My weapon cylinder is like a living thing, like a part of my arm. I realize that instinctively Luka, Jackson, and I have arranged ourselves in a tight group with the wall at our backs.

We're surrounded.

There are so many of them.

And it isn't just our lives at risk. Everyone who hasn't yet evacuated the dance is only a floor away.

They have no clue what we're up against.

I don't want them to have a clue.

I'm just praying Carly and Kelley and Dee made it out. Maylene. Aaron. Shareese. So many kids I've known almost my whole life.

I have to win. Have to take out the enemy.

Lives depend on me.

I surge forward, my blade sweeping across my attackers. Shards of light fall on me, penetrating skin and muscle, the pain bright and sharp clear through to bone.

Black ooze pulses from my weapon in a powerful stream, eating a Drau, pulling it in headfirst. The way it screams is familiar now. I cringe, then lock those feelings away.

Them or me.

There's a commotion to my left. I can't see what it is.

"Reinforcements!" Luka yells, but I'm shorter than

him and I can't see what he sees.

Jackson leaps forward and cuts a Drau in this freaky underhand sideways maneuver that leaves the Drau's throat slit open, head lolling back. I catch a glimpse of white bone and very dark blood, and then the Drau's gone, digested by the surge from Jackson's weapon cylinder.

That Drau was inches from me.

"Focus," Jackson snarls.

I yank my cylinder up and fire over his shoulder, taking out the Drau that was coming at his back.

"Focus," I snarl back.

I lunge, thrust, making up moves as I go because this sure as hell isn't anything I ever learned in kendo. This is a miserable, wretched slaughterhouse where I hack at limbs and chests and heads, stab at torsos—anything to hold them off.

Sweat trickles along my spine. My arm feels like a thousand-pound weight is dragging it down. I can't stop. I can't rest. I lift my sword. I pull everything I've ever learned and funnel it into each move. I time my strikes, taking advantage of the Drau's forward movement, using its momentary focus on its own attack against it.

But I'm tiring. Fading. We all are.

How long have we been down here? How long can we go on?

"Now would be a great time for a plan," Luka yells.

A plan. We can't go in either direction along the hall. The Drau are coming at us from both sides like converging swarms of locusts. The only place we can go is back into the room with the boilers.

I shoot a split-second glance in that direction. No chance. They've herded us away from the door and we're stuck here against the wall, a tiny island of three in a churning sea of Drau.

"The reinforcements . . . is it Tyrone?"

Luka shakes his head. "I don't think so. Can't be sure. I caught sight of a human head, but I can't say whose."

So another team's here. Maybe we can coordinate somehow, strengthen our position.

"Can you still see them?" Jackson asks, which means that even though he has height advantage, he hasn't caught sight of them, either.

Luka shakes his head again, dashing my hope for a coordinated team effort.

Jackson steps and turns so he's at ninety degrees to the wall as he shoots a Drau dead ahead, while at the same time flipping his knife blade up and jacking his fist back over his shoulder like he's throwing salt, slamming a Drau right between the eyes.

His expression is set in grim lines. He seems leaner and harder than I've ever seen him, his cheeks hollowed, his jaw taut. His lips draw back from his teeth in a snarl as he turns his body and takes a spray of Drau fire across his back, sheltering me from the worst of it.

"Every man for himself," I remind him as I lunge and hack at his attacker.

Jackson doesn't say anything back. I don't really expect him to.

We fight until my brain is numb. My entire being is comprised of my hands, my sword, my weapon cylinder.

The Drau keep coming, wedging us apart. Every move we make to try to stay together, they counter. Exposed, outnumbered, we don't stand much chance. Then I think of my friends, my teachers . . . and not just them. The whole community's at risk if we don't stop the Drau here. The whole damn world.

It seems ridiculous, a handful of teens against a monster invasion.

And thinking like that might get me killed.

So I don't think. I just lean against the wall, not bothering with footwork anymore; my rubbery legs aren't up to the challenge. My whole body feels like it's on fire, pinpricks of pain bursting bright as the Drau shower droplets of light—droplets of agony—on us. I'm breathing too fast, too hard, and I can't slow it down. My movements are growing sluggish, sweat dripping in my eyes, blurring my vision. I don't dare look at my con.

I don't know where Jackson is. He was separated from us. I can't see him. But I know he's alive. He has to be alive.

Luka grunts and jerks. He presses right up against me. At first, I think it's because he's trying to protect me. Then I realize it's because I'm helping to hold up his weight.

He's in bad shape.

We're in trouble.

I hack at bodies.

There's movement to my left and I turn, aim, shift my weapon at the last second as I see a human head bob up beyond the sea of Drau.

Too short to be Jackson. Someone else. The reinforcements Luka saw earlier. They must have been fighting one end of the mass of Drau while we tackled the other.

I almost shout in relief.

There's a spray of light so bright it makes me see spots. Pinpoints of pain erupt on the side of my face, my neck, my shoulder. Luka's body jerks against mine; then he stumbles, almost falling. Almost taking me down with him.

I get my shoulder under his, panic biting at me.

"Got him," Jackson says, coming up on Luka's other side. Before he can take Luka's weight, he spins to the left, throws his knife.

It plants solidly between a Drau's eyes.

Jackson leaps forward and pulls the blade free, then comes back and gets his shoulder under Luka's.

"The boiler room," he says, and I realize that somewhere in the past few minutes, we've worked our way back toward that room.

"We'll be trapped."

"We can pick them off as they come through the door."

He half drags, half carries Luka backward through the door. I stay in front of him, offering cover, shooting, hacking, one step back and another until we're all in the room.

Trapped.

I check Luka's con. Dark orange tinged with red. His eyes are closed, his breathing shallow. Where's he hit? Where's he bleeding?

Everywhere.

Jackson stands in front of us and covers me as I unzip Luka's vest, check his chest, his abdomen. Wounds, but nothing that's bleeding too much. Then I see the shine on his black pants at the very top of his thigh.

"There's an artery there," Jackson says, tossing me his knife, hilt up. "Cut his pants. If the blood's spurting, we're in deep shit. If it's oozing, it's not as bad."

I slash Luka's pants, terrified of what I'll find, expecting a spray of blood.

Instead, I find a trickle.

I exhale sharply. Then I set about slicing off a piece of his shirt, forming a pad, slicing off a second length, and tying it all down.

Luka's lids flutter. His gaze sharpens. He glances down at the location of my hands.

"Hey," he says. "If you wanted me that badly, all you had to do was ask."

I snort.

He lifts his hand and shoots, taking out a Drau that was charging the doorway.

"Any closer and that shot would have hit my hip," Jackson says.

"You're welcome," Luka says, trying to pull himself up

to a sitting position against the pile of ratty cushions. Third try's the charm. Panting, he sends me a pained grimace.

I leave him there and move to Jackson's side, my weapon cylinder humming as we take down any Drau that fill the doorframe. We may be trapped in here, but it's a pretty good bet we can hold them off out there, at least for a while.

Stalemate. I'll take it, for now.

"We need a location on the other team," Jackson says. "It'd be nice if I knew how many there are and exactly where our backup's positioned."

"The Committee's not telling you anything?"

"No."

I cover Jackson as he peers around the doorjamb, then steps through, motioning me to move forward.

There's a girl just to the right of the door. Her back is to us, light brown hair falling over her shoulders. She takes out a Drau with a spray of light, the weapon in her hand smooth and metallic and jellylike.

"That's the girl who helped me on the last mission," I say, recognizing her posture, the way she moves, the set of her shoulders.

"Go," he says. "I'll cover you and Luka from here."

I dart forward so I'm with her, side by side.

A Drau comes at me, moving too fast. Terror claws at me. I fire. It fires. Pain erupts all the way up my arm. My fingers go numb and lax and my sword clatters to the floor.

I lift my cylinder, but the Drau's gone.

Point for Miki.

I squat, retrieve my blade, and realize the hall's clearer now. Three Drau run away toward the far end. The girl sprints after them. She's close enough to shoot, but she doesn't. Just like last time.

The pain in my arm makes me feel woozy. I force my unresponsive fingers to close around the hilt of my sword. With a groan, I lift it, but I won't be using it—not with this hand, not anytime soon.

"Miki," Jackson says, grabbing my good arm and dragging me back toward the room where Luka's holed up.

"Is it over?" I whisper. "Do we make the jump now?"

He shakes his head.

So there are more Drau here somewhere. We need to smoke them out.

Jackson stops in the doorway and aims his weapon down the hall at the fleeing Drau. They're almost at the end now. He doesn't shoot. The girl's in the way.

He curses under his breath.

She stops dead, spins back toward us. Her hair obscures her face, then settles to her shoulders.

"No," she says, the inflection familiar.

My world jerks to a stop.

I've seen a close-up of that face framed in brushed nickel.

I've seen those features on rows and rows of clones as I

pulled out tubes and turned off machines.

I've spoken to this girl in my dreams.

I've seen those eyes. Green. Lizzie green.

Jackson makes a choked, horrified sound.

"Miki! Miki!" Carly's voice, behind me.

I turn, a reflex. Jackson turns with me.

"You have to leave the building." Carly's standing at the end of the hallway next to the stairs we originally took to come down here. Her body's tense, her face pale. I stare at her in horror, words locked in my throat. *Get out. Get out now. Get away. Go!* "They're evacuating," she says, oblivious to my panic on her behalf. "Everyone out. Didn't you hear the fire alarm? You're lucky I saw you duck out and come this way."

Carly followed me. To keep me safe.

She waves her hand in a frantic, beckoning motion. "Come on! We have to go."

She can't be here. I don't want her here. I don't want her anywhere near the Drau.

Now I understand what Jackson felt when he saw me outside his window. He wanted me gone. He wanted me out of the game. He wanted me safe.

That's what I want for Carly. But here she is.

Because *she* wants *me* safe.

Only, she has no idea what monsters lurk down here.

"Go," I yell, finally rediscovering my voice. "Carly, get out. Go!"

My words sound strange in my ears. Slow. Heavy. Like I'm underwater.

I shake my head, completely disoriented. It's like this whole scene is playing out in slow motion. But it isn't just that. It's like time's passing differently in different compartments of the same reality.

How long did it take Carly to get down here?

It feels like we've been battling the Drau for hours and hours. But Carly's acting like I just ran down here moments ago.

There's a sound behind me. Running footsteps.

I turn my head, my torso, looking back over my shoulder. The movement takes an eternity.

The green-eyed girl's gone. Jackson's halfway up the hall, running after her.

Again, the sensation that time is distorting hits me. The hallway must be as long as three football fields for him to still be running.

"Miki! Come on!" Carly yells.

I turn back toward her.

Light flares behind her.

Light shaped in human form.

A red flower blossoms on the yellow spandex of her suit, just below the Dijon mustard label she has tacked to the cloth.

Her eyes widen. Her brows rise. Her mouth forms a round *O*.

She looks confused, startled. Afraid.

The moment hangs suspended.

She doesn't drop to the ground. It's more of a long, slow crumple, like a coat sliding off a hanger.

Or a final exhalation.

CHAPTER TWENTY-THREE

I'M MOVING BEFORE I REALIZE THAT THE HORRIBLE, HOWLING sound is coming from me.

My arm lifts. My sword's above my head, point back, blade up. I run at the Drau, swinging with all my might. As I connect, there's a tug of resistance, like I'm separating a chicken leg from the thigh. Then the Drau's head flies up, up, its body dropping like a sack, its head splatting on the ground to one side. A spray of dark blood marks the wall, the floor. Me.

I toss the sword. It clatters across the floor in one direction as I fall to my knees and skid in the other, coming to rest at Carly's side.

She's not moving. She lies there, a broken doll in bright yellow spandex and a cheery yellow wig.

"Carly," I scream. "Nononononono." I take hold of her shoulder, shake her.

There's the sound of footsteps pounding behind me. I twist at the waist, my weapon cylinder in hand, my will gathering to annihilate whatever's coming.

It's Jackson.

With a cry, I drop my weapon. I have the split-second thought that he didn't go after the girl, the green-eyed girl. The girl who looks like Lizzie.

He came to me.

"Check her pulse," he says, lips taut, his whole body humming with tension as he drops to his knees on Carly's other side.

Tears stream down my cheeks, blurring my vision, my hands shaking so hard I can barely rest my fingers against her throat, never mind find her pulse.

"I'll do it," Jackson says. He grabs my wrist to move my hand out of the way and puts his fingers flat on her neck.

Carly's face is grayish white, her eyes closed, red blood pooling on the floor beneath her. I splay my hand over her belly, put pressure on her wound. Her blood leaks through my fingers.

Jackson holds his fingers on her pulse for what feels like an eternity. Then he leans over and rests his ear on her chest.

I wait, my heart slamming against my ribs. One second spins into forever.

Pleasepleasepleaseplease.

Jackson rears back, his shoulders sagging, his head bowed.

"No!" I fling myself on Carly, my ear pressed over her heart. I hear nothing. Nothing at all. And her chest isn't moving, not even a little. She isn't breathing.

I tip her head back and try to breathe for her.

Jackson layers his hands and starts chest compressions like he's done this before—one more thing I didn't know about him. Blood spurts from the wound in an arc. Every time he presses, she bleeds.

"Stop," I say, tears choking me. "We're killing her."

But we're not. She's already dead.

I jerk back, grab her shoulders, shake her. "Carly!" I scream. "Carly!" I can't breathe. I can't think. This is my fault. She came down here for me. To save me. She didn't even know what she was trying to save me from. "Carly!"

"Call 911!" I yell at Jackson. "Call 911! Call them. Call—" He doesn't reach for his phone. Doesn't move. Because we can't call anyone, not while we're in the game.

I swipe the tears from my cheeks, then look at my hands. Red. Blood. Carly's blood. The whole front of her yellow spandex bodysuit is dark with it.

Luka's shouting from the room up the hall where we left him. He's asking what's going on. Yelling Carly's name. Jackson's. Mine.

I'm dying. My soul is dying. Because Carly's gone. She can't be gone.

"Fix it!" I scream at Jackson. "Fix it!"

But he can't fix it. No one can.

I did this. I killed my best friend.

I should have stayed with her. Should have made sure she got out. Should have defended her against the Drau invasion.

That's the whole reason I'm in the game. To keep my world safe.

I failed. I failed.

"Jackson," I sob, crumpling onto Carly's chest.

"Get off her, Miki," Jackson says, icy and calm. His tone's enough to grab my attention. I look up as he pulls his glasses off.

"What are you doing?"

"Get up."

I do, obeying the rigid expectation in his tone, sitting back on my heels, my whole body trembling.

I'm on one side of Carly and he's on the other. His gaze meets mine, his eyes Drau gray, swirling, endless, mercury bright. So beautiful. I can't look away.

But he looks away, hunching over Carly, his hands on her cheeks.

For a second, I just stare at him, bewildered and numb.

"What are you doing?" I grab his arm, confusion bleeding into wariness.

He doesn't lift his head, doesn't shake me off. But the tension in his muscles ramps up as he says, "Seeing if it works both ways."

I stare at his bowed head. Then I gasp in horror as I get

what he means. He's going to bring Carly back. He's going to do what he did with Lizzie, with me, only in the opposite direction. Give electrical energy instead of take.

I stare at the top of his head. His thumbs slide to Carly's eyelids, resting there for a second.

"What—"

"If I can keep her alive until we jump, maybe she'll be okay when we respawn. Maybe she'll still be alive."

He'll save her the way we saved him.

And he'll pay the price.

"You can't." My fingers curl tighter, digging into his arm. "I can't let you."

He cuts me a glance. "My choice, Miki. Not yours."

"They'll kill you. The Committee. They won't allow this."

He lifts his head and his lips shape a dark, predatory smile. "Let them try."

They won't need to try very hard. They're the Committee. They bend time, shift us between realities. He's no match for them. The thought makes agony burst inside me like a broken pipe.

"I can't lose you, too. And I will if you even try this. The Committee will take you. Kill you. This time there will be no reprieve. You'll be dead. And if what you try here doesn't work, Carly will still be dead. You'll both be gone."

I can't lose them both.

"Then I better make certain this works."

Jackson lifts Carly's eyelids so she's staring, sightless, at the ceiling.

I'm torn, sick, horrified, terrified. I can't let him do this.

I can't not let him do it.

Luka's still yelling at us to tell him what's going on. There's a scraping sound, like he's dragging himself across the floor.

"Jackson," I whisper.

Please don't do this.

Please do it.

Save her.

Save yourself.

"You—" I choke on my words, feeling like my insides are being shredded.

Jackson ignores me. He leans close to Carly's face.

I'm going to lose someone I love tonight. Right here. Right now. Either Carly dies, or Jackson saves her and the Committee takes him. And kills him.

I can't live with either loss.

I'm shaking so hard my teeth clack together.

"J-J-J-J-J-Jackson—"

He looks at me, his eyes swirling silver.

"She dies, and a piece of you dies, Miki. I can't let that happen," he says. "I'll take my chances with the Committee."

But we both know his chances are bleak.

I can't make any words come out. I shake my head.

"What makes you think you get a choice?" he asks, one

corner of his mouth lifting in the barest hint of a smile that breaks my heart. His eyes swirl and draw me in. I gasp, feeling the pull, feeling the pain.

He tears his gaze from mine and focuses on Carly.

"Please, Jackson, please—" *Please make this all go away, make it better. I can't lose her. I can't lose you—*

"Oh my God. What happened?"

My head jerks up. Lien and Kendra and Tyrone are standing at the far end of the hall, staring at the scene, identical expressions of horror etching their features stark and tight.

When did they get here? Sometime during the battle, I'm guessing, if their bloody clothes are any indication.

Tyrone looks beyond me, his weapon cylinder lifting, the muzzle erupting with its greasy, black stream. I don't need to look behind me to know there are more Drau creeping out of whatever hole they were hiding in. I can sense them. Enemy.

Where did they come from? I thought we got them all. But no . . . we couldn't have or we would have been pulled.

Tyrone runs at them, darts around us, firing. Lien's right behind him and Kendra behind her. Jackson hasn't moved. He's still hunched over Carly, his eyes locked on hers.

I stare at them for a millisecond. I'm no good to anyone kneeling here on the floor, whimpering. Jackson's risking his life for Carly, for me. The least I can do is buy him time, keep him alive long enough to do the deed.

270

I have one working arm. The other hangs useless by my side, a vortex of pain thanks to the Drau hit I took earlier. I grab my sword, surge to my feet, and chase after my team.

Light zips up the hallway toward me.

I don't think, can't think. I move on autopilot, letting instinct guide me. I bring the blade down with all my might, splitting the Drau's skull like a melon.

The second wave of Drau surges out of a room at the far end of the hall. Lien wings one, despite the fact that she had a clear shot to take it out. She steps aside and it's Kendra who claims the kill with a head-shot.

Proof that Luka was right.

Tyrone glances at them and snarls; then he surges forward, shooting. Drau fire rains down on him, hitting him with a thousand tiny points of pain. He jerks but keeps moving.

"Miki!" Jackson shouts. "Get down."

But his warning comes too late.

CHAPTER **TWENTY-FOUR**

THERE'S AN EXPLOSION OF LIGHT AND A SHATTERING DETONA-tion of sound. My retinas burn, the light tearing into my skull, the sound pulverizing the tiny bones inside my ears.

I'm blinded and my equilibrium is shot. The floor feels like it's falling out from under me. A hand catches my elbow and guides me down before I fall. Lien? Kendra?

Words come at me in disjointed sound bites like bits of coherence couched in radio static. I string them together as best I can. "I—ot—her."

I know that voice. It's the girl. The same girl.

"Lizzie?" I whisper. Or maybe I yell. My hearing's so messed up I can't tell the difference.

No answer.

I can't see, can't hear. I can't defend myself. Or Jackson.

Or Carly. I almost slash wildly, blindly, in case I manage to hit something, but what if that something is Tyrone or Lien or Kendra?

In the end, I just sit there on the floor, chest heaving, trapped inside myself with only my fear for company.

The Drau? Where are they?

I open myself to the gut instinct that always screams the alarm when they're near. I get nothing. Radio silence.

Panic threatens. I shove it down, push the lid onto the pot, but it's bubbling and twitching, trying to break free.

I can't just sit here, doing nothing. I get up on my knees, push my palms along the floor, sweeping them side to side, hoping I encounter Jackson . . . Carly . . . someone.

I don't know how much time passes. A second. A year.

The roaring in my ears fades to a buzzing, then to a faint hiss.

I'm scared to call out. Instead, I shimmy along the floor in the direction I think will take me to Jackson.

How long have I been doing this? It feels like an hour, an agony of waiting for my vision to come back online in spangled increments, for the buzzing/roaring in my ears to dull and fade. I'm terrified the Drau will get us, that my team is already gone.

I bump up against something. A shoulder.

I feel a vest with pockets but no big, round circles. Not Jackson. Luka. I find his hand. Squeeze. He squeezes back.

Now what? Wait it out? Keep moving?

I feel around until I hit the doorframe—Luka must have dragged himself this far. Then I create a map in my mind of where Luka was in relation to Jackson and Carly.

Using my elbows, I drag myself along, combat style, relying mostly on one arm because the other's still weak and numb.

On the floor in front of me, a small shadow shifts, dark against the light floor. I freeze. It freezes. I move. It moves.

My hand.

I'm seeing my hand as I drag myself forward on my belly. It isn't much, but it's something.

Relief trickles through me in a weak stream. I focus on my hands, willing myself to be able to see my individual fingers.

I do. I see them.

I lift my head and manage to make out a doorway, the subtle shift in light enough that I can see a dark rectangle.

I try to make out any bright flares against the background, a hint of the Drau.

Nothing.

Pushing to my feet, I sway, dizzy. I take a step, stumble, almost fall, but catch myself at the last second as my shoulder bumps something solid. The wall.

Blinking, I stand there, enraged by my helplessness, desperate for control.

"Miki?" Jackson's voice, camouflaged by the drone of a thousand nonexistent bees. I turn toward the sound, toward him. His arms come around me, solid, safe. I close my eyes.

"Carly?" I rasp.

"I don't know. I didn't get to finish what I started."

"The Drau?"

"If there were any still here, would we still be breathing?"

He has a point.

"Can you see?" I ask.

"Just shadows."

"Same as me. Where's—" I swallow against the lump in my throat. "Where's Carly?"

"Back here." Jackson shifts me a few feet forward, but Carly's not there. Not that I can find.

"Are you sure she's this way?"

"Yeah."

"Where?"

He hesitates. "I don't know."

I get down on my knees and move forward, hands outstretched. I turn right. Left. I can't find her. Without my sight, I can't find her.

"Wait," Jackson says. "Stay still. Just let your eyes adjust. We'll find her. Just give it a minute."

He sounds like he's strung so tight he's about to break.

Not just because of Carly.

Because of the girl with the green eyes. Lizzie.

God, what must he be feeling?

"Did you—" I reach for him, find his hand, twine my fingers with his. "Did you see her? The girl? Lizzie?" I whisper.

He doesn't answer right away, and when he does, his voice is so low I have to strain to hear him. "The Drau took my sister. They kept her body alive, hooked to machines. They tried to create an army of shells in her image. Three times, I've gone in and killed Lizzie all over again. Unplugged the machines. Pulled the tubes out of the army of clones the Drau created from her DNA." He pauses. "Looks like I'll be doing it a fourth time."

I tighten my hold on his hand, feeling sick.

"She saved my life," I say. "Maybe—"

"Don't say it. Don't *say* it, Miki. Lizzie's gone. Has been for five years. That thing was not my sister."

I nod, clinging to him, sick at heart, confused, scared. I remember her weapon, a Drau weapon. I remember her taking off after the Drau, but not shooting even when she was within range. Like she didn't want to kill her own kind.

But she did, didn't she? On the last mission, when I was bleeding out, I could swear she shot at the Drau that came at us.

"If that girl was a shell, why did she save my life?"

"That's what they do. Keep humans alive long enough to harvest their DNA, turn them into an army of shells."

I shiver, horrified.

As I lift my head, I see clearer shadows and light. My vision coming back online.

Carly.

I wrap my arms tight around my waist, pressing them against my belly. I don't want to look, don't want to see her like that, broken and bloody.

Jackson has his glasses on, hiding his eyes. His Drau eyes. Did it work? Did he save her?

I swallow against the bile that's crawling up the back of my throat. Trembling, I turn to where I left her lying on the floor.

My vision sharpens and tunnels to the dark splotch of blood on the light floor, to the hand-drawn, cardboard mustard label lying at the edge of the crimson stain, to Carly's yellow wig lying two feet away.

But there's no Carly.

She's not there.

"Carly!" I yell. Did she simply get up and walk away? I jump up and run along the hall, looking in doorways. Jackson snags me from behind.

"Jump in thirty," he says. "She's not here, Miki. We can only hope she respawns when we do."

"But—" I shake my head. This makes no sense. Nothing makes any sense. "Everything about this mission has been wrong." I stare at Jackson. "How can you be so calm?" I whisper. "How can you take all this in stride?"

"Miki?" Not Carly's voice. Luka's, very weak. I turn my head to find him sitting up, leaning against the doorframe, his face so white he looks like he's been dipped in wax.

"Man, it's like I've been staring straight at the sun,"

Tyrone says, walking toward us along the hall, trailing one hand along the wall, still feeling his way. "What *was* that?"

"Flashbang," Jackson answers.

Tyrone nods. "Stun grenade. Meant to incapacitate, not kill. So whoever used it wanted us out of the picture for a few minutes, but not hurt or dead. Why? And who?"

He turns. His eyes narrow as he glares at Lien and Kendra. They're leaning against the wall, Kendra's head bent forward, buried in her hands. Lien has her arms around Kendra's shoulders.

"Are you looking at *us*? Are you seriously looking at us?" Lien asks. "Why would we do that?"

"To steal points," Tyrone snarls. "You think we don't know you're griefers?"

Lien looks back at him, completely calm. "How could we steal points if we're equally blinded? I can still barely see you. And think about it," she says. "We'd have no way to smuggle a flashbang or whatever you called it into the game."

"That's crap," Luka says. "You can't bring anything out of the game, but you can bring shit in. Case in point, our clothes."

"We didn't do it," Lien says. She glares at Tyrone. "And as for being a griefer, yeah." Her chin kicks up a notch, like she's daring him to comment. "I'm setting it up as much as possible for Kendra to get points. She needs to get out." She swallows, and to my shock, her eyes fill with tears, all her bravado melting away. "She isn't going to last. I need to get her out before the game breaks her. Or she ends up causing someone else's death." She holds out a hand to Tyrone. "You don't understand. The game *will* kill her."

"Yeah," Tyrone says, "I understand. I understand way more than you think."

Lien looks at Luka, then me, then Jackson.

Tears trickle along her cheeks, and she holds Kendra, her chin resting on the crown of the shorter girl's head. "You don't understand," Lien says. "You don't understand."

But we do. We all understand.

We respawn in the Jeep in my driveway. I'm disoriented, sick at heart.

I feel like the car's spinning round and round, skidding out of control. Except, it isn't moving.

I pick a spot out the side window—a light post halfway up the street—and stare at it, waiting for the spinning to stop. Two older kids pass my house, looking to trick-or-treat at houses that haven't turned out the lights yet. They're moving impossibly slow, each step exaggerated, like they're wading through Jell-O. This is what happens when we respawn back to real life. A momentary disorientation. A lack of synchronization between worlds.

In the seat next to me, Jackson reaches for the ignition. He and I are the only things moving at normal speed.

A dull throb builds behind my eyes. My jaw aches. Then my ears pop and—*snap*—everything speeds up. A car drives past going exactly the speed it should be. The kids speed up and walk at a normal pace.

"Call Carly," Jackson says, his wrists resting on the top of the steering wheel, shoulders relaxed.

How can he be so calm? How can he even think? My brain feels like it's growing green fuzz like three-week-old bread.

I yank out my phone. Dial.

No answer.

"Carly, call me." I barely manage to choke the words out.

My heart feels like it's been skewered.

Hands shaking, I try Dee's number and Kelley's.

"They're not answering." My thoughts are sluggish. All I can focus on is the memory of Carly, covered in blood. "I'll try Amy. Shareese. Maylene. Sarah—"

Jackson reaches over and closes his hand on mine, stilling my frantic movements.

"If they're at the dance, they won't hear the phone, and if they do, they might not answer," he points out.

"They could have their phones on vibrate. They could—" I press my lips together and turn my head to stare out the window, unseeing.

He backs out of the drive.

After a few minutes I ask, "Where are we going?"

"The dance." He sounds so cold. So remote. His walls—his shields—are firmly in place. I think that if I reach over to try to touch him, I'll slam against an invisible barrier, just like I did when we were in the amphitheater in front of the Committee.

I'm hurting, but he's hurting, too. I'm not the only one who's been ripped open and flayed tonight.

"Do you want to talk about Lizzie?"

He turns his head toward me, his face expressionless, his eyes hidden behind opaque shades. "No."

"Do you want to talk about how much you knew?" When he doesn't say anything, I clarify, "Before we got to the dance? Before the rest of us knew the Drau pushed through into our world?"

"No."

Part of me is relieved by that. I don't know if I'm up for a heavy conversation when the most important thing to me right now is finding out if Carly's okay. And it will be a heavy conversation, because I'm pretty sure Jackson knew a lot more than he let on and I don't like the idea that he purposely kept me in the dark.

We drive the rest of the way in silence.

He's barely parked when I tear out of the Jeep and run for the school doors. He catches up, catches me around the waist, holds me back. I slap at his hands, and struggle to get free. "Carly. I need to—"

"I know," he says. "Stay calm. Don't draw attention. Hopefully, we'll walk in and she'll be on the dance floor in all her blinding yellow glory."

He's right.

I don't want to ask. But I have to. "And if she isn't?"

"We'll figure it out, Miki."

I don't know how he can sound so sure. How will we figure it out if she's dead?

We walk toward the front doors of the school, Jackson looping his arm over my shoulder and setting the pace.

"Have you ever heard of something like this?" I ask. "Of a civilian being pulled into a mission? Getting hurt? Dying on a mission?"

A muscle in Jackson's jaw tightens. "No."

I think back to the first time I was pulled, to Janice Harper's little sister almost getting hit by the truck. She could have been killed. And Jackson . . . he was twelve when he and Lizzie were in that car accident . . .

"You were hurt in the car accident. You almost died," I say.

"That wasn't on a mission."

"No, but you were a civilian when it happened and you ended up in the game. They made an exception for you. They could make an exception for Carly. Maybe she can be part of it. Part of the game. We could train her. Watch out for her. We could—"

Jackson squeezes my shoulder. "Yeah, they made an exception, but they had something to gain by keeping me alive, putting me in to fight. I offered a specific genetic blueprint they happen to be fond of." With his index finger, he pushes his shades up the bridge of his nose, a subtle reminder of exactly what he brought to the table when the Committee decided to conscript him. "Carly's human."

"So are we," I snarl.

"For the most part. But we're also part something else."

For a second, I'm blindingly furious with him. But he's right. And it isn't his fault that he's right.

"Would I even want this for her, if I had a choice?" I ask.

Would I? Would I want her to be part of the game, to face what I face every time I'm pulled?

"Better than dead," Jackson says softly. "And it isn't your choice to make, Miki. If it's even possible, it'll be Carly's call."

Just like it was Jackson's call to do what he did, to risk everything to try to save her.

He broke every rule for her. Risked his life and the Committee's wrath for her.

No, not for her. For me.

"Let's hope there's no call to make," he says. "Let's hope she's already respawned fully healed."

Together we walk to the auditorium doors. Everything is tinged with a strong sense of déjà vu. Marcy eyes Jackson. Maylene chats with him and smiles. Jackson does the cash-for-tickets exchange. Kathy stares at her hands while she counts the bills.

Then we're inside. The dance floor's packed, music pumping, lights flashing. It looks exactly as it did when we arrived before. I turn to where I saw Carly last time I got here. There's Kelley and . . . there's Dee. Jackson and I push our way through the crowd to them.

Before I have a chance to ask, Dee yells in my ear, "Have you seen Carly? She's late and I can't reach her!"

"She's not here?" A band of steel crushes my ribs, stealing my breath.

Dee shakes her head.

"When was the last time you spoke to her?" Jackson asks.

She glances at him, frowning. "I don't know. About an hour ago?"

I round on Kelley, trying not to show how frantic I feel. "What about you?"

We're all yelling to be heard over the music.

"Haven't spoken to her since I got here. What's wrong, Miki?"

Before I can figure out what I'm supposed to say, Jackson grabs my arm and, using his body as a wedge, gets us back through the crowd to the doors. We practically slam into Luka coming in as we're going out.

There's a split second of sheer joy at seeing him whole, unhurt, his massive injuries left behind in the game.

Then he asks, "Carly?" His expression is haunted, and I'm hurtled back into a reality where my best friend may be dead because she came after me. To warn me. To keep me safe.

My fault.

"She's not here," Jackson says. "And no one's heard from her since the dance started."

Luka looks at me and asks, "Ideas?"

My brain feels like a lead brick.

"We check her house," Jackson says.

There's an idea.

Luka nods. "You drive," he says, his tone grim, and we head for the Jeep.

The second Jackson rolls up in front of Carly's house, I don't wait for the boys. I leap out of the car while it's still slowing, tear up the front walk, and ring the bell. I hear someone walking around inside; then the door opens.

My words catch in my throat, clogging my windpipe, stopping my breath.

Carly's mom stands there, her shoulders sagging, her expression grim.

CHAPTER TWENTY-FIVE

THE EXPRESSION ON MRS. CONNER'S FACE SENDS DARTS OF terror straight to my heart. If it wasn't for Jackson coming up behind me and grabbing my elbows to hold me up, I might collapse.

"Miki," Carly's mom says. "Did she call you?"

I can't talk. I can only shake my head.

"I thought we were done with this." She sighs. "It's been years since she had one of these fits. Maybe you can get through to her." She throws her hands up. "I'm all out of ideas."

I try to align my thoughts and expectations with Mrs. Conner's attitude. She isn't grief stricken. She isn't in a panic. She's upset, yeah, but she seems more . . . annoyed than anything else. Then her words filter through my fear.

"Carly's . . . okay?" I ask.

She shrugs. "As okay as she ever is when she locks herself in the bathroom for an hour, sobbing her guts out, refusing to talk to me or unlock the door."

My relief is so acute that my knees give out completely. Jackson presses against my back, keeping me upright.

"She's not—" *Dead.*

Carly's not dead. She's locked in the bathroom. Whatever's wrong with her, we can fix this.

Mrs. Conner narrows her eyes at Jackson and Luka, who stand behind me. "Is this because of one of you? Did you break her heart?"

Embarrassing mom question. I feel an acute pang of longing, a wish my mom were here to ask every embarrassing question under the sun.

"No," I say. "This has nothing to do with either of them. Maybe she's upset about her costume. Did she say anything? Anything at all?"

Mrs. Conner shakes her head. "Other than 'go away'? No. She's been in there for over an hour. She won't come out. Won't talk to me. I could hear her crying. I threatened to get one of her brothers to break down the door, but she just told me not to come in, no matter what. And now they've all gone out and it's just her and me, and she hasn't made a peep in about twenty minutes." She sighs. "Not that I've been standing outside the door listening. Just checking on her now and then."

"I—" The word comes out as a croak. I wet my lips and

try again. "Let me talk to her," I say.

Pulling the door wide, Mrs. Conner motions us inside. "Give it your best shot, Miki."

I toe off my boots. Jackson and Luka do the same and the three of us head up to the bathroom, Mrs. Conner watching us warily. Okay, this is weird. Me and Jackson and Luka hunting Carly down in the toilet.

I knock on the door. "Carly?"

No answer.

"Carly? Open up. I'm here with Jackson and Luka. We're worried about you." I just need to see her. I need to know she's okay. "And Kelley and Dee want you at the dance. Ketchup and relish aren't quite the same without mustard."

No answer.

Luka reaches over and rattles the doorknob. Locked.

We exchange *so-what-do-we-do-now* looks. I glance over my shoulder at Jackson to see if he has any ideas, but he's not there. He's standing at the top of the stairs, talking quietly to Carly's mom.

I turn back to the door and tap on it. "Carly? Listen, you don't need to open the door if you don't want. Just answer me. Tell me you're okay. Otherwise . . ." I try to think of a threat. Again, I glance at Jackson. He's standing there, watching me, arms crossed over his chest. Mrs. Conner has now left us alone, so no help there. I sigh and turn back to the locked door. "Otherwise, your mom said she's going to call 911. She's really worried. We all are."

I press my ear to the door. Not a sound. I try to decide what to say next, minutes crawling past, my exhausted brain coming up blank.

"Let me," Jackson says.

I turn to see that Mrs. Conner is back. She hands something to Jackson. I can't imagine that Carly will be any more responsive to him than she was to her mom or me. But I step aside, hoping I'm wrong.

Of course, Jackson takes a completely different tack. He uncoils the paper clip he must have gotten from Mrs. Conner, squats down to eye level with the doorknob, and slips the end of the paper clip into the hole at the bottom. He wiggles it for about three seconds, and then turns the knob. The door opens a crack.

Jackson gets to his feet and steps back. As Luka reaches for the doorknob, Jackson catches his wrist. "Maybe let Miki," he says.

I glance at Mrs. Conner, who's standing by the top of the stairs again. Her arms are folded over her chest, her brows drawn in a frown. For all that she was trying to come off as annoyed, she really is worried.

I offer what I hope is a reassuring smile, slip into the bathroom, and close the door behind me. It's dark, just a sliver of ambient light leaking through the edge of the blind that's pulled down over the window.

"Carly?" I say as I flip on the light, which also happens to turn on the overhead fan. They're wired together to a single switch. Carly and I have a running joke that the fan's louder than a jet, so we can always tell if one of her brothers is in the can.

As it roars to life and the sudden light hits her, Carly lets out a squeak and throws her forearm across her eyes. She's curled up on the floor in a corner of the bathroom, dressed in her yellow bodysuit. The yellow wig's nowhere in sight and her mustard label isn't tacked on.

I hunker down beside her and lean over, trying to give her a hug. In this position, it's more like a pro-wrestling cross-body block.

She squirms and says, "What are you doing?" The words are muffled in my shoulder.

"Me? What are *you* doing? You scared the shit out of us."

"What?" She sort of curls to a sitting position and pushes away from me, then scuttles back until her back's pressed to the wall, her legs straight out in front of her. Her eyes are puffy and red, swollen almost completely shut, her cheeks tear stained.

She looks around, then drops her face into her hands. "Did I cry myself to sleep on the bathroom floor? Could I be any more pathetic?"

I settle on the floor next to her, remembering times when she was twelve and going through major mood swings and she'd lock herself in the bathroom for hours on end and just cry. Sometimes she'd let me in. Sometimes she wouldn't. But she's not twelve anymore and this is something else entirely.

"Did you . . . um . . . drink something?" I ask.

"No."

"Smoke something?"

"No!"

"Get your period?"

She shoves my shoulder. "Shut up."

We sit like that, shoulder-to-shoulder, my back to the wall, my legs stretched out next to hers. Mine in black. Hers in yellow. Like a bumblebee. Finally, she says, "I had the worst nightmare. It was so real."

"Do you . . . want to tell me about it?"

"I died."

My stomach knots and I wait for her to continue, a million questions on the tip of my tongue. I don't want to push her, but I need to know. The game is spilling into real life and now that I know Carly's okay, that she made it through, I need to think strategically. Any info she can give me might help us against the Drau.

My head's clearer now, and the implications sparkle deadly bright. The Drau were at the dance at my high school. They almost killed Carly. Next time, there might not be any *almost* in that sentence. And the number of victims might not be in the single digits. The number of dead could number in the hundreds . . . thousands . . .

"I thought you're not supposed to die in your dreams," Carly says just as I'm about to fire off a question or two, "cuz if you die in a dream you die for real."

"I think that's a myth. Tell me about the dream."

She takes her hands from her face and stares at the

floor, pulling on alternating strands of the fluffy blue bath mat. "I was at the dance. We were doing 'The Time Warp.' There were these lights flashing, really bright, right in the middle of everything. Lights in the shape of people. I thought someone came up with a really cool costume. Then there were a bunch of little lights, like falling stars, and when they landed, they burned holes through people's skin. Everyone started screaming. Running. It was crazy."

She pulls at a strand of carpet, lets it go, pulls at another. "You were there. You and Luka and Jackson. Someone pulled the fire alarm. You ran down toward the gym instead of running out. I was scared you'd get hurt. Get killed."

She shrugs, still staring at the carpet, pulling and pulling at the threads. "I knew I had to follow you, save you. It was like there was something driving me to follow. You went to the basement and I knew that if I didn't go down after you, something terrible was going to happen to you." She pauses. "It was so *real*. Not like any dream I've had before."

I put my hand over hers and squeeze. She stops pulling at the rug, just sits there, tense and rigid.

"I found you," she says. "I was telling you to get out. And then I died."

My fingers tighten on hers.

She looks down and spreads her free hand over her abdomen. "It didn't hurt. It was just sort of dull. Numb.

But there was a lot of blood." She takes a deep, shuddering breath. "Like, a *lot* of blood."

She lets her hand fall away. She tips her head back against the wall, eyes closed. "You know I hate the sight of blood."

I wait for her to keep going, and I'm about to push when she starts speaking again.

"Then Jackson was there, bending over me, looking in my eyes. But he was a girl. And then this laser beam went right through my eyes into my brain. It hurt so bad. Like my eyes were exploding. A gray laser, silvery, really freaky. It was—"

She tips her head forward and starts picking at the carpet again.

I don't know what to think, what to say. She remembers everything that happened in the game. But she doesn't know she remembers. She thinks it was a dream, a really bad dream.

I want to tell her everything. The Drau. The Committee.

I want to tell her nothing.

I hope she keeps thinking it was just a nightmare, and actually, from her description it sounds like a blend of nightmare and memory.

Finally, I say, "Sounds pretty crazy. Jackson was a girl?" I laugh because I'm wound so tight that if I don't laugh, I'll crack. And because the thought of Jackson as a girl *is* pretty funny. But mostly I laugh in pure relief, because Carly's okay. Somehow, she's okay and I'm so damn grateful for that.

I lace my fingers with hers. "Come on. Come out of the bathroom. Your mom's worried. Luka and Jackson are worried. Dee and Kelley must be freaking by now. Come on."

I tug lightly on her hand, but she doesn't move. She just sits there on the bathroom floor staring at the carpet.

"The nightmare was bad enough. But you know what's worse?" she asks.

I stop tugging. She isn't ready to budge; there's more to the story. Unease slithers across my skin, raising goose bumps. "Tell me."

"When I looked in the mirror . . ." She pulls her hand from mine. "When I looked in the mirror, the nightmare was still there. My eyes—"

I gasp. I can't help it. I know what she's going to say even before she says it.

"My eyes were like theirs." She shudders. "Gray and scary. With slitted pupils instead of round ones. Not human. Like theirs."

My turn to shudder.

Carly's describing the Drau's slitted pupils, but she never saw the Drau that killed her. It hit her from behind. She saw Jackson's eyes when he did his Drau trick, but his pupils are human; they're round.

My thoughts shift while I try to rearrange the pieces of the puzzle. I stare at the top of her bowed head, more than a little freaked out, trying to make sense of everything she's saying.

She said she cried herself to sleep on the bathroom floor. . . . "Wait, when did you have the nightmare? Here, on the floor? After you locked yourself in the bathroom?"

She shakes her head. "I fell asleep on my bed. It was so weird." She's picking at the carpet again. Faster. Rougher. A thread pulls free and she throws it down, then pulls out another and another. "One second I was getting ready for the dance." She pauses, her whole body motionless; then she starts pulling out threads again, even faster. "Then I was waking up on my bed. I don't even remember lying down on the bed. I came in here. Washed my face. Looked in the mirror, and—"

I need to see her eyes.

"Look at me," I order. And when she doesn't, my unease ramps to full-on fear.

What if this isn't Carly? My Carly. What if this is a different Carly, a shell?

No. That's not possible.

Could they even have cloned her and made a shell so quickly?

Or maybe it wasn't quick. Maybe the whole time-jump thing worked in their favor. Time passes differently inside the game and out.

But she's acting like Carly acts when she's upset. Would the Drau know that? Would they be able to program it into a clone?

Adrenaline spikes, sensitizing my skin, making my pulse gallop, my breathing harsh.

She balls her hand into a fist and presses it against her stomach, like she's feeling sick.

That's my opening. Only one way to be sure.

"Feeling queasy?" I ask, laying my hand just below hers.

I need to know if Carly's a shell.

I curl my fingers a little, searching for proof. My index finger finds her navel.

She slaps at my hand. "What are you doing poking in my belly button?"

"Sorry," I mutter, grinning like a Cheshire cat because the spandex clings to her and I can still see the indent. Shells don't have umbilical cords, so they don't have navels. One question answered.

"Freak," Carly says without venom. She nods and sniffs, then scrubs her nose with the back of her hand. I unroll a few squares of toilet paper and hand them to her.

"I'm scared to look at my eyes," she says.

Yeah . . . I might have a harder time explaining that away. I need to see them. See how bad they are. I don't even want to begin trying to figure out how or why her eyes are Drau gray.

Is it because Jackson healed her? Fixed her? And now she has some connection?

But then why didn't my eyes go gray when I healed him?

Because the flow of energy was in the opposite direction?

And if Jackson healed her, why hasn't the Committee pulled him to face the repercussions of that?

My brain's hurting from trying to figure this out.

One thing at a time.

"That's why you locked yourself in? You didn't want your mom to see your eyes?"

She gives a harsh laugh. "You're giving me credit for actually thinking of a reason. I didn't. I just freaked out and hid in here."

"Show me," I say.

"I'm scared," she says, sounding young and lost and forlorn.

"I know. Let me see." I cup her cheeks, tipping her face up so I can see exactly what she saw.

Carly's hazel-green eyes look back at me, mascara streaking her cheeks in lurid black stripes.

Relief is like a hydrogen-filled balloon, floating up, up, up. "You're nuts, you know that, right?" I ask.

"What?"

Laughing, I bound to my feet, grab her makeup mirror off the shelf, and hold it up so she can see.

"There's nothing wrong with your eyes. It was just part of the nightmare."

"Oh." She moves closer to the mirror and stares at herself. Then she smiles. "Oh!"

I put the mirror down and hold my hand out to her. "You freaked yourself out for no reason."

She huffs a short laugh. "I swear I'm never going to eat a giant Hershey bar in one sitting again. Ever."

She grabs my hand and I yank her to her feet.

And for a millisecond, I swear her eyes flash Drau gray.

CHAPTER **TWENTY-SIX**

WE DON'T GO TO THE DANCE. CARLY JUST WANTS TO COME TO my place and chill, so she heads into her room to change while Jackson and Luka and I sit on the front step, waiting for her. The screaming match between her and her mom carries to us through the walls and the glass of the closed windows, muffled but still audible.

None of us says a word. I can feel the tension radiating from Jackson like heat from a fire.

Luka glances over at me, lifts his brows. I lift mine back. I'm not sure what message he takes from that, but he says, "I can't sit here." He slaps his palms against his thighs and stands. "I'm just gonna walk to the end of the block."

I watch him go.

"Thank you," I say to Jackson, once Luka's out of ear-shot.

"For what?" He doesn't look at me, just hunches forward, his forearms on his thighs, his hands loose between his spread knees.

"For what you did for Carly," I say.

"I didn't do it for Carly," he says.

I nod. He did it for me. *And* for Carly, though he's not the type to admit the last part.

"Truth is, I don't think I did anything at all," he continues, straightening and tipping his head back, his face toward the night sky. "There wasn't time for me to do any kind of energy exchange. And if I'd succeeded, the Committee would be having a field day with me right now." He drops his chin and turns his head a little toward me. "I wouldn't be sitting here with you."

Everything he says is true, but hearing it out loud makes me afraid. Because if Jackson didn't fix things . . . "You think *they* saved her?" The Committee.

"Something did." He offers a hint of a smile. "I don't get to take credit for this one."

I take a deep breath, hating myself for what I'm about to ask, needing to ask it. "Do you get to take credit for lying to me again?"

The smile vanishes. He's quiet for a bit; then he asks, "Which lie are we talking about here?"

"There's more than one?" I shake my head. "No, don't answer that. Of course there's more than one."

"I don't consider them lies."

"Because they're omission rather than commission?"

"Something like that." He rests his forearms on his thighs again and dangles his hands between his legs.

"You knew, didn't you? You knew while we were in the lobby that we were going to respawn at Glenbrook."

"We didn't respawn at Glenbrook."

"Not at first, no, but somehow that's where we ended up. And you had forewarning. You knew."

"Yeah."

"Did you know the Drau would be able to hurt people?"

"The Drau always hurt people."

I exhale in a rush. "That's not what I mean. Did you know they would be at the dance, that they would *be* there, really be there, in the same reality or dimension or whatever? Did you know that they could hurt people *at the dance*? Answer me, Jackson. The truth, not one of your versions of the truth."

"I knew when we were in the lobby that we were going to Glenbrook. I knew before Luka went into the dance that worlds were about to collide."

"And you didn't tell me."

"I did what was best for the team. Kendra was already losing it. Lien's focus was on her. You were freaked that we were at Glenbrook, never mind that the Drau were about to attend the Halloween dance with us." He turns his head toward me and continues in a flat, even tone. "When we're there, on a mission, I can't be Jackson, the boy trying to work things out with Miki. I have to be Jackson who gets everyone in, then gets them out. It's the only way I can do this, Miki."

"When—" I begin, then pause, trying to figure out exactly what I want to say. "You said you had to do what's best for the team. That's the key word. *Team*, as in collaborative effort. You aren't a lone gunman, Jackson. When we're on a mission, I can't be the girl who blindly follows orders, no questions asked. You should have told me."

"And if you freaked out? Drew attention to us? Jeopardized the mission?"

"Because telling me would have been so much more likely to freak me out than letting things blindside me, letting me see it all happen right in front of me?"

"Miki, you're a control freak. If I'd told you in advance, you would have second-guessed yourself, seen each scenario before it played out. Tried to twist it to conform to your mental plan. And that could have gotten you killed." He pauses. "The way it panned out, you were confronted by a situation; you reacted without overthinking. You're trained for battle, Miki. That's what kendo did for you. So I let your training take over."

Anger flickers and flares. I hate that he did this. That he high-handedly made decisions for me. But that's his job—at least, it is when we're in the game. He's the leader. He's supposed to make decisions.

I doubly hate it that I know he's right about the control thing.

"So you did it because I'm not capable of knowing the truth and thinking it through?" I snap, not even meaning to. It just comes out. "Because I'm just a bundle of raw nerves? Is that what you think of me? Is that who you think I am?"

"No."

I push to my feet, pace away, then back again. He's not totally wrong. I do get panic attacks. I do have anxiety. But not when we're on a mission. On every mission, I've done what I had to, done it with a cool head and a fair amount of logic.

Because I've been dumped right into the thick of things. No forewarning, no time to agonize and second-guess.

Which backs up Jackson's claim that his way was the right way. I ball my fists, angry with him. Angry with myself.

He catches my hand and draws me back down next to him on the step.

"It isn't just about me. Or you," he says. "It's about the rest of them. Was I supposed to tell them, too? Drag you aside and whisper it in your ear?"

"However you want to spin this in your own mind, whatever justifications you have, you didn't just omit information, Jackson. You lied. When we first respawned in the hallway, you said it was like Vegas. You said no one outside the game would get hurt."

"Did I say that?"

I stare at him, thinking back, dissecting my memories.

"No," I say slowly. "You didn't. You said one word. *Vegas.* You let me fill in the rest. And you didn't correct me when I filled it in wrong."

"I made a judgment call."

"Do you understand how wrong that is? You making decisions like that for me?"

He shrugs. "Blame it on a heavy dose of caveman genes."

Caveman genes that have kept us all alive. I'm torn. I see his side, but I also see mine. We're both right. We're both wrong. "You told me you wouldn't lie to me anymore."

He doesn't say anything.

"If we don't have honesty . . . if we don't have trust . . . what do we have?" I whisper.

"I trust you, Miki. I trust you with my life."

It's my turn not to say anything. If I say I trust him, I negate all my arguments and this will never be resolved between us. If I say I don't trust him, then I'm the one who's lying. Rock and a hard place.

He sighs. "If you can't forgive me"—he holds up a hand when I start to interrupt—"if you can't forgive me, Miki, then what do we have?"

"I forgive you."

"Do you? For what? For not telling you everything on this mission? For doling out details on a need-to-know basis? Or is it that you forgive me for tricking you in the first place? Dragging you into the game?"

I open my mouth. He shakes his head and keeps going. "What is it you forgive me for, Miki? For being the leader I've been forced to be for the past five years? For making the choice to risk my life so your friend could live, making that choice so you didn't have to? For not being perfect? For not being the boy who tells you absolutely everything, and never will?"

I recoil from him, stinging like he struck me. "Is that how you see me? Is that what you think of me? That I'm so shallow, so weak . . . so foolish?"

His laugh is bitter and dark. "I see you as strength incarnate, a warrior forged of steel, the single bright light in my effed-up world. But it's how *you* see us. It's about what you can and can't accept."

He pushes to his feet, his back to me, and says, "Some buildings sway when an earthquake hits, and they're the ones that are still standing when it's over. Some buildings don't. They're too rigid. They snap. You're lucky, Miki. You get to choose what sort of building you want to be."

I stare at his back, feeling sick, wondering how we got to this place when we ought to be hugging and jumping for joy because he just got our whole team out alive, got me out alive, got Carly out. Sent the Drau back to the hole they crawled out of. Saved the team. The school. And for the moment, the world.

"Jackson." I jump to my feet, lay my hand on his shoulder, feeling sick and hurt and confused, not wanting to let this conversation end like this.

"I'll drop you and Carly at your place," he says. "I just need some time on my own."

"He says he'll never be the boy who tells me absolutely everything," I say to Carly. She's lying on my bed. I'm lying on my back on my floor.

I didn't tell her what my fight with Jackson was about. How could I? When she asked why he and Luka weren't coming in, I just told her Jackson and I had a disagreement, that he isn't always completely truthful with me.

"That is completely unacceptable," she says in her best imitation of Mr. Shomper. "I mean, how can he not tell you what toothpaste he uses? Or what he ate for breakfast? Or . . . wait, no," she says in a horrified tone, "if he forgot to do laundry and didn't have any clean socks so he's wearing the same ones as yesterday." She tips her head to look at me. "Does he do his own laundry? Did he tell you?"

"Not funny." But I smile anyway because she's here, lying on my bed, eyes still puffy from her crying jag, but other than that looking healthy as can be.

Puffy eyes are a vast improvement over bone-white and bloody and dead.

"Do *you* tell *him* absolutely everything?" she asks. "Like, did you tell him about the time you pooped in the bathtub and it floated and you called it a boat?"

"I was three!"

"But did you tell him?"

"No."

"What about the time you barfed all over Allen's lap on the bus on the class trip to the zoo? Did you tell him that?"

"Those are disgusting and ridiculous examples. Is there a particular reason you're choosing to be as gross as possible?"

"I guess I just feel like it."

"Well, unfeel."

"*Unfeel?* Is that a word?" She laughs at the look I shoot her and says, "Okay. Answer this. Did you tell him all about the nightmares and the panic attacks?" Her voice gentles. "Did you tell him about your mom? Or about how worried you've been about your dad and his drinking?"

I take in a breath, ready to answer, and then I stop. Carly knows all that. Some, because she lived through it with me. Some, because she knows me so well I don't need to tell her. The stuff about Dad's drinking, because I confided in her. In the beginning, she even helped me count the bottles on the counter and the ones in the fridge.

But Jackson doesn't know—at least, not everything. Parts of it we've talked about. And parts of it, like the anxiety stuff, I think he pretty much figured out. But some of it, I just didn't talk about because . . . I just didn't. "Not all of it, no."

"Why not?" Carly asks. "Shouldn't you tell him everything?"

"I . . ."

"Double standard much? He's supposed to bare all for

you"—she pauses and looks at me and grins—"which I'd like to be present for if it's all the same to you. Anyway, he's supposed to bare his soul for you, but you get to keep secrets?"

"They're not secrets. It's just, I can't tell him everything. I don't always think about explaining stuff like that. It's just part of . . . I don't know . . . part of *me*. And other stuff, I guess I don't think he really needs to know. Or maybe I don't think he'd want to know."

"And you don't think maybe it's the same for him?"

"No, it isn't the same. The stuff he doesn't tell me is different. It's important. It's—" *About the game.*

And I can't tell Carly that.

So I'm doing exactly what Jackson does. Keeping secrets. Or, at least, avoiding certain topics. Because sometimes that's just the way it is.

I sigh, thinking about our argument and about Jackson, the way he was there for me, the way he came to me when I needed him, when Carly needed him, instead of going after the girl with the green eyes.

"I made it all about me," I say, covering my face with my hands. "I knew he had a rough evening, too, and I just focused on my stuff."

Rough doesn't begin to describe it. On top of everything we all went through on that mission, Jackson had to deal with being responsible for all our lives and facing down a shell wearing his dead sister's face.

I could have cut him some slack.

I could have started the argument another day.

I just didn't think. No wonder he said he wanted some time to himself.

"What's wrong with me?" I ask.

Carly rolls facedown and slides off the bed headfirst so she ends up half-on, half-off, supporting her torso on her straight arms, her face above mine.

"Nothing's wrong with you. Actually, you're the least wrong that you've been in two years. Couples argue sometimes. No biggie." She slides the rest of the way off the bed, so we're lying side by side. "It's not like he broke up with you. I mean, he didn't, did he?"

"No."

She rolls on her side and stares at me. "Do you love him?"

I study the ceiling, trying to decide how to answer. Do I want to say it out loud? I've told Jackson that I love him, but that was under duress while he was dying in a deserted building in Detroit after he took a Drau hit meant for me. And I qualified that declaration by telling him I didn't forgive him, that he had to live so he could beg forgiveness. On the romance scale, that'd have to score a negative ten.

And maybe I've said it once or twice since then in a joking way—I can't even remember if I have or not. But I haven't actually *said it* said it. Maybe I'm afraid to love him. Or maybe I'm just afraid to admit it out loud.

Bad things seem to happen to people I love.

I haven't told anyone else how I feel about him. Not even Carly.

"It's okay," she says. "You don't have to answer. Not out loud. But you have to answer it in your own head. In your heart." She pauses, then says in a slow, sonorous tone, dragging out each word, forcing a huffing exhalation into each vowel, "Love . . . means never . . . having . . . to say . . . you're sorry."

"Did you seriously just say that to me?" I surge up and grab a pillow off my bed and whack her with it. She grabs another and whacks me. "Did you really just tell me that love means never having to say you're sorry?"

She's laughing so hard, she's gasping for air as her pillow smacks me upside the head. I get her on the arm. She gets me flat across the back.

In the end, we're both gasping and snorting as we let the pillows drop.

"I love you," she says. "There, I said it."

Everyone leaves.

She almost left me tonight, almost died. I never would have had these moments with her, never would have had the chance to tell her. Just like I'll never again have the chance to tell Mom. But I have the memories of a thousand times I did tell her, and the thousand times she told me. Those memories matter. "I love you, too, Carly," I say.

She puckers up and makes kissy-face noises. "I really do forgive you for killing my fish," she says.

"I really do forgive you for bringing that up yet again," I say.

She shrugs. "You deserve it."

"You plan to milk it for eternity."

"Pretty much."

"Okay."

She grabs me and hugs me, and I hug her back, holding tighter than I probably should, the memory of her lying on the floor covered in blood too fresh, too raw.

There's a tapping at my door. "Miki? Carly?"

We both flop on the bed. "Come on in, Dad."

He looks at the pillows on the floor, then at us. If I look anywhere near as bad as Carly, whose hair is standing out in all directions from static electricity, then Dad'll have no trouble figuring out what we've been doing.

"I'm heading out to get milk," Dad says. "Do you want a ride home, Carly?"

"Yeah, thanks, Mr. Jones. My mom's not speaking to me. Again. So calling her for a ride probably isn't my best plan."

"Right. Okay." Dad holds up his index finger, punctuating each word. "Ready to go when you are."

CHAPTER **TWENTY-SEVEN**

I STAND AT MY BEDROOM WINDOW AND WATCH THE EXPLORER pull out of the drive. Carly opens the window and hangs her arm out to wave wildly. I wave back, feeling like the whole night was surreal, but it isn't until the car disappears around the corner that I slump against the wall.

It's like Carly took all my energy with her when she left.

Between the Drau, and Carly almost dying, and the fight with Jackson, there just isn't much left of me. I should take a hot shower or flop in front of the TV and watch a show or maybe just crawl into bed and sleep for a week.

But I don't do any of those things. I stay where I am, my cheek resting against the window frame as I unpack the crazy that's crawling around in my head like a bunch of centipedes.

I start with the things I know.

The Drau pushed through into my world, my real world.

Everything the Committee said about how big of a threat they are is true.

Carly almost died.

Someone healed her, but Jackson doesn't believe it was him. Which leaves the possibility that the respawn did the trick. Except, Carly isn't part of the game. She doesn't respawn. And even if she did, it wouldn't explain the hint of Drau gray I saw flash in her eyes.

Which brings me to all the things I don't know: Who healed Carly? Exactly how trustworthy is the Committee? If the green-eyed girl is a shell, why does she keep helping me? Because the Drau want to use me as an original donor?

I guess Jackson could be right about that, but if that's what she wants, she could have fought my team the first time I met her, when I was lying on the ground, bleeding, dying. She could have fought them and killed them— maybe—and taken me then. But she chose to run away.

A quick tapping snares my attention, and only then do I realize I'm drumming my fingertips against the window-sill. I force myself to stop. Then I force myself to mentally catalogue what I know, starting from the beginning. I end up with questions and more questions, like an infinite circle spinning around.

But at least I have a few answers now, too. I know more about the game and about the Committee and their limitations. I know more about myself, my weaknesses, my strengths.

The chill from outside penetrates the glass. I shiver, but I don't move away. It's like I'm waiting for something but I don't know what.

Lie.

I do know.

I'm waiting for the prickle of awareness that will tell me Jackson's there, on my street, watching my window. I've felt it before, more than once. Not in a creeper way. He had good reasons. I kind of wish he'd find a reason right now.

Once, he left me a gift—a copy of my favorite manga, wrapped in a plastic bag to protect it from the weather—on the flat roof of the overhang that covers the front porch.

Once, I looked out my window to find him sitting cross-legged on that same porch roof, his honey-gold hair gleaming in the moonlight, shades firmly in place, even at night.

That was the night he snuck in my bedroom window. The night he lifted his shirt and bared his abs—and his navel—to prove to me he wasn't a shell.

The night he kissed me for the first time.

Not on my lips. That came later. The first kiss was something else entirely.

I remember it. I remember the way he grabbed my

wrist and turned my hand over, then lowered his head and pressed his lips to my palm.

I remember the shock of electricity that danced through me.

Then he moved his lips to the crease of my wrist. I stood perfectly still, my blood hammering through my veins.

I remember the way he made me feel; I'd never felt like that before. I wanted him to do it again. Instead, he climbed out the window and took off into the night.

I close my eyes now and press the inside of my wrist against my mouth, wishing Jackson were here, wishing we hadn't parted the way we did.

He just faced down what amounted to his sister's ghost. I hate that I know he has to be suffering. And I hate that I know I added to his pain. I wasn't there for him, didn't offer much in the way of comfort. I'm not feeling very proud of that.

I grab a hoodie, climb out my window, and sit on the roof with my back pressed against the bricks, just like Mom and I used to do when I was little. We'd sit out here and stare at the stars. She'd try to name them. She didn't always get them right, and it really didn't matter.

Staring up at the stars now, I can't help but wonder how many of them support worlds like Earth. Worlds like my ancestors came from. Or the Drau.

I wish Mom were here right now. I wish I could talk to her. I wouldn't be able to tell her about the game, but I could tell her about the gray fog, the panic attacks, the way I try so hard to control everything in my life, as if that will keep me safe.

I could tell her about Jackson.

She could help me figure it all out.

But she isn't here, and I haven't felt this alone in a really long time. I haven't let myself feel this alone.

I play with my phone, trying to decide if I should call him or not.

Not.

He said he needed some time on his own.

An hour? A day? A month?

There's no one for me to ask.

I love Dad so much. But I can't talk to him the same way I talked to Mom. It's just different. They're different.

I bend my knees up and hug them. "I miss you, Mommy," I whisper. "I miss you so much."

It isn't until I'm shivering from the cold that I realize Dad's been gone way longer than the twenty minutes it should have taken him to drop Carly, get milk, and make it back home.

Maybe he got caught up talking to Mrs. Conner when he dropped Carly off.

I pull out my phone and call him. Through my open window, I hear the faint sound of his ringtone inside the house. He forgot his phone. Again.

And the battery's probably almost dead. Again. He has a habit of forgetting to charge it.

316

I duck back in through the window and head to his room. No phone on the dresser, but there's a low oval dish that Mom used to keep potpourri in. I stare at it for a minute, really seeing it for the first time in ages. It's full, but not with aromatic leaves. There are matchbooks in there.

I exhale a shocked breath. Dad wouldn't smoke. He wouldn't. He quit as soon as Mom was diagnosed. I don't believe he'd start again.

I pick up a matchbook and open the flap. All the matchsticks are there. Same with the next one and the next. So he's just collecting them; he's not using them. I run my fingers over the glossy covers. Blue Mill Tavern. Dante's Inferno. La Ronda Bar. Elk Bar. Dad must like that one; he has at least a dozen of their orange matchbooks.

My stomach clenches. I feel like I'm going to puke. All those nights Dad's been out, he hasn't been going to AA meetings. He's been going to bars.

Is that where he is now? Is that why he's so late?

I remember what Dad said to me back at the beginning of September, the words playing through my thoughts. *I don't have a problem. It's all under control. I'm not one of those after-school specials, passed out on the couch, with three empty bottles of gin on the floor.*

No, he's not passed out on the couch. And the bottles aren't gin. They're vodka, like the one I found in his office when I was vacuuming.

He's been lying to me. Lying to himself.

Am I supposed to forgive him for that? I need him. And

he's nowhere to be found. Not even when he's sitting right across the dinner table from me.

I give up on finding his phone and stalk downstairs to the den. I pace to the front window, pull back the drapes, and stare at the empty street. Then I pace back to the couch.

I dial Carly's number. She doesn't answer.

I put my phone on the coffee table, line it up parallel to the converter, rearrange Dad's fishing magazines so they're perfectly straight. With a cry, I draw back my arm and swipe the surface, sending everything tumbling to the floor.

Then I pace back to the window and just stand there, waiting for the flare of headlights.

When the cruiser turns into my driveway, I'm not surprised. When the two police officers get out and walk to my front porch, settling their hats on their heads as they move, I'm not surprised.

And when I open the door and they start to speak, I'm not surprised.

I'm numb.

I don't hear their words. They run together into a blur of sound.

I struggle to focus.

I pull the door wide as they step inside, removing their hats. Why did they put them on just to take them off again? It feels like such an important question.

"No shoes in the house," I mumble.

I think they ask me my name, or maybe who I am.

"Miki," I say. "I'm Miki Jones."

One of them asks me something else. I blink. Stare at them. He asks again. They want to know who else was in the car. She didn't have ID. Do I know who she is?

"She didn't need her wallet because she was just coming here," I say. "She didn't need money or anything. She didn't want to go to the dance."

The officer nods like I'm making perfect sense, but I think that maybe I'm not.

"Can you tell me her name?"

"Carly Conner." I pause and stare at them and they stare back at me like they want something more. I rattle off her home phone number and address because that's all I can think to do.

They keep talking. I stop listening. Not on purpose. I just . . . shut off.

Then one word jumps out at me: *hospital.* I nod. Out of habit, I pull a coat out of the front closet, get my key, lock the door.

But I'm not here.

I'm not living this moment.

It's just a shell of me walking to the police car, staring straight ahead, feeling nothing. Nothing at all.

I sit in the waiting room, my forearms on my thighs, my head hanging down. There's a TV in the corner, set to some local news show, droning softly. I can't hear the words. I don't care about the words.

I'm alone. Just me and my thoughts.

The two officers were in the hall until a few minutes ago. I heard little snippets of their conversation.

. . . head-on collision . . .

. . . blood-alcohol level point one eight . . .

. . . more than twice legal limit . . .

They've left. I don't know when. I don't even know how long I've been here.

I don't know how bad things are. I don't know anything about Dad or Carly other than they were both alive when they were brought in. I can only pray that's still the case now.

When we got here, the officers spoke to someone, a woman, maybe a nurse. She pointed us here. They deposited me in a chair and went out in the hall.

I haven't seen or heard from anyone since.

Not a nurse or a doctor. I want to go try to find someone to talk to, but I'm afraid to leave this spot in case someone comes to talk to me.

Burying my face in my hands, I try to make sense of things. How can it be that Carly survived a Drau attack only to be in a car crash a few hours later?

How could that happen?

It doesn't make sense. Nothing makes sense.

I need it to make sense.

There's a commotion in the hall. I lift my head. Carly's parents come into the room, clutching each other's hands, clinging to each other. They look old. Really old. As if twenty years have passed instead of the handful of hours since I last saw Mrs. Conner.

I cringe inside.

This is my fault. I could have stopped it.

If I'd driven Carly myself.

If I'd made her call her mom for a ride.

If I'd made her sleep over.

If I'd checked to see if Dad had been drinking.

He said he wouldn't drink and drive. Promised me. I believed him. I really believed him.

This is on me and I'm never going to be able to forgive myself.

I force myself to my feet, meeting Mrs. Conner's gaze, expecting . . . I don't know what. That she'll scream at me? Hit me? Lose it totally?

She lunges forward. Grabs me. Drags me against her chest, her whole body trembling as she hugs me tight. "They'll be okay," she whispers. "We have to believe that. They'll be okay." Then she starts sobbing, holding me and sobbing, and all I can do is stand there and stare over her shoulder at the poster for flu vaccines that's on the wall, because if I do anything else, I'm going to burst into a million tiny specks of nothing.

Pulling back, she studies my face. She's talking, but I can't hear what she's saying. My ears buzz. My head feels like it's going to explode. For a second, I'm terrified that I'm getting pulled. Then I realize it's my anxiety taking over my senses. I'm just a bundle of raw nerves.

"What do you know?" she asks. I get that more from focusing on her lips than actually hearing the words.

What do I know? Not much.

"Did you talk to the police?" I ask. Silly question. Of course they talked to the police. How else would they have known to come here?

Mrs. Conner nods. "They phoned us as soon as you gave them Carly's name. Have you seen a doctor? A nurse? Has anyone said anything?"

I shake my head.

"Did they tell you anything?" I ask.

"Not much at all. A nurse brought us here and they said someone would speak with us as soon as possible. She said Carly's being sent for a CT scan and it could take a few hours for the results."

"And an MRI," Mr. Conner says, his voice gravelly and rough. "They told you nothing about your dad?"

How can he sound so kind? So concerned? Carly's here. My dad was driving. I don't know any details of the accident. If the police said, I don't remember. All I know is what I overheard . . . that alcohol was involved. But here's Mr. Conner, being so kind.

"Just that he's alive. And doctors are with him." I try to remember anything else the nurse said. "That he has two IVs and they need to do tests."

With her arm around my shoulder, Mrs. Conner steers us both to the chairs opposite the TV. She keeps one arm around me and reaches her other hand across to hold my hand.

"I yelled at her," she says.

It's my turn to say, "She'll be okay," mostly because I have nothing else I *can* say.

Carly's dad shoves his hand in his pocket and jiggles his change. Then he takes his hand out, stalks into the hall, stalks back in, jiggles his change some more.

"Coffee," Carly's mom says. Her husband stops pacing and looks at her. "I think we could all use some coffee."

He nods, his face grim, and heads into the hall. "I'll see if I can get any more information out of them."

"He needs something to do," she says once he's gone.

So do I. I need to run. Or hit something. I need to make this better. Change it. Fix it.

And I can't.

So I just sit beside Carly's mom and stare at the flu-vaccine poster.

CHAPTER TWENTY-EIGHT

"HEY."

I open my eyes, disoriented and achy. My neck's twisted to one side, my shoulder pinched. I sit up, rubbing the ache, trying to figure out where I am.

Then it all comes back to me like sewage spewing from a drain. The police. The hospital. I fell asleep in the waiting-room chair. I don't even get how that's possible with how wired I am by worry and strain.

Jackson slouches into the chair next to me and takes my hand.

I shove my hair out of my face. "What are you doing here?" That didn't come out the way I meant it to. I want to add, *Thank you for being here. I need you.* The words get stuck inside me.

"Sitting." He squeezes my fingers a little. "In a chair."

"Not in a tree."

"Maybe later."

"How did you know?" I whisper. *How did you know I needed you? How did you know to come here?*

"Luka came to my place after we dropped you off. We hung out. Played a few games. I was driving him home and we saw a bunch of police cruisers detouring traffic. Luka recognized your dad's car." He exhales, a slow, controlled movement, and his fingers tighten on mine. "I wanted to come straight here, but Luka's dad called and said he needed him home to stay with his sister." He pauses. "The rest of the way to Luka's, I kept thinking it was you in that car."

"No, not me," I whisper. My dad. Carly. "Did you see Carly's parents?"

"Yeah. Her dad's pacing the hall. Her mom's trying to get him to stop."

"Did you talk to them?"

"Mrs. Conner said they're still doing tests." He takes a slow breath, like he isn't sure if he should say more.

"Tell me."

"Carly was unconscious when they brought her in. She hasn't woken up. Mrs. Conner said she has some broken bones but she didn't say which ones and I didn't push."

I can't speak. I can't breathe. I taste salt on my tongue and it takes a ridiculously long time for me to realize I'm tasting my own tears. "Daddy?" I rasp.

"They told Mrs. Conner they were taking him to surgery." I clutch his hand tighter. He glances at our joined hands and continues, "She said he has a ruptured spleen." He leans over and presses his lips to my forehead. "You can live without a spleen, Miki. Live a perfectly normal life."

"How do you know?" I whisper.

"This guy I knew in Texas wracked up his bike. They had to take out his spleen. He walked away with a big scar on his left side and a warning not to play contact sports." He bumps me lightly with his shoulder. "That'll be okay with your dad. Fishing isn't a contact sport."

I try to offer a watery smile, but I can't. I'm fresh out of smiles.

"So it's just his spleen? That's all?"

"I don't know. That's all Mrs. Conner told me. That might be all they told her." He shifts in his seat, angling his body; then he draws me against his chest, my head lolling on his shoulder. "I'm sorry I woke you," he says. "I just wanted you to know I'm here. Try to sleep. I'll wake you if anyone comes."

Tears clog my throat. He held me like this in the caves, ordering me to sleep while he watched over me.

"Thank you," I say. "Thank you for being here."

"I'll always be here, Miki."

My heart clenches. "Don't say that," I say, my tone fierce. "Don't make a promise you might not keep." *Everyone leaves*. "It's enough that you're here right now. This moment. You taught me that."

And I can't think beyond this moment, because what the moments to come might hold is terrifying and dark and horrible.

We're both quiet for a bit.

I keep thinking of Carly, lying on the floor of the school basement, covered in blood. Like a portent of what was to come.

"It doesn't make sense," I say. "How could she survive the Drau, and then d—" I can't say it. Can't say the word. Like saying it might make it real.

"She isn't dead, Miki. She's still alive. Your dad's still alive. Hold on to that. Hold on tight."

I push off Jackson's chest and twist in my seat so I'm looking at him. In this second, I hate his dark glasses. I desperately need to see his eyes, to know what he's thinking when I say what I have to say. But he can't take them off—not here, where someone might walk in any second.

Maybe I shouldn't tell him. Maybe if I keep it a secret inside it won't be true. But it's already true. That's why we're here, in this waiting room with its brown, cloth chairs and scratched coffee table and flu-vaccine posters on the walls.

"My dad . . ." I say. "I heard the police out in the hall . . . they were talking about blood-alcohol level." I jump up and just stand there, wanting to run far away, but having nowhere to run to. And knowing that no matter how far I run, this will still be real.

I start shaking and I can't seem to stop. Jackson grabs

me, pulls me onto his lap, and wraps his arms tight around me.

"It's my fault," I say, turning my face into the curve of his neck, clinging to him because if I let go I'll be swept away by the raging current. "I should have checked if he'd been drinking. Should have driven Carly myself. Should have never fought with you because then you would have been there, you would have been driving her home, you—"

"Would have been the one lying in the hospital right now," Jackson cuts me off.

I rear back and stare at him. "What?"

He cups my cheeks. "Miki, I don't know what you're thinking, but if you think the cops were talking about your dad, you're wrong. It's the driver that hit him who blew something like point one eight. He was on the wrong side of the road. Hit your dad head-on."

"What?" I ask again, parroting myself.

"Your dad isn't at fault. They were hit by a drunk driver. That's why I said if I'd been driving Carly home at exactly that second, through that same intersection, I would have been the one the guy hit. I'd be the one in surgery instead of your dad."

I stare at him, uncomprehending, and then understanding hits like a wave, crashing over me, dragging me under.

My dad wasn't the one who was drinking.

I have a flashback of Carly when we were maybe ten, standing with her hands on her hips in my kitchen, laughing and pointing at me. *When you assume it makes an ass of u and me.*

I jump to my feet and back away.

The sounds from the hall—conversations, beeping, the hiss of an automatic door opening—expand and echo, too loud, like a power sander in my head. I clap my hands over my ears. I can't breathe. I can't think. The air rasps my lungs like shards of glass.

The brown chairs turn bronze and glow too bright.

The red type on the posters on the walls turns to bloody claws, reaching for me.

Colors too bright. Sounds too loud.

The antiseptic hospital smell burns my nose.

No. Not now. It can't be now.

Jackson gets to his feet, so slow.

"Miki!"

My name's dragged out, the syllables pulled like taffy.

The world tips and tilts.

Jackson leaps forward, grabs my hand.

And we're tumbling, tumbling, falling through nothing.

We respawn in a room with no floor, no walls, no ceiling. I mean, I know they're here—I can feel the floor under my feet and when I stretch out a hand, I can feel the smooth, cool wall—but I can't see them. Everything is just a bright, blinding white.

This isn't the lobby.

Were we pulled directly on a mission?

Terror bites at me. I can't do this—not now. I don't know what shape Dad and Carly are in, don't know if they'll live or die, don't know anything about their injuries. I'm a scattered mess. How am I supposed to fight Drau like this?

I'm a danger to Jackson, my team, myself.

Jackson grabs my hand and pushes me behind him, using his body as a shield. Except, am I behind or in front? Hard to tell when the room has no doors or windows, no beginning or end.

The light ramps down. A door appears. Not because it was always there and the light was making it hard to see. It literally appears, a piece of wall sliding open to reveal a rectangle of complete blackness.

I freeze. I know this place. I've been here before. In my nightmares. I stare at the dark doorway remembering the fear I felt, the certainty that danger lurked on the other side. Remembering that when I walked through, Lizzie was there with her Drau weapon in hand.

I'm about to signal Jackson to see if he thinks it's okay to talk; then I realize of course it is. We have no weapons, so we're not here to fight. And if the open door is any indication, whoever—whatever—brought us here knows we're here.

Whoever brought us here . . . the Committee? How could they? How can they think I can do this now? I make a low sound—part moan, part howl.

Jackson pushes his glasses up on his head and turns to

me, his expression intent. He grasps my upper arms. "Miki, I know this is rough—" He shakes his head. His jaw tenses. "I know your mind isn't here. But we don't get a choice. Do you understand? We don't get a choice."

I nod. Jackson shrugs out of his jacket and wraps it around me. Only then do I realize how cold I am. I have the incongruous thought that he was wearing his jacket when we got pulled, but mine was on the seat beside me.

"You can do this," he says. "We make it through. We go back. Your dad and Carly will be waiting for us."

I stare at him, into his mercury-bright eyes. "Will they?" I whisper, not so sure. "And if they *are* alive when we get back, what shape will they be in?"

New guilt swamps me. I don't feel like the accident was my fault now. Jackson disabused me of that. Now I feel guilty because I doubted my dad, blamed him, suspected him.

But he's as much a victim here as Carly.

"They'll be alive when we go back because they were alive when we left."

Of course. We'll respawn in the exact instant we left.

I notice he doesn't make any comment about the shape they'll be in. We have no way to know and there's absolutely nothing either one of us can do about that.

"I'm scared," I whisper. "I don't trust myself to keep it together."

A muscle in his jaw jumps.

"You cannot do anything for them from here. The

only thing you can do is keep yourself safe. Focus on the moment, this moment, just this one. Then on the next one. Then the next. You can't change the situation, so work with it. Think only about this."

I catch my tongue between my teeth and nod. "I'll try."

I will. I just don't know if I'll succeed.

I think of Dad and what it will be like for him if he wakes up and I'm not there. I think of Carly and all the things I want to do for her when I get back. And I realize I have to do more than try. I have to succeed. I can't die in the game. I won't be the one who leaves.

"I will keep you safe, Miki," Jackson says, and then presses his lips to mine. "I swear it." He pulls back; his expression shifts, growing harder, colder. He tips his glasses back down, clasps my hand tight in his, and heads for the door.

"You stay close," he warns.

"Close enough that you can hear me breathe," I say.

"Stay behind me."

I slide my fingers between his, then curl them in. "I'll stay beside you."

He glances at me and smiles, a spare curl of his lips that hints at the dimple in his cheek. "Beside me, then."

"What is this place?"

"Don't know," Jackson says, his tone terse. "Never seen it before."

"I have. In a nightmare."

He turns his head and I can feel him studying me even

though I can't see his eyes. "Tell me."

"It was exactly like this. The walls. The floor." I jut my chin forward. "The door. When I went through—" I break off, hesitate.

"Tell me," he says again.

"When I went through, the girl with the green eyes was waiting for me. She had a Drau weapon. She aimed it. Fired." I shiver, remembering, and as I do, I can see the spray of tiny droplets of bright pain shooting toward me. Skimming my left shoulder. Missing me. "She wasn't firing at me," I say. "She was firing at something behind me."

Jackson nods. "We'll count your dream as a warning."

Cautious, we make our way to the door, separating just before we get there, Jackson going to one side, me to the other. I'm not sure why we bother. We have no weapons and there's no doubt that whoever brought us here knows we're here.

I'm about to say exactly that when Jackson says, "They know we're here. Let's just do this. Find out who they are and what they want."

"Great minds think alike."

We walk through the door to a curving corridor. The sight lines suck. We can't see what's waiting around any corner, because there are no corners.

Despite Jackson's jacket, I'm shivering. The air's cold and dry and smells artificial, like there's a hint of air freshener being pumped in.

We don't pass any windows or doors, just smooth,

white walls, white ceiling, white floor that all meld together seamlessly so I can't tell where one stops and the other starts.

At one point I pause and stretch my hands out to both sides, wondering how wide the corridor is. My fingers extend as far as they can go, but I don't hit anything solid. So it's wider than my arm span.

We keep going, following the curve, until ahead we see a massive arced bank of what appears to be computers. There's a person there with her hands on some sort of control panel. She's dressed all in white, her back to us, her hair pulled in a high ponytail.

She twists at the waist and turns her head back toward us until we have a three-quarter view of her face.

Jackson stops dead.

Her nose. The shape of her face.

Her eyes.

"There you are," Lizzie says, and smiles.

CHAPTER TWENTY-NINE

JACKSON PRACTICALLY VIBRATES WITH TENSION. HIS BREATHing's shallow and faster than normal.

He wants to kill her, this shell who wears his sister's face.

I can feel his emotions like they're my own.

"Stop," Lizzie says, her smile turning to a glare. "No one's killing anyone. Typical Jackson, bristling like a hedgehog."

I blink at that description. Not one I would have thought of. "We don't have much time. I can't keep you here for long," she says.

"Where's here?" I ask.

She shoots me a look so reminiscent of one of Jackson's looks that it hurts my heart to see it. "Does it matter?"

"What do you want?" Jackson asks, his voice harder than I've ever heard it, his expression liquid-nitrogen cold.

"I know things. You need to know them, too." Her expression shifts to one of concern, and she turns back to the control panel ahead of her, touching things, skimming her hands over molten, glowing surfaces. "We have to hurry."

"And why would I believe anything you tell me?" Jackson asks.

"That's a problem, isn't it? I have about three minutes to gain your trust." She pauses. "The box of candy we were sharing the night we got in the accident . . . it was chocolate-covered peanuts."

Jackson crosses his arms over his chest. "Good guess." He doesn't seem impressed.

"The summer you were twelve, we took a family trip to the Grand Canyon. I was scared of heights and didn't want to go near the edge. You held my hand."

This time, Jackson doesn't say anything.

But I'm not convinced that info is something only his sister would know. I saw pictures of his family at the Grand Canyon. Maybe somehow, a Drau did, too.

Lizzie glances back at the panel in front of her and her breathing speeds up. "You were born with an opaque layer over your corneas," she says, talking very fast now. "But you could see perfectly well. Your eyes changed a little at a time until you were about six, and then they've been Drau gray ever since."

I remember the day Jackson told me that. We were sitting at the top of the bleachers. "You knowing that doesn't prove anything," I say. "Jackson told me that story. In fact, he told it to me in an open, public space. You could have been listening."

"I could have been?" Lizzie asks, her brows shooting up.

"You," I say. "The Drau. Same thing, right?" I glance at Jackson. He's rigid and silent and I can't imagine how hard this is for him, facing down Lizzie's clone, a shell with a Drau consciousness inside it. "That's why we have to be careful what we say outside the game. They can always listen."

"Not quite always." She turns back to the panel. "You're a harder sell than I expected, Jax. I thought you'd be so happy to see me, that we'd have this awesome reunion."

"It isn't a reunion," he says, his voice flat. "It's a first meeting. You're not my sister."

"No?" The word sounds strained. Like she's in pain. "Okay . . . how about this? You had a fuzzy brown bear with a blue ribbon around its neck that you slept with until you were nine. You got it when you were three. You called it Calcaneus because Dad busted his heel falling off a ladder and that was the bone the doc said he broke. Believe me now, Jax?"

337

His breath hisses through his teeth. Was that Lizzie's nickname for him? Jax? And that story about the bear . . . is it true? And if it is, there aren't too many ways she could have known it.

With her hands still on the panel, she twists again to face us, and I get a clearer glimpse of what's in front of her.

I gasp as I realize her hands aren't just on the panel, they're *in* it. Part of it. I can see her bones through her translucent skin, and crawling all over them are what appear to be tiny spiders.

"Nanoagents," she says. "They don't really hurt, just sting a little. They connect me to the machine. Efficient, if a little weird. And they're much smaller than they appear here. They're magnified by the panel." She pins me with her gaze. "Miki, right?" She cocks her head in a beckoning gesture. "Come here."

I take a step forward without really thinking about it.

Jackson grabs my arm and stops me.

"I don't think so," he says.

She makes a dismissive noise, the kind Carly makes when her younger brothers annoy her.

"I can't leave the panel or you'll move through to the lobby."

"Explain," Jackson says.

"I need to show you something before I explain."

"Why?" Jackson asks.

"Because it's the only way you'll believe a word I say."

338

"Show us from there. We'll stay here."

Again, she makes that sound.

She closes her eyes for a second and shakes her head rapidly from side to side. "You haven't changed much in five years. Still arguing with everything I say."

"And you haven't changed much in five years," Jackson clips. "Which is why you can't be my sister. You look exactly as she did the night she died. Like a teen, not a girl in her midtwenties. Lizzie would have aged. A shell wouldn't."

She sighs, glances at the panel again, then back at us. "I need a hand. Mine are occupied at the moment."

"Use my hand. Miki stays right here," Jackson says.

Lizzie smiles. "Right. Because she'll be perfectly safe there as opposed to here."

She has a point.

Jackson doesn't move, and his grip on me doesn't loosen.

"Fine," she says, gritting her teeth now, thrusting her hands deeper into the panel, her skeletal fingers grasping some unseen thing. "I was just trying to spare your modesty, Jax."

Her hands move quickly. She hunches forward.

"Now, Jax. Right now," she barks, her hands jumping right, left, right again. "Hurry!"

I don't know if it's her tone or her use of his nickname, but something makes Jackson move. He sprints toward her as she says, "Lift my shirt. Do it!"

The white walls burn my eyes. The sound of her voice is so loud it hurts.

"I'm losing you!" Her words come at me way too slow, but the urgency isn't lost. She's panicked. Frantic.

"Shells don't have navels. No umbilical cord. No belly button. You remember when I taught you that, right? I told you in the lobby, right before your first mission."

She cries out and thrusts her hands deeper into the mass of skittering, clawing nanoagents. "Crap," she snarls. "You're gone. And I didn't get to tell you a damn thing."

Jackson grabs her shirt.

"Lift it," she orders.

After a split-second hesitation, he yanks it up.

The world tips and tilts, but not before I see exactly what I knew I'd see. Her belly button. Lizzie isn't a clone, a shell, a Drau.

But as I stare at her skeletal fingers enrobed in the moving layer of spidery nanoagents, I don't think she's quite human, either.

"The Committee," she says, her tone tight and pained and urgent. "Don't trust them, Jax. They aren't what you think. Neither are the Drau, the battles, the game." She jerks her hands from the console with a cry.

"Lizzie," Jackson rasps.

I catch a glimpse of his stricken face and then I'm falling, falling, falling away.

▲▼▲

I respawn in the lobby. Grass. Trees. Boulders.

I feel like I'm going to puke, like my head's going to explode. I haven't felt this awful since the first time I got pulled.

Swallowing, I push to my feet, just in time to see Jackson push to his.

His face is sheet white, his lips drawn in a taut line.

He opens his arms and I run to him, heart pounding, pulse racing.

He pulls me close. Holds me tight.

And whispers against my ear, "Incoming. Gear up."